*Angie Turner hopes her new farm-to-table restaurant can be a fresh start in her old hometown in rural Idaho. But when a goat dairy farmer is murdered, Angie must turn the tables on a bleating black sheep . . .*

With three weeks until opening night for their restaurant, the County Seat, Angie and her best friend and business partner Felicia are scrambling to line up local vendors—from the farmer's market to the goat dairy farm of Old Man Moss. Fortunately, the cantankerous Moss takes a shine to Angie, as does his kid goat Precious. So when Angie hears the bloodcurdling news of foul play at the dairy farm, she jumps in to mind the man's livestock and help solve the murder. One thing's for sure, there's no whey Angie's going to let some killer get *her* goat . . .

# Also by Lynn Cahoon

# Who Moved My Goat Cheese?

*A FARM-TO-FORK MYSTERY*

## Lynn Cahoon

**LYRICAL UNDERGROUND**
Kensington Publishing Corp.
www.kensingtonbooks.com

Lyrical Underground books are published by
Kensington Publishing Corp. 119 West 40th Street New York, NY 10018

All Kensington titles, imprints, and distributed lines are available at special
quantity discounts for bulk purchases for sales promotion, premiums, fund-
raising, and educational or institutional use.

To the extent that the image or images on the cover of this book depict a
person or persons, such person or persons are merely models, and are not
intended to portray any character or characters featured in the book.

Special book excerpts or customized printings can also be created to fit
specific needs. For details, write or phone the office of the Kensington
Special Sales Manager:
Kensington Publishing Corp.
119 West 40th Street
New York, NY 10018
Attn. Special Sales Department. Phone: 1-800-221-2647.

First Electronic Edition: March 2018
eISBN-13: 978-1-5161-0381-2
eISBN-10: 1-5161-0381-5

First Print Edition: March 2018
ISBN-13: 978-1-5161-0382-9
ISBN-10: 1-5161-0382-3

Printed in the United States of America

*To the little girl who turned into the writer. Who knew all the bits and pieces we picked up along the way would be useful someday?*

# Acknowledgements –

Farm to Fork came out of a need to write about the place where I grew up, the Treasure Valley in Idaho. I lived most of my life within 40 miles of the place I was born. They say you only have so many memories you can keep in your brain before you write over them with new experiences. This is one way of downloading the love I feel for this rural farm area. Big thanks to my Mom and Dad (Viola and Robert Gardner) for moving their growing family in true pioneering spirit out of South Dakota to Idaho. If not for that one move, this book might have been completely different.

Thanks to Esi Sogah and the Kensington crew for taking a chance on a new cozy concept. And thank you to Jill Marsal, my agent. Welcome to the family.

# CHAPTER 1

Angie Turner knelt in the grass beside Nona's herb garden, loosening the soil around the rosemary plant and cutting back the chives, the beat of June sun on her back reminding her of childhood summer days. Back then, she'd loved visiting her grandmother. On warm mornings, Angie would lie in the tall grass, listening to the bird songs in the trees and the cattle wandering around the pasture near the house. Later in the afternoon, her dad always saddled the horses and took her riding after lunch. Growing up in rural Idaho had reminded her of the stories from those Little House books.

Dom, her newly adopted St. Bernard puppy, sat nearby, watching Mabel, the lone surviving white and black hen from her grandmother's flock. She was inching closer to the garden, probably looking for the worms Angie disturbed while she turned the soil. She stood and brushed the dirt off her hands.

"Time to make dinner." Angie held the back door open for the dog and he trotted inside. Then she loaded her arms up with russet potatoes and a large onion from her storeroom. River Vista farmers' market had just started carrying the sweet Vidalias, so last visit she'd bought several and had been playing with different recipes all week. She would have to refill her stock soon. The star of today's menu was her version of Nona's potato soup. She'd take that and a fresh onion sandwich over to Mrs. Potter's house, her only neighbor on the mile road.

The recipe for the onion sandwich consisted of thickly sliced sweet Vidalias, the last of the herb bread she'd baked on Sunday, and Miracle Whip. The only upgrades she'd made from her grandmother's recipe had been to change the white bread to whatever homemade loaf she had on hand and adding sea salt.

While she cooked, she was serenaded with snores that came from Dom's puppy bed in the corner of the kitchen. Right now, the world made sense. Buying a St. Bernard puppy might not have been the smartest idea, especially if she ever had to go back to apartment living. Yet, as she worked in Nona's newly remodeled kitchen, Angie didn't think staying here in River Vista would be a problem at all. Especially if her new restaurant became successful.

The previously agriculture-based town of River Vista had become a bedroom community for Boise. As a small town filled with corporate working couples who didn't have time to cook dinner, it was just the right time and place to open The County Seat. While the soup simmered on the stove, she checked her tablet. Since that morning, she'd received ten new emails from Felicia Williams, her best friend and now, business partner.

This wasn't the first time they'd opened a restaurant. The trio of friends from culinary school, Felicia, Todd Young, and herself had opened their first place, *el pescado*, five years ago, after working for some of the best restaurants in the San Francisco area. When the lease on their location expired, the landlord wanted more than what the restaurant could afford so they'd closed the establishment. Todd had gone back to Jersey and the two women had moved north to Idaho and the farmhouse Angie had inherited.

She sent Felicia a quick text telling her to come over for dinner and that soup was ready. Then Angie finished packing her basket and took it across the road to Mrs. Potter. When Angie returned to her own kitchen after a few minutes of idle gossip, Felicia had arrived. Her business partner was the light to her dark. Blonde and thin, she looked like the typical California valley girl. Angie had her grandmother's Italian features and thick black hair. Felicia already sat at the table, a bowl of soup in front of her and Dom at her feet, watching her take each bite.

Holding out the spoon, she pointed it at Angie. "This is good."

Angie went over to the counter and made a couple of tuna fish sandwiches since neither of them loved the onion sandwiches like Mrs. Potter did. After pouring her own bowl of soup, she finally sat. Blowing on the too hot soup, she studied her friend. "You've been burning up my email today. Tell me what's got you all worked up. We have three weeks before opening, everything is on track, and we're meeting with the city council for our liquor license next week. Nothing's going to go wrong."

Felicia set her sandwich down on her plate. "That's where you're wrong. Something already has. The guy that runs the farmers' market is refusing to work with us. He says we're too 'corporate' for his liking."

Angie almost spit out the spoonful bit of the soup she'd just put in her mouth. She grabbed a napkin. "What do you mean we're too corporate? He realizes the 'company' is me and you, right?"

"Apparently, he has a strong no-corporation policy, so when he found out you'd filed papers to incorporate the restaurant, he got nervous." Felicia fed the crusts off the bread to Dom, who swallowed the bite without tasting it. "It's an easy fix. All you have to do is sweet talk him into changing his mind. No harm, no foul."

Angie pulled out her phone and made another notation on her already growing list for tomorrow. "Who did you talk to? The owner or the manager?"

"One and the same." Felicia took a business card out of her oversized designer purse. "Here's his deets."

Angie looked over the formal business card. Ian McNeal was listed as the owner/manager of River Vista Farmers' Market. He'd made the market a 503(c) nonprofit for the local farmers. She'd have to remind him that it was almost the same thing for little businesses. If she had to build her own vendor process, opening day needed to be pushed out at least a week. She could use a local produce supplier, except it was hard to claim farm-to-table when the tomatoes for the caprese salad came from California.

Felicia stood, taking her empty bowl to the sink and put a hand on Angie's shoulder. "Don't worry about it. You can talk the devil into serving ice cream as an afternoon snack in hell. You'll be able to handle this guy, no problem."

"When I was talking to Mrs. Potter just now, she mentioned I also need to charm Old Man Moss. He has a goat dairy up on the river canyon and only sells to people he likes. She told me not to mention her name, because he doesn't like her. Some old argument that's festered for years." Angie laughed at the memory of the woman's chatter. "What was I thinking when I agreed to a farm-to-table concept? I'm going to spend all my time chatting up every farmer in the Treasure Valley."

Felicia paused at the kitchen door. "That's what the executive chef does. I'm just front of the house. Which reminds me I still need to find a local craft beer or two to add to our bar stock. Maybe I'll get lucky tonight."

"You mean with the beer, right?" Angie motioned Dom to come sit next to her.

Felicia shot her a wicked smile. "Whatever do you mean? Anyway, thanks for dinner. I'm going into Emmett for the Cherry Festival. Do you want me to pick up samples?"

Felicia had already been on more dates in the last month than Angie had since high school. "Get business cards from some of the local farm stands. I might need to reach out directly."

Felicia threw her a cockeyed salute as she opened the screen door, keeping her gaze on Dom who had left Angie's side to find his food bowl, deciding it was his dinnertime as well. The dog had a habit of thinking he needed out every time the door opened. She paused briefly. "You could come along."

"I don't want to be part of some blind date setup. You go have fun and be careful. This may not be California, but it doesn't mean bad things don't happen here." Angie opened the business plan for The County Seat and started scanning for things she'd have to change if she couldn't talk the farmers' market guy into being reasonable. Besides opening day.

She'd taken a loan to start the restaurant, buying the small building where she'd be cooking four nights a week for the rest of her life, hopefully. Her projections were all based on opening in three weeks. They'd already been taking reservations and had bookings for at least two weeks after opening night. If she had to push it back, she shook her head, not wanting to go down that road. Dom had cleaned out his dinner bowl and was looking at her unfinished dinner.

"Sorry guy, I'm not as much of a soft sell as Felicia." She took her dishes to the sink, putting a cover over the soup pan. Even though she'd fed only four people tonight, she still cooked as if she was in el pescado's kitchen. She'd freeze the leftovers as soon as they cooled.

The evening light had softened the kitchen. Angie picked up the blue leash hanging on the corner. "What do you say, want to go walking?"

He sat in front of her, motionless except the constant wag of his tail.

"I should rent out your talents as a floor cleaner." As Angie locked the door and tucked her key into her capris pocket, Dom strained on the leash. Mabel was still clucking around the front of the coop. "You're in charge," she called to the hen, who looked up at her like, "Aren't I always?"

The evening was still warm and the light that pulsed in the valley appeared soft and inviting. June had always been her favorite month. Not deep summer, but out of the chill of the spring. The good thing about River Vista is they got all four seasons. Winter, spring, summer, and fall. And the area residents celebrated each one. If Felicia liked the small local festivals, she'd have her choice year-round. Since high school, the Cherry Festival in nearby Emmett had been one of Angie's favorites. She'd met her first love there, had her first kiss, and it had been the first festival her grandmother had let her go to with friends rather than as a family. Of course, nothing got past the woman and at the breakfast table the next morning, her grandmother asked her about the new friend she'd met. Grandma's spies had been everywhere.

As they crossed the empty highway to the next mile of their walk, Angie considered the field to her right. Whatever was growing wasn't corn. Instead, the plants were more bean like, but didn't seem to be green beans. She took out her phone and snapped a picture of the field and one close up of the plant. The crunch of tires on the gravel side of the road made her freeze as a vehicle rolled to a stop behind her.

"Can I help you, miss?" The southern twang in his voice told Angie the man wasn't a local. She turned and a well-used red Chevy Silverado with a pile of silver siphon tubes piled in the bed sat parked on the side of the road. The man's appearance screamed farmer, from his worn Levi's to his flannel over shirt unbuttoned to show a sweat-covered tank underneath. Worn cowboy boots and an old Chevy baseball cap finished the look. He could be a model for *Rural Farmers Quarterly*, if there was such a magazine. "It's not safe for a pretty little thing like you to be out alone after dark."

"Not quite dark yet. We're just out for a walk." As to emphasize the point, Dom wiggled by her side, wanting her to release his leash. The puppy thought everyone was his friend, and wanted to get a whiff of the guy to add to his catalogue of humans. "Sit," Angie said, the command in her I'm-serious-voice and for once, Dom listened.

"Beautiful pup. My friend Cindy's girl just had a litter a few months ago. This guy's not from her litter, is he?" The guy stood still, leaning on the hood of his truck, watching Dom. He squatted down to the dog's level. "You mind if we meet?"

Angie could feel the shiver going through her dog. Dom seemed to like the guy, but what good was getting a dog for protection if he liked the entire human race. She released the leash and Dom bounded over to meet his new friend.

"I'm Kirk Hanley." He looked up from one of Dom's full body hugs. "Local vet so I would have met you guys sooner or later." He glanced at Dom's tags. "I guess I must have met this guy before since this is one of my tags. You are one of Cindy's boys, aren't you?"

Dom wiggled in agreement, apparently overjoyed that the guy who'd done his puppy shots for the breeder remembered him. Her dog did know everyone.

"I'm Angie Turner. We have an appointment in a couple of weeks for his boosters." She stepped closer and held out her hand. "Nice to meet you."

"Well, welcome to the neighborhood Miss Angie. I'm sure you'll love it here, But you might want to be careful walking out here alone. I'm not sure your pup's much protection." He rubbed Dom's tummy.

"We'll be fine." She looked around the too empty space, finally settling her gaze on the bed of the pickup filled with silver irrigation tubes. "Don't tell me you farm too?"

"Guilty as charged. This whole eighty acres is mine, although since it didn't come with a house, I'm living in town over the vet clinic." He stood and Dom sat by his foot, leaning into his new friend's leg. "Someday I'll build a place out here, but student loans are a blessing and a curse."

Angie nodded. "I just paid mine off, now I'm back in debt for the new restaurant I'm opening, The County Seat, next month."

"You're the one opening the new restaurant in town? I've heard good things." He glanced at the setting sun and put out his hand. "Nice to meet you and Dom. I need to get water set before it gets too dark to see."

She shook his hand. "I'm sure we'll see a lot of each other."

"Why?" He looked down at Dom, "Is he okay?"

Open mouth, insert foot. "No, I mean, yes, he's fine. I just meant since River Vista is so small…" She shook her head and changed the conversation. "Before you go, I don't recognize this plant. What are you growing?"

He paused before he got into the cab of his truck. River Vista Vet Clinic had been stenciled on the side of the door, but the paint had faded over the years. She wondered how long Kirk had been the local vet. "Soybeans. According to the grange guys, I'm growing the new cash crop of southern Idaho. You be careful now, you hear?"

"Soybeans," she said aloud as they continued their walk. She smiled at the vet's warning to be careful. Hadn't she just said the same thing to Felicia? Pot, meet kettle. The little town of River Vista had changed a lot since she'd been gone. And not all for the better, apparently. Dom, oblivious to any danger, sniffed at a gopher hole he'd found by the side of the road.

She wondered as the truck disappeared over the hill if her new friend knew either the farmers' market guy or the cheese guy. She should have asked. Everyone seemed to know everything around here, even where she bought her dog.

They finished their walk and as Angie got the kitchen cleaned up before bed, she touched Nona's basil plant, growing in a colorful pot on the kitchen windowsill. Being in River Vista felt right. The house felt right. Now, all she had to do was convince the rest of the town that she and her restaurant deserved to be here.

# CHAPTER 2

The next morning, the first thing on her list was a trip into town and the farmers' market. Based on what she found, lunch could be interesting. She put a handful of shopping bags into the back of her crossover and returned to the house to get Dom's leash. The dog sat at the front door, looking out the screen, whining. "Hold, on, you can go, but you have to use your good boy manners today."

Dom was a sweetheart. At his worse, he'd sit on someone's foot or slobber them to death. Kirk was right. Dom was not quite the guard dog she'd been planning on getting, but as soon as she'd seen the litter, Angie knew that she wasn't leaving without one of the pups.

They drove the ten miles into town with the radio blaring and the sunroof open. There on the edge of the city limits sat the old high school gym. The school district had kept the gym and the land where the high school originally sat and now rented it out for community events. Like the weekly farmers' market. Just a little farther down Main Street, on the other side of town was the building she'd bought for the restaurant. River Vista was tiny as far as cities went, more like a village. Angie sighed as they passed the town limit sign. She'd always felt a special connection with River Vista even before she'd moved here full time to live with her grandmother. The town sign boasted 400 residents, but the majority of the population lived outside city limits, enjoying the weekend farmer lifestyle while still keeping their corporate jobs in Boise.

The market was almost all set up and customers were starting to arrive and park on the roads. Across the street sat the only grocery store in town. Angie could get most things she needed for the restaurant right here in

River Vista. As long as Ian McNeal got off his high horse and decided to sell to The County Seat.

She clipped Dom's leash on his collar and started through the stands. As she strolled, she purchased Idaho walnuts, a bag of fresh baby spinach, more onions, and a couple large bags of different types of cherries. From the large sweet Bing cherries to a smaller, sour cherry that would be perfect for a tart, her bag was heavy before she found Ian McNeal standing at a booth, arguing with an older man who was setting out ice. As she watched, the man sat plastic bags filled with a curd type cheese in the display. She stepped closer to examine the offerings.

"All I'm saying is you can't sell the aged cheese until you get permission from the Department of Agriculture. You know Mildred just wants to examine your cheese cave." Ian's voice seemed too Scottish for the rural Idaho scene. Angie expected him to rip off his t-shirt and jeans and let down his kilt. She tilted her head down as she tried to get the smile off her face and the image out of her head.

"I'm not letting those vultures anywhere near my cave. You know all they want to do is shut me down. Mildred's been looking for an excuse to get me out of the goat cheese business for years. She's in cahoots with the Simpson Dairy in Meridian." The other man put the wheels of cheese back in the cooler. "I bet they pay a pretty penny for her protection."

"No one is trying to shut you down." Ian took a step toward Angie and Dom inserted himself between the two, barring his teeth and growling. "Seriously? Whose dog is this?"

Angie pulled Dom's leash and moved him to a sitting position next to her. "Mine." She put her hand on Dom's head. "He doesn't like loud arguments."

Ian ran a hand through his hair. "We weren't arguing."

"Seemed like it to me," the man she now knew had to be Old Man Moss mumbled. "Dogs are good judges of character. Like goats."

Ian took a step back. "Look, I'm just trying to keep the market open. I'm not the bad guy here."

"But you are Ian McNeal, right? I'm glad I ran into you. I need to talk to you about something," Angie took her business card out of her jacket. "I'm the new chef/owner over at The County Seat and I understand you are banning the market from selling produce to me."

He took the card, looked at it and her for a long minute, then slipped it into his pocket. "That's not exactly what I told your business associate, Mrs. Turner."

"It's Ms. Turner. And good, I'm glad Felicia misunderstood. I'm opening in less than a month and I need your produce to even come close to the restaurant's concept. Can we sit down early next week and set up an ordering process?"

"Ian, the guy from Marsing Fish Farm is here with the trout, where do you want him to set up?" A voice called from down the line of booths.

"I'll be right there." He turned back to Angie. "I didn't quite say she misunderstood my meaning. Look, call me on Monday, we'll talk about my hesitations. I'm a little busy today."

Before he walked away, he turned back to the man in the booth. "Don't be selling that aged cheese here. All you have the permit for is the curds, okay?"

Old Man Moss fell into a lawn chair with a travel cup of what Angie was sure wasn't just straight coffee. "Who died and made you king?" He frowned at Angie, just noticing her still at the counter. "You want to buy something or what?"

Angie nodded. "I need two pounds of your curds. And I'd love to talk to you about supplying my restaurant." She fumbled for one of her cards. "Can I visit you tomorrow?"

"Turner? You Margaret's granddaughter? She was a Turner." He peered at the card, then tucked it into the front pocket on his overalls.

"Margaret was my Nona, yes." Angie smiled at the man, thankful her grandmother had been well known in the community before her passing. "I'm Angie."

"Well, Angie, I owe your grandmother enough that I can give you a few minutes to talk." He placed two bags of the cheese in a plastic bag that had seen better days. "We'll finish milking about six tomorrow morning. If you wanted to bring out some coffee and Ding Dongs, I'd give you some time."

"Ding Dongs? Like the chocolate cupcakes? Do they even still make those?" She took the bag and handed him a twenty.

"Of course they do." Glaring at the bill, he pulled out a thick wad of paper money and put her bill in the middle, then counted her out ten dollars in change. One five, and five ones. "You can get them over at the market." He nodded to the grocery store across the street. "They have lots of good stuff in there."

Dom woofed and waged his tail, apparently agreeing with the cheese guy. For the first time that morning, Angie saw a smile come across the old man's face. A few missing teeth didn't dim the real feeling behind the emotion. "You can bring him too. I bet he'd like to meet my blue heelers. Now, those are herding dogs."

"Dom's more of a lap dog." Angie tucked the cheese into her already overfilled shopping bag.

"I suppose that Potter woman who lived next door to Margaret is still alive? Evil tends to live forever, yet angels like your grandmother go too quickly." He paused, watching her reaction.

"My neighbor? Mrs. Potter?" Angie felt confused at the change of subject. "Yes, she's still alive."

"Too bad." With that, he walked away to talk to the man in the next stall. The conversation was apparently over.

Angie wandered through the booths, picking up a few more items, letting her mind work on the salad she'd been thinking about all morning. Good thing she'd brought Dom today. He'd been her good luck charm with the cheese man. She had accomplished both things on her must do list for today. Now all she needed to do was pick up some of the old man's treats and head home to play with the salad recipe. She'd talk to Mrs. Potter and see why Old Man Moss didn't like her one bit. Probably an old feud that neither one of them could remember how it started.

Angie ran into the grocery store after parking in the front row and rolling down all of the windows halfway. She'd found the packaged cupcakes on an endcap and headed to the front to check out. Angie could see Dom sitting in the driver's seat, watching her through the plate glass windows. The clerk rang up the two boxes and bagged them as she called out the total. "I don't sell a lot of these except to the teenagers and Mr. Moss. He buys them by the case when he comes into town."

"I'm going to visit him tomorrow at the goat barn, so I was warned to bring treats." She swiped her debit card and took the receipt and bag from the clerk.

"I haven't been out there since high school. Our FFA teacher took us out to show us the cheese making facility. The lesson was something about small businesses being worth supporting. My dad almost blew a fuse when he found out. We run a big dairy farm west of town. Apparently, goat cheese is too subsidized in the dairy guys' minds." The girl leaned against the checkout stand and pointed to Angie's SUV. "That your dog? He's going to be huge."

Angie laughed. "I might have to buy a truck just so Dom can keep going places with me."

The young girl shrugged. "Well, no one's going to mess with your stuff while you're gone. Even if he doesn't bite, he could lick someone to death. Or sit on them."

Angie made her way out to the car. She put the bags in the back where Dom couldn't get access due to the dog restraint she'd had installed between the back of the car and the back seat. Not that Dom ever went in the back, but at least she could buy stuff and get it home. The iron bars reminded Angie of her one and only time in the back of a cop car after joy riding with Brad Moore, junior year.

She turned the car back onto Main Street, toward the restaurant. Felicia was living in the apartment on the second floor of the building. There was a chance she was home. And a slimmer chance that she was alone.

Angie didn't have to worry about meeting the latest man of the moment. Felicia sat outside on the benches they'd built for overflow customers to use while they waited. She'd wanted to set up café tables on the sidewalk but the city council hadn't been swayed by her argument. Benches would have to do until she had the numbers to back up her need for more seating. Felicia opened the passenger side door and took Dom's leash, leading him toward the bench.

There wasn't a lot of traffic on River Vista's Main Street, especially not at ten in the morning, but Dom needed the consistency, especially since he ran free out at the farm. When he left the property lines, he was on the leash. Hopefully that would keep him from straying. Angie had only had the dog for a few months, but she'd be lost without him.

"Come for a walk through? The kitchen guy is supposed to be here sometime this morning so I thought I'd take my coffee out here and get a little sun while I waited." Felicia waved her hand at the travel cup sitting on the built-in end table along with one of those romance novels with the guy in the kilt. The cover made Angie think of Ian McNeal, and heat bloomed in her face. She shook the thought away and focused on the subject of the book. Lately Felicia had been reading anything she could get her hands on that had time travel involved in the story line. Angie's reading had consisted of foodie cookbooks and memoirs, with an occasional murder mystery thrown in the mix.

"Actually, I was in town at the farmers' market. I've got an appointment to meet with Ian on Monday. I think he's warming up to me." Dom looked at her and barked his disapproval of the idea. "Okay, maybe not, but at least I have an appointment. Tomorrow, I'm meeting with our cheese supplier."

"So you've completed your to do list. Why don't we head over to Emmett for the Cherry Festival later this afternoon? I'm sure we can rustle up a group to come along." They were now in the kitchen. The main remodel had been finished, now all that needed done was to refurbish or replace the kitchen fixtures and appliances. She hadn't kept much from the original building, mostly because the Mexican restaurant that had occupied the space had been closed for years. She didn't know if she could trust any of the appliances. Besides, she had the money now, no need to be penny wise and pound foolish as Nona used to say.

Angie brought her attention back to her friend. "Sorry, I'm going to play with some salad recipes for opening day. I bought the sweetest Bing cherries that are screaming at me to make them into some type of vinaigrette."

"If I didn't know you better, I would think you were teasing. The kitchen guy's going to be here until about five, but after that, I'm heading back out to play. That festival was rocking last night. Today, it should be amazing sauce."

"Just be careful." Angie looked around the shiny, new, empty room. "I can't believe we're doing this."

"Again."

She turned toward Felicia. "What did you say?"

"You said you couldn't believe we were starting up a restaurant and I said, again. You tend to forget we made el pescado a success. We can do this. And before you mention our third partner's name, you know Todd just showed up when the pictures were being taken." Felicia crossed her arms, challenging Angie to disagree.

"That's not true, Todd was there at the beginning." Angie tried to remember the work before the opening, but the only scenes she could wring out of her memories of that crazy time had her and Felicia scrubbing the old tables, down on their knees scraping the years of wax buildup off the floor. Where *had* Todd been? "Okay, so maybe not."

Felicia put her arm around Angie. "We can do this, we did it before."

Angie walked Dom out to the car. "Call me tomorrow morning and let me know you're okay. Or text me when you get home tonight. I worry about you."

Felicia followed her out to the car and leaned on the passenger side door, one hand patting Dom. "I'm a big girl. I can take care of myself, especially here in Hicksville."

"It's not all sunshine and roses, just remember that. I grew up here. Some of the guys are real jerks." She wanted to add paternalistic, male dominant, rednecks, but since she'd been gone more years than she actually lived in River Vista, she kept those descriptors to herself.

"You worry too much." Felicia mussed Dom's hair and he lay down in the seat. "Talk to you soon. Have fun with that salad."

And that was the thing Felicia didn't understand about her, Angie thought as she pulled the car into the street, waiting for the older Ford truck filled with a load of alfalfa bales to pass by. She slowly followed him out of town until she could see far enough ahead to pass, then she hit the gas.

She *would* have fun trying new tastes and textures for the salad. For some people, making one version was enough. Angie liked to take okay to fabulous. And the only way to do that was to try a few different versions. The County Seat would be the destination restaurant for not only local foodies, but she hoped she could draw in diners from all over the Gem State. At least, she'd put up her best attempt at wowing them with food. If it didn't work, she'd done her best and she'd look for a job cooking at one of the high-class spots in Boise.

But the restaurant was going to be successful so there was no need for a plan B.

# CHAPTER 3

A baby goat ran full bore at her and Dom as Angie walked toward the goat barn. Several older cars and trucks were parked by the side of the faded red barn. Dom hid behind her legs as the baby reached them. "Bah," the almost all-black goat bleated. The much larger puppy whimpered and leaned into Angie.

"Hey, sweetheart." Angie leaned down, keeping her tote in view so Dom wouldn't take off with one of the boxes of cupcakes. She'd also brought Mr. Moss a loaf of homemade focaccia bread that she'd baked yesterday to round out the salad she'd perfected by dinner. She'd brewed the coffee this morning after grinding the beans she planned to serve at the restaurant. Angie was certain the food bribe was perfect. The tiny goat nuzzled her outstretched hand.

"Precious likes you. That's a good sign." A gruff voice called from the barn door and she looked up to find the cheese man standing watching her. "Legend has it that currying a newborn's favor bestows luck on the recipient. Why don't you drag that dog of yours over here to the porch and we'll have some breakfast? The crew is almost done with the milking and the goats will be heading out to graze in about an hour."

The sun had just risen over the mountain ridge to the east. The view included the river flowing through the canyon below as well as the first rays of sunshine filling the valley. The air smelled sweet like hay and grass and goats and milk, all mixed together. Angie set up the coffee, pouring cups for both of them, and opened a box of the prepackaged bakery goods. Then she pulled out the loaf of bread. "I can see why you love it out here. The view is amazing."

"According to you and all those blood-sucking realtors." Moss frowned at the plastic-wrapped loaf. "What's that?"

"I made it last night. I thought you might enjoy a loaf." She leaned back into the wooden Adirondack chair, a little worse for wear but still sturdy. Dom lay at her feet, keeping his gaze on the baby goat who now was trying to climb a rock in the middle of the driveway.

"No, I mean what is it?" He poked at the package. "My wife used to make bread. But that can't be bread, it's all round."

"Focaccia bread. I mixed herbs from my grandmother's garden into the dough. Your cheese complements the taste. I made a tomato caprese sandwich with it last night for dinner." She sipped her coffee and closed her eyes for a moment. This place was heaven. No loud noise, no people, and no traffic, unless you counted the goats.

"I typically eat Wonder bread." The old man shrugged, "But if you say it went good with the cheese, who am I to question. I'll give it a go tonight with my stew."

"I guess you want to know why I'm here." She didn't look at him, using her free hand to scratch Dom's head.

"I asked around about you. You're opening that fancy restaurant. You know you're going to go broke. No one around here can pay that kind of price for a meal. Especially if you cheat them on the serving size. I swear, new places don't know how to feed folks." He unwrapped a cupcake and put the entire thing in his mouth. After a few swallows, he sipped on his coffee. "I guess I can't stop you if you want to buy my cheese. As long as you treat it kindly. Some of these people haven't eaten anything but that processed cheese spread you buy in loafs at the store. Even some of my milkers hadn't ever tried it before they started working for me. Of course, now I can't keep them out of the stuff."

"I was hoping you'd show me around. The barn, the production shed, and maybe even the cheese cave if you think you'll be selling the aged stuff sooner or later?" She took another long, deep breath. The place was hypnotic. She could feel the stress leaving her.

"Maybe someday." His voice choked on the words. "I told your grandmother if I was ever going to share my secret, it would have to be with her. Since she's gone, I guess it will have to be with her kin. I've kept that promise for over twenty years now. We can wait a few more months before I let you go inside."

"The cheese cave? Is that what you're talking about?" Angie didn't sit up or open her eyes. The more she got him talking, the more she'd find out about him and his relationship to Nona.

"Secrets are meant to be kept, little girl." He chuckled as he unwrapped a second cupcake. Angie could hear the cellophane wrapper crunching. She turned and looked at him before he spoke again. "You mark my words, nothing good comes of a leaked secret."

A car pulled into the driveway and Reana Whiting waved from the driver's seat. Angie sat up, wondering why the realtor who sold her the building for the restaurant would be out here on a Sunday morning. "That's Reana. I wonder what she's doing out here?"

"Must be the first of the month, if the gold digger's here. She comes by once a month or so to give me an update on who wants to buy my land and for how much. I swear, I can see money signs in her eyes as she explains the offers." He put his wrapper back in the box.

"I didn't realize your place was up for sale." She glanced around at the wide expanse of land. She could see either a group of overpriced condos hugging the cliff area and maybe some larger estate homes dotting the landscape. People would pay big for this view, even if it was a good forty-five minutes from Boise.

"It's not. And I've told her that over and over." Old Man Moss winked. "I think the girl's gone a little sweet on me. She brings me out homemade cookies when she comes."

Dom barked at the newcomer and Angie held on to his leash. "I guess we'll be going then. Maybe I can come back and visit sometime soon?"

"I hope so. At least I know what you want, not like her or that no good nephew of mine." He shook his head. "I'm not going to bore you with my family troubles. I know Margaret said you had your own tragedies in your life. And yes, I'll sell you as much cheese as you want to buy, so just call me and leave a message with your order on my answering machine. We'll deliver each Saturday to your shop."

"I appreciate it. I do still want to do a tour of your place soon. As a farm-to-table chef, I like to know where my product is coming from." Angie stood and gathered the coffee carafe into her bag. "And I'd really like to see your cheese cave."

Old Man Moss shook his head. "You aren't going into the cave. Not yet. Didn't you listen when I said it was where the secrets stay? I'll show you the barn processing plant, that's the only cheese they'll let me sell anyway."

Angie blew out a breath. She wasn't going to change his mind. At least she wouldn't without a bribe that probably included a whole truckload of the individually wrapped cupcakes. "I didn't mean to upset you," she began.

"Then don't bring it up again. I don't see what the big deal about my cave is. Last month, someone snuck into it and made a mess of things."

He didn't get up from the wooden chair. "Come by next Sunday and I'll take you on a tour of the place. We might even hike down to the river if you're up for the walk."

Angie hitched her tote onto her shoulder, unable to keep the smile from curving her lips. "That would be nice. I hope you enjoy the bread." She stepped away from the chairs and met up with the realtor as she slowly approached, her gait uneven on the dirt driveway in her platform heels. "Hey Reana, didn't know I'd see you this morning."

"Gerald and I are old friends." Reana leaned down to Dom and cradled his chin. "Nice to see you again too, big boy."

Dom's tail wagged so hard he almost pulled his leash out of Angie's hand. She tightened her grip and aimed Dom toward the car and away from the expensive suit before he could leave paw prints on Reana's pants. "I've got to get back to town. I have a lot to do before opening."

As she started up the car, she watched Reana and Gerald Moss greet each other. There was a tinge of familiarity in the way the two hugged, not quite friends and especially not lovers. But something. "None of our business, right Dom?"

She backed out of the driveway and turned back on the narrow dirt road that would lead her back to the highway. Precious stood at the edge of the property and watched her go. At least she'd gotten the goat's blessing. Now, she just needed to sweet talk Ian into letting her source her foods supplies from his bank of farmers. Then she'd be able to finalize the menu, pull off her first family tasting meal for the staff, and actually make opening night, which was less than three weeks away.

"That's all," she said as she adjusted her rearview mirror to make sure the goat wasn't following. She'd hate to let her good luck charm out and have her become road kill her first week on earth.

* * * *

Monday morning, she was deep into making some strawberry jam when a knock came on her kitchen door. Wiping her hands on a towel, she looked out the window over the sink. A large new Ram truck sat in her driveway next to what appeared to be a police cruiser. Her gut twisted. Felicia must have gotten hurt on her trip to the local festival. She hadn't texted last night and Angie had been giving her some time before she called. A car accident? Or maybe something at the festival? Or someone? She squared her shoulders and went to open the door. As she'd expected, a police officer stood in his uniform next to Ian McNeal. What in the world was he doing here?

"Miss Turner? I'm Sheriff Allen Brown. I understand you've already met Mr. McNeal here?" The sheriff nodded to Ian, but neither man met Angie's gaze.

"I have. What's going on? Did something happen to Felicia? Or the restaurant?" Oh God, maybe the building burned down. Or the guy working in the restaurant had been hurt. Had she paid the insurance on time this month? If she got sued without even opening The County Seat's doors, she'd never dig out of the legal costs.

"Can we come in?" The sheriff took off his wide brimmed hand and pulled out a handkerchief from his pocket, wiping the sweat beads off his too wide and too tall forehead. "It's mighty hot already. I think summer's going to be a scorcher."

"Of course, I'm sorry, come on in." She pointed to the dining room table where her jars were set up for the jam that bubbled on the stove. She looked around the room and said the obvious. "I'm making jam."

"My mama used to make strawberry jam every summer. I loved that stuff." The sheriff didn't sit, standing near the door with his hat in his hand. "Look, ma'am, I hate to do this, but I need to ask you some questions."

"About?"

The sheriff looked at Ian who raised his eyebrows and nodded. "I need to know if you met with Old Man, I mean, Gerald Moss yesterday."

"Yes. I wanted to set him up as a vendor for the restaurant. He invited me over Sunday morning for an early breakfast to talk about the proposal." She squinted her eyes at both men. "That can't be illegal."

Ian pulled out one of the chairs from the kitchen table. "Why don't you sit down, Ms. Turner."

"Why should I sit down?" She looked from Ian to the sheriff. "I don't understand. Visiting him wasn't against the law. I mean, seriously? Why are you making my life so difficult?"

"No ma'am, visiting isn't illegal, but, well, I'm afraid murder is." The sheriff turned his hat over and over in his broad hands.

She sank into the chair Ian had pulled out for her, her energy sapped. "Murder?" She repeated the word, knowing she sounded like a magpie. "Who was murdered?"

The sheriff took a chair and sat next to her. "Gerald Moss. Hikers found his body at the bottom of the canyon just a few hours ago."

# CHAPTER 4

By the time the sheriff and Ian had left, Felicia had arrived at the farmhouse. She shut the door after the men and sat next to Angie. "I heard about Mr. Moss in town so when you didn't answer your phone, I came right out. What happened?"

Angie stood and went to the stove to check on her jam. She'd forgotten to turn off the stove when the men arrived, so the mixture had kept cooking until she pulled the pan off the heat. If the jam wasn't burned, it was at least scorched. And definitely ruined. She brushed tears away from her eyes. "I shouldn't be feeling bad about jam when a man has lost his life."

"You make really good jam, but I'm not convinced that's why you're upset." Felicia put her hand on Angie's shoulder. "It's okay to feel sad about Old Man Moss. I didn't meet him, but everyone in town said he was quite a character."

Angie turned around to see her friend smiling at her. "He just had such a great life out there. He had the most amazing view from his front porch and the goats were a riot. You should have seen baby Precious. You would have fallen in love."

"Then let's toast to his passing and send him on his journey with good wishes that his path to heaven is error free. I have just the place." Felicia turned on her phone and opened up her task list. "I want you to come with me to the Southside Winery later today. I've decided that we'll highlight their product as our house wine but I'd like you to check it out first."

Angie put the pot in the sink. She'd clean up the mess when she got back. She returned to the table and opened her tablet to her calendar. "Sure. I have to meet up with Ian at his office in thirty minutes, then I'll swing by and pick you up and we can drive out together. That way you can update me on the hiring you've done."

They made plans to meet up and Felicia gave Angie a quick hug before she left. "Don't think too much about Mr. Moss's death."

But that was all she could think about. As Angie got into the SUV to drive into town, she saw Mrs. Potter sitting by her mailbox on a bench her husband had made for her before he'd passed on. Now, the wood was weathered and the bench needed a coat of paint, but structurally, it was still sound. She pulled up next to her and rolled down the window. "I'm heading to town. Do you need anything?"

"Can't think of anything, except maybe for Delores to show up soon. This bench is giving me hemorrhoids." Mrs. Potter squinted into the cab. "Where's Dom? Don't tell me you left him home. You won't have a stick of furniture left when you come back."

"He's locked in the kitchen with his bed. I'm sure he'll be fine." Just in case, Angie had left out not one but two chewy toys for Dom's entertainment. "Hey, Old Man Moss died yesterday, did you hear?"

"Good riddance to bad rubbish. I can't believe I even sent you out there to talk to him. He never was any good." She adjusted her walker closer to her. "I guess karma does work in mysterious ways."

"Did you two have a fight?" Angie wondered if Old Man Moss had been part of a love triangle with Mr. and Mrs. Potter. The thought made her lips try to turn up, but she pressed them together to keep from chuckling.

Mrs. Potter stared down the road. "You need to get going because Delores is speeding up the road and her brakes aren't very good." Finally, she turned and looked at Angie. "We didn't have a quarrel. The man killed my sister."

\* \* \* \*

Things were getting curiouser and curiouser, as Alice would say. Except this wasn't Wonderland and Angie hadn't fallen down a rabbit hole. Or maybe she had. She glanced around Ian McNeal's cramped office and wondered if she was only dreaming. Angie pinched her arm just as Ian returned with a glass of iced tea.

"I'm afraid this is reality. No use getting all bruised up." He sat the tea in front of her and then instead of going around the desk, he sat in the other visitor chair next to her. "I'm sorry about this morning. When Allen asked me if I'd seen anyone else talking to Old Man Moss, you popped into my head. He thought me being there might help when he questioned you."

Angie stared into Ian's deep blue eyes. "Why? Because I'm some female who needs taken care of?"

The jerk of his head was almost imperceptible, but she'd seen her words had the effect of a slap. "We—I didn't mean to be insensitive. Allen's just not good with people. His deputy typically handles the interviews and I don't think they've had a murder in River Vista for over twenty years. And that was a bar fight."

She was winning friends and influencing people. The way she was going, she might as well put a closed sign on the restaurant and get that chef job in Boise. "You and the Sheriff seem close. Are you friends?"

"It's complicated. He's kind of family."

When Ian didn't continue the story, Angie figured that door had been closed. "I'm still a bit shaken over the news. I didn't know Mr. Moss well, but he seemed so settled. I was looking forward to getting to know him better as he knew my grandmother."

"He could be a bit of a curmudgeon, especially when it came to his cheese. The other farmers thought he was cheating by taking on several government grants to build his barn and set up that darn cheese cave." Ian glanced at his watch. "Sorry, I hate to move this on, but I've got another appointment in Boise early this afternoon. What did you want to talk to me about?"

Angie set the tea aside. "I need your approval to use your farmers' network for our supply chain. Yes, The County Seat has filed corporation papers, but that's just about business. My friend and I are the owners and we're not hiding behind some legal maneuvering. We're here for the long haul and I expect to make The County Seat one of the premier farm-to-fork restaurants in Idaho before we're done."

"That's a lofty goal." He glanced out the window that faced Main Street. "River Vista is kind of a small community for you to be expecting that kind of attention. Maybe you should look for property in Boise or even Sun Valley?"

"I grew up here." She pushed back her hair from her face, a habit she'd tried to stop but had failed. "I know we can pull in from the surrounding areas. Besides, I have a few more tricks up my sleeve to bring in more business. Including takeout for busy couples. The only thing I need now is the produce and supplies to make the food. And that's where you come in."

"You don't understand. I can't just approve everyone who comes in here with a sob story. I have to protect the integrity of the food." Ian sighed. "I'm going to be honest with you. We just had an issue with a guy who said all the right things, but once he set up shop, he conveniently forgot to pay his debts. Then, he moved on to another town where he could pull the same scam. The farmer group lost a lot of money. I just want to make sure you are going to be part of the community, not just a fly by night drifter."

"I'm not going anywhere. I know a farm-to-fork concept will thrive out here. I studied the demographics before I bought the building and took out the loan. But I need locally sourced produce and protein sources to make it successful. I'm hoping to be 100 percent local, but there may be products I might have to use from at least organic sources. Like olive oil."

"You could use local butter. There's no reason to break your farm-to-table pledge if you are really committed to local sourcing." Ian glanced at his watch again, standing to end the meeting. "I really have to go. I'm expected at the cheese commission in Meridian at two. We're discussing a memorial for Gerald."

"What about my suppliers?" Angie stood and watched as Ian opened the door, holding it for her.

"I'll send out an email to the group. If you insist on trying, I can't stand in your way. But don't think that it's going to be easy. Most of these guys don't like change. And they really don't like new ideas. Just talk about honoring their food and they might choose to work with you." He tossed his head toward the door and Angie followed him out. He locked the small office, turning the in sign to out. "But I can't make them sell to you. You're on your own there."

"I'm sure I can be convincing." Angie put on her best smile.

He stopped in the hallway. "Please, take this the way it's intended. But don't smile like that when you're talking to the guys. You look creepy." He turned around and headed out to the street.

"I do not look creepy." She called after him. She examined her reflection in the glass of the doors, trying out her smile again. Okay, so it looked a little creepy. Her cell rang. "Hello?"

"Where are you? I thought we were going to the winery for lunch?" Felicia whined. "I'm starving."

"I'm right down the street." Angie pushed open the door. Ian was getting into an older wagon with logos on the side announcing the River Vista Farmers Market. She supposed she should thank him, but he hadn't been particularly supportive of her ideas. In fact, he'd insinuated she'd fail. Well, she'd show him. Creepy, he was creepy, not her. She spun left and headed to the restaurant.

The short walk did nothing to cool the steam. That man was infuriating. If he wasn't key to The County Seat being successful, she'd show him what he could do with his concern about her smile. This is why she liked being in the kitchen. There, no one bothered her, except maybe a waitress with a bad attitude or a sous chef who wasn't pulling his weight. Those things she could handle.

She found Felicia sitting outside with a book in her hand. Another Highlander romance from what she could tell by the cover. When her friend saw her, she popped up. "I'm so hungry, I could eat this book."

"Sorry, I got tied up." She motioned to the back of the building. "I parked in the back. Let's go before I decide to go back and trash his office."

"I take it the meeting went badly? What are we going to do about supplies?" Felicia followed Angie around the building, trying to keep up.

"Oh, he's letting people sell to us. He doesn't think I'll be very effective working with his farmers though. He treats me like..." She paused and considered the last hour. "A helpless female."

"Oh, boy." Felicia climbed into the passenger seat.

Angie started up the car and looked over at her friend. "That's all you got? Oh, boy?"

Felicia squirmed in her seat. "It's just that I know how you can get. If you think you've been slighted, well, you go a little overboard to fix things."

"I've never gone overboard." Angie pulled the car out of the small lot and drove out of town.

Felicia turned toward her. "What about the time you sent 12 dozen cookies to the reviewer who didn't like your dessert?"

"She deserved them. She wouldn't know a good dessert from a store-bought cookie."

"And the time you bought out every avocado, lime, and tomato the market had on hand because they refused to special order your produce?"

That had been a little extreme. They'd been making some sort of salsa special for the next week, trying to use up all the produce before it went bad. "It worked didn't it? The manager called me the next day and set up an ordering process."

"You can't always get what you want by bulldozing people. You need to find some charm and use that." Felicia smiled. "Like me. I've made a lot of new friends since we moved here. There was a rocking band down at the bar last night. I love that I can just walk home when I stay out too late."

"You really should be careful. Bad things can happen here, just like they do in the big city." Angie snuck a look at her friend. Man, she sounded like an old lady. Or maybe like Kirk, the vet. And from the look on Felicia's face, she was taking the unsolicited advice just as well as Angie had from Kirk.

"I'm a big girl. If I want to be griped at, I'll call my mother." Felicia slumped in her seat. "What has your goat today? Did Ian really tick you off that bad?"

The car was quiet for a while, then Angie blew out a breath. "I don't know if it's Mr. Moss's death, or just being home. Maybe a combination of everything. He was so sweet, and he knew Nona. I wish I'd known him when I lived here as a kid. But I was too busy doing kid stuff. If she'd offered to take me out there, I probably would have begged off to read or go to the town pool."

"Kids think everything's going to be the same forever. They don't have the ability to think past the next swim party." Felicia leaned forward. "Speaking of swimming, did you know they float in rafts and on inner tubes down Indian Creek? There's a park where people leave their vehicles, then they float downstream to another spot where someone drives them back. I was talking about floating the Boise River soon and Tank told me about the creek just outside town."

Angie smiled at the memories that came flooding in. She'd been a teenager the last time she floated the creek. Who had she been dating then? She couldn't remember his name but he was tall, dark, handsome, and the captain of the football team. The summer romance hadn't lasted past fall when she'd gone off to college, but he'd been fun.

"By the look on your face, you did know about the creek. You have to tell me the story behind that blush." Felicia crossed her leg under her and turned toward Angie, leaning back against the door.

"Just memories." Angie ignored the plea in her friend's voice and turned up the radio station. She hadn't had a country station set on her vehicle for years. Now that she'd returned home, she found the station she used to listen to was still going strong. "Tell me about the hiring. Any hiccups?"

"I'm still looking for your sous chef, but the college says they might have someone locally who would be interested. I guess they graduated a few years ago but haven't worked in the field." Felicia pulled out her phone. "Good news is I'm fully staffed for front of the house. We have our first training next week. I was hoping you'd come."

"That would be perfect. We could do a trial run on a few of the menu items the same day if you can get my kitchen staff in for a few hours before and we'll do a family meal together." Angie started humming along with the song playing on the radio. Everything was going to work out. She could feel it.

"So what was the old guy like? I've heard stories he could be mean." Felicia put her phone away after making a few notes on her calendar. "All fire and brimstone?"

"He was a little brusque at first. Dom liked him and you know he's a good judge of character." Angie thought about Dom stuck in the kitchen. Maybe they should run home first and let him out for a minute. She glanced at her watch. They had an appointment with the winery owners at two and if she made the detour, not only would they be late, they might miss the lunch serving. She sent positive thoughts to her dog and hoped he was sleeping rather than using her kitchen table leg as a chew toy.

"Dom is still a puppy. He hasn't had a chance to meet any truly evil people. Maybe he just likes everyone?" Felicia narrowed her eyes. "Where is he by the way? Did you get that fence installed and I didn't notice?"

"The crew's coming tomorrow but I decided to leave him in the kitchen. I put everything away." Including the clean jars she'd gotten ready for the failed strawberry jam that morning. "The doors are shut tight to the rest of the house."

"You like to live dangerously." Felicia grinned. "Anyway, I heard Mr. Moss killed a girl when they were young."

"Mrs. Potter's sister."

Felicia sat straight in her seat. "What? You're kidding, right?"

Angie told her what she'd heard from Mrs. Potter. "I'm sure it was just sour grapes. I mean, the Sheriff didn't say anything about Mr. Moss being a murderer. And besides, if he was, he'd be in jail, not running a goat farm."

"Maybe they isolated him because they couldn't prove it but he was shunned from all human contact." Felicia sat up straighter in her seat and Angie could see the wheels turning as she concocted a story.

"You read too much fiction. Especially stories about wounded heroes." Angie tapped the steering wheel with her fingers, thinking about how she might find out. "Maybe we should go visit the library and see if they have the old newspaper articles on file. If she was murdered, it should have made the paper."

"If she stubbed her toe on the sidewalk it would have made this paper. Have you read it yet? I can't believe the things they call news around here." Felicia grinned. "In California there would be too many murders to do an article about each one. Here, they do articles on the local festivals and new businesses opening in town. And by the way, a reporter named Doris will be calling you tomorrow. I pushed her off a day since we were so busy today."

"Why didn't you handle it? You're part owner too." Angie grumbled, her good mood disappearing as fast as it came. Burning the jam this morning had started off a run of bad luck. She needed to get home and try again so at least the day would end on a positive note.

"She wanted to interview the successful chef coming home." Felicia shrugged. "I thought it was a good angle. Oh, there's the winery. Isn't this location lovely?"

It definitely was lovely. The winery sat on the ridge of the canyon. The road they were on would wind its way down to the riverbank and cross the new bridge that had been constructed a few years ago. The old bridge had been turned into a walkway for bicyclists and pedestrians to get to the trails on the other side of the river.

The winery hadn't been here when she left. Or if it had, she hadn't thought about it as a place to go. Of course, she'd still been too young to drink when she went off to college. A fact that didn't seem to stop her from drinking too much, especially her freshman year. She'd straightened up during her first culinary class during sophomore year. When she'd found her calling.

She found a parking spot near the door. The lunch crowd had already left which would make it easier to talk business with the owners. Walking into the building, she was reminded of the Napa Valley wineries she'd visited the summer before they'd left California. Same lovely flowers planted in large half barrels. But here, a row of white rockers sat on the porch. "Kind of looks like Cracker Barrel, doesn't it?"

Felicia shot her a 'be quiet' look and pulled open the door. They entered the winery and walked toward the hostess table that doubled as a cashier station for the wine that was displayed throughout the room. Little signs on tables suggested food pairings to go along with the wines. Angie picked one up. "This is a great idea. We should think about a suggested wine or drink pairing with the entrees."

"Do we hire a sommelier? Or a sous chef? Because we can't afford both." Felicia nodded to the hostess stand. "Let's get a table. I'm starving."

The hostess led them to a small table covered with a white linen tablecloth. Empty wine glasses sparkled in the sunlight. The woman set up a small chalk board. "These are our lunch options. The soup and salad are always popular as is the grilled salmon sandwich. Take your time, Connie will be with you in a few minutes."

"I guess this saves money printing up menus." Angie picked up the menu board. "But you'd have to come in early every day and write out the different selections."

"Maybe that would be the sommelier's job. He would need something to occupy his time since we'll be paying him an arm and a leg to pair wines." Felicia smiled up at the woman pouring water in her glass. "I think Mr. Harris is expecting us. Can you let him know Angie Turner and Felicia Williams are here to see him?"

"Sure, hon. Can I get you something else to drink besides good old Snake River water?" The woman's eyes twinkled.

"Bring us the local white zinfandel. Glass only. We're on business." Angie was scanning the wine list that had several options from the winery as well as other local sources. "This is a good sign. It looks like they're used to working with other local businesses. There's even a beer that's brewed in northern Idaho. Did you know they grow hops there too?"

"I'm more of a domestic bottle girl." Felicia grinned at her. "You are such a food snob. I'm kind of embarrassed that I don't know all the stuff you do about food and beverages. You should write a blog. It would be good for the restaurant. You could spread the gospel on locally sourced food and how it's going to save the planet."

"You're funny." Angie sipped her water.

Felicia shook her head. "I'm dead serious. That's a great social media angle for The County Seat!"

"I heard you two were out here." A man approached their table. He leaned down and kissed Angie on the cheek. "It's so nice to see you again. We were all so saddened by the passing of your grandmother. The winery sent flowers, but you probably already knew that."

"Mr. Harris?" Felicia held out her hand. "I'm Felicia Williams and apparently you already know our chef/owner, Angie Turner."

"Ms. Williams, so nice to meet you. Call me Rob." He turned toward Angie and put a hand on her shoulder. "Of course I know Angie. She broke my heart at the senior prom."

# CHAPTER 5

Angie almost knocked over her water glass. The weird thing is she didn't know this guy. Seriously, how could she not remember who she went to prom with. Then memories started to flow back. "I didn't go to senior prom. I had a college tour that weekend back east."

Rob Harris held up his hands. "Exactly. You probably didn't realize this but I was planning on asking you to go with me. I had the whole scenario planned out in my head. Music, flowers, even a large bottle of Coke with plastic champagne glasses they sell at the party stores, even though I'm more of a Pepsi person, I still remember you loving your Coke."

"We went to school together?" Clearly this guy knew her and her inappropriate love of the too sweet soda. It was almost a guilty secret now a day. She kept a stash hidden in the bottom drawer of her fridge, just in case she had a craving. "I'm sorry, I don't quite remember."

He put his hand over his heart in fake dismay. "So you're not here to rekindle our fiery teenage love that never quite worked out for either of us?"

When neither she or Felicia responded, Rob pulled up a chair and sat next to the table. "I'm just kidding with you. I don't think you even knew I existed, but man, I did have a crush on you. As soon as you showed up sophomore year, I was your slave. Or could have been, if you ever talked to me."

"I was shy." Angie remembered arriving at River Vista High School that spring after her parents died. All she'd wanted was to wake up from the nightmare and be back in her canopy bed in Colorado. Instead, she wandered like a ghost through the halls and cooked with Nona at night. The only thing that kept her going was knowing that she'd be going off to college in a few years and she had to cherish every day she had with her grandmother. Especially since she hadn't given her folks that respect before they died.

"You were amazing." Rob grinned at the two women. "Anyway, enough of my teenage wounds. So you're opening up a dinner place in River Vista? Tell me about it."

Angie went through the concept, how she wanted to locally source all of the main proteins and most of the ingredients from the area. Seasonal and fresh. She hadn't worked through a winter menu, yet, but she imagined it full of soups and chowders unless she could find a local greenhouse that would grow her greens inside. When she paused, lost in thought about options, Felicia took over.

"And we'd love to feature your wines. Of course, we'll have some local microbrews on tap as well, and maybe some locally produced liqueurs, but I'm sure the wines will be the focus for the food pairings." She picked up the glass that the waitress had brought her while they were talking and sipped. She winked at Angie. "Maybe you could even help us choose the pairings?"

Rob chuckled. "Not sure that my girlfriend would be on board with me spending so much time over at your new place, especially since she runs the lunch restaurant here at the winery. That being said, we're excited about your new venture and would love to partner with you."

"That's wonderful." Angie held up her glass in a toast. "Felicia will handle all the ordering and I'd love to have you and your girlfriend attend opening night, my treat."

"Tasha and I will be there." Rob lowered his voice, scanning the room to see who could overhear. "Tough luck about Old Man Moss dying. I hear you were the last to see him alive."

"Actually, no. There were a lot of people still at the barn when I left. Including my realtor, Reana." Angie wondered where that particular piece of gossip was coming from. Ian and the Sheriff had been under the same assumption. "I guess the Sheriff just wanted to know what I was doing out there."

"The guy had more enemies in town than friends." He shrugged. "I hate to speak ill of the dead, but the guy was a tool. He hated everyone. My mom said your grandmother used to take the church visitation every month when his name came up. No one but her ever wanted to go visit, even if it got them in good with the big guy upstairs."

Angie remembered her grandmother doing visitations to different church members as part of her woman's group. Nona had tried to get her to go, but even when she talked her into driving, Angie had stayed outside in the car and waited. The memory made her smile. "She loved going visiting."

"She was an amazing woman. Everyone loved her." He looked at his watch. "Sorry, I've got another meeting. It was great to see you again Angie. And Felicia, I'm sure we'll talk soon. Call me tomorrow and we'll figure out what you need for your first order."

As he walked away, Felicia sank back into her chair. "That went better than I'd expected. When I'd called to set up the meeting, he was less than enthusiastic about partnering. Who else had a crush on you in high school that we can use?"

"How am I supposed to know? I didn't even remember Rob." Even now, she couldn't quite place the dark-haired, good looking man with any of the boys she'd remembered from her three years at River Vista High. She was going to have to review her yearbooks so she wouldn't seem rude the next time a former classmate came up and wanted to revisit the glory days. "I was a loner. I didn't have many friends and mostly, I just counted the days until I could get out of high school and back to what I'd considered home. Of course, I never did return, even after college."

"I'm on a Facebook page with my class. We chat all the time." Felicia took a bite of the sandwich they'd ordered before Rob had descended on their table. "This is good, but I don't think they are really focusing on their food."

Angie shook her head. The tomato soup had seemed a good choice, but the taste was flat. Definitely not made in the kitchen. She held up a card. "The menu is pretty limited. Mostly it looks like they are providing lunch just for people who drive out for a wine tasting. Although they will put a picnic basket together for you if you want to head to the river and eat there."

"That's a great idea." Felicia grabbed her notebook out of her purse. "Maybe we can steal it for The County Seat."

Angie pushed the soup away and tore off a bit of the French bread. "We'd have to advertise it as a BYOB. I don't think our alcohol license allows people to take wine off the premises for consumption." The picnic idea was a good one though. Maybe she could find some cheap baskets that they could afford to provide as well. So many ideas, and they only had a few weeks before opening night. She looked at Felicia's half-eaten sandwich. "Get that to go or hurry up. I've got to get you back to town and me home before Dom eats his way through the back door."

"He wouldn't do that, would he?" Felicia waved the waitress over for their check.

The young woman shook her head. "Sorry, Rob said your lunch was on him today. No charge."

"Well, wasn't that nice of him? Tell him thanks the next time you see him." Felicia stood, brushing crumbs off her lap. She followed Angie out to the car. "Wine list done. Now I just have to nail down the microbrew guy. Before you look at me like that, I had a guy lined up, but he bailed on me. Something about his licensing. So I went to this new guy who's been highly recommended, but he's been out of town. Don't worry, I have a backup plan in place in case we can't get this deal closed. But we'll be serving domestic beer for a few weeks."

"I guess we could open without a beer selection, but it's not ideal." Angie opened the car doors. As she looked past the winery down the road that lead to the cabin, she realized she could reach Mr. Moss's ranch from this side too. Maybe she'd bring Dom out for a walk this afternoon. If she was going to be asked about the guy's death, maybe she should know more about how he really died.

"Earth to Angie, what are you thinking about?" Felicia stared at her friend.

She started the car and pulled out of the driveway and away from the river canyon. "I think I'm taking Dom for a long walk this afternoon."

By the time she got Felicia back to the restaurant and drove the rest of the way home, she had started to worry that she'd really tested Dom's patience. When she opened the back door, he came bounding outside, ran to the patch of grass and did his business. Then he came and gave her loves. She peeked inside the kitchen and was surprised to see no major damage. "What a good boy you were."

Mabel squawked like she totally disagreed then scratched at the dirt in front of the garden again. "Not a fan, are you?" Angie asked the chicken, but got no response. The paper had been delivered and was in the small box attached to her mail box post. She and Dom walked out toward the road, with Angie checking to make sure there weren't any cars coming, then hurried back to the house. Dom went inside first and headed to his food and water bowls. Angie sat at the table and spread out the paper.

"Long-term Local Citizen Killed in Freak Accident." She read the headline aloud. Glancing through the article, the reporter said that the body had been found by an early morning hiker coming up the hill from the riverside park below. The article didn't mention that the police were investigating anyone. She looked at the small map showing the area where the body had been found. As she suspected this afternoon, the winery was just minutes away. When she looked up at Dom, the puppy was watching her closely. Maybe it was for Nona, or maybe she was just curious, but she made a decision. "Let's go see what we can find out."

It was one of the perfect June afternoons she'd remembered from her childhood. Warm, sunny, with a sky the color a painter could only imagine. Coming home to live after losing Nona and closing el pescado had been the right decision. Now, all she had to do was make The County Seat successful and she could stay. Dom barked out the window at a field full of bored Black Angus cows as they drove past.

"You told them." Angie glanced at him in the rear-view mirror and grinned at the happy look on her dog's face. She turned up the tunes and thought about the idea of murder. She wasn't a trained investigator, but just something in the way everyone apparently knew she'd been out to see Mr. Moss on Sunday made her uneasy. Besides, she was just taking her dog for a walk. If she happened to see where he fell, maybe she could confirm the paper's report that the death had just been an accident. That would make her feel better at least. *Sheriffs don't come knocking on your door when there's been an accident.*

She pushed the voice away as she drove by the empty winery parking lot. Apparently, they didn't get much traffic on weekdays. Even the dining room had been almost empty when they had lunch. Angie had assumed the crowd had already left, but maybe lunch times were just slow. Thankfully, she'd planned on opening only on weekends for the first couple months until they had their feet under them. Once the reservations started filling, she'd add a day or so during the week.

Angie angled the car down the winding road and just before the road crossed the bridge, she turned left into the park that was supported by the state parks department. Celebration Park was a great place for hiking, cycling, or even fishing. She'd hung out here on many nights with her high school gang, talking about what they were going to do once the graduation bell rang and they were released from their educational prisons. Had Rob Harris been one of that group? Of course, most of the kids talked about getting jobs or leaving town. Angie knew she wanted to go to school, but had no idea for what. General studies, her counselor had suggested, hinting that a major might find her while she tried different careers. The woman had been right.

She parked the car near the unmanned visitor center and went to the back door to click a leash on Dom and let him out. The center had a map of the hiking trails posted on the front of the building and she paused there, trying to determine where Mr. Moss's farm was located on the ridge. She ran a finger across the line indicating the path, then angled it down to where she stood. All the trails were named after native birds and the one she thought she wanted was named Red Hawk. She pulled Dom's leash tearing him away from his watching a bee perched on a wild flower and they started their walk.

The trail gently angled upward, but Angie could feel the grade increasing as they made their way away from the parking lot. Her throat tickled, making her wish she'd grabbed a bottle of water from the house. Next time, she thought as she pushed her hair out of her eyes. And she wished that she'd put on a baseball cap as well. She knew better than to come hiking unprepared, but then, she wasn't really hiking, was she?

Angie paused at a switchback in the trail to glance around. They were about halfway up the hill. Farther down the riverbank, the ridge broke off into a rock canyon wall instead of this hill that allowed them to hike to the top. Of course, rock climbers could probably make the top there, but they didn't have a hundred-pound St. Bernard on a leash. Dom sat next to her and nuzzled her hand. He was breathing hard as well.

"You can have some water as soon as we get back to the car." Angie scratched behind his ear. She kept a bottle of water and a bowl in the car for Dom, just in case. She glanced around one more time. What had she expected to find? All she saw was vegetation and the dirt trail leading farther up the hill. As she examined her surroundings, the sound of someone running down the trail made her focus above her.

Reana Whiting ran down the trail, alone. Or ran as fast as she could in a pair of stilettos. She was dressed in a red skirted suit that matched her red pumps. Her hair was disheveled and her face looked almost as red as the fabric in her clothes. She saw Angie and skidded to a stop, almost face planting forward when her shoe hit a patch of loose gravel.

"What are you doing out here?" Angie held Dom close. The woman was excited enough, she didn't need a large dog giving her the once over. "You really need to learn what casual means."

"What?" Reana brushed her hair back with her hands and then pulled on her skirt. "What do you mean?"

Angie noticed that her realtor had ignored the question she'd asked. She pointed at the woman's shoes and clothes. "Those aren't approved for hiking. Unless I missed the memo."

Reana paused, straightening her jacket as she apparently thought of what to say. "I should have waited to come down here after work. I just needed some time to think after hearing about Gerald, and this was the first place that came to mind. Then I started walking and before I knew it, I was on the ridge. Now, I'm late for a showing."

"I'm sorry about Mr. Moss. The two of you were friends?" Angie knew she was blocking the trail and with those shoes, Reana couldn't very well just move around her.

"Not really. I mean, he didn't like anyone. When I saw you up there Saturday—"

Angie interrupted. "Sunday. We saw each other Sunday."

"No, it was Saturday. I know it." She looked at her watch again, then stepped toward Angie. "Anyway, I really need to be going. I'm sure I'll see you soon."

Angie stepped aside and let the woman pass. She and Dom watched as Reana disappeared down the trail. As they returned to their own walk, Angie paused and peered downward, trying to see the parking lot. "I didn't see another car in the lot, did you boy?"

Dom didn't answer as he was too busy sniffing at pile of dirt.

"Never mind, let's go." Angie took two steps and then Dom froze. She pulled on his leash but he wouldn't budge. "What on earth is wrong with you?"

She knelt beside him and looked at his paws, wondering if he'd gotten a sticker. Nope, nothing. Then she heard a small whine. And she felt something on her back. She spun around and there was Precious, the baby goat, staring at her.

"Where did you come from?" She reached out her hand and the goat came and stood next to her, leaning in for what Angie thought of as a hug. Dom whimpered.

"It's okay, boy, she's just a baby." Angie stood and glanced around. No sign of any other goat. And she had no idea how to get to Moss Farm from the trail. She made a decision and picked up the little goat. "I'll get you home."

Precious bleated again. And this time, Angie saw a scrap of red fabric in the side of her mouth. Apparently Reana had been running from the goat and Precious had gotten a bite of the woman's suit. So where had Reana been? And why was Precious out here all alone?

Angie had too many questions, but the first thing she needed to do was get the lost goat back to its mother.

She put the goat in the back of the crossover behind the dog barrier. Then she let Dom in the back seat. He stared at the goat, now in his car, and whined again.

"Hold on, it's not far to the farm." She got back on the road and was relieved when both Dom and Precious laid down for the ride. Her cell rang and she picked up using the car's Bluetooth.

"What are you doing? Do you have time to talk about schedules?" Felicia's voice boomed through the car. Dom sat up, looked around, then laid back down, apparently convinced his friend wasn't actually close by.

"I'm taking a goat back to Moss Farm. Let me call you when I'm home."

Instead of a response, all Angie got was silence. Maybe cell service was spotty out here.

"Hello? Are you there?" Angie turned onto the road where the farm sat.

"I'm here. I'm not sure I want to ask, but why do you have a goat?"

Angie caught a glimpse of Precious in the cargo hold. Her lips curved into a smile. "Long story. I'll call you back when I get home."

She found the farm, but when she drove into the driveway, there were no cars near the barn and the house appeared to be locked tight. She walked over to the barn where a sheet of paper flapped in the wind. She got out of the car and went over to read the sign. MILKING IS AT FIVE AM AND FIVE PM. IF YOU ARE HERE OTHER THAN THOSE TIMES, YOU ARE TRESPASSING. PLEASE CALL THIS NUMBER WITH ANY QUESTIONS. 208-922-4111.

Angie hurried back to her car and grabbed the phone. When she dialed the number, she got one of those voice mails that had a robotic response. She left her name and number and added, "It's an emergency!" at the end.

She looked back at Dom who looked hopeful that they might be dropping the offending goat off where it belonged. She reached back and scratched his ear. "Sorry buddy, we can't just leave her alone here. Something might happen to her."

The look in Dom's eyes made her think he wasn't too sure that wouldn't be the best idea but when Angie started up the car, he sighed and laid his head on the seat. Precious was curled into a ball sleeping, apparently happy with her first car ride.

What on earth was she getting into? Angie headed toward home and some semblance of normalcy.

# CHAPTER 6

Precious went into the small back yard and went straight to trimming down the grass Angie hadn't mowed that week. After she went into the house and got the goat a water dish, she scanned the fencing and decided that it would be good enough to keep the baby goat inside. She didn't leave Dom out alone in the fenced yard as the picket fence was way too short and not very sturdy in places. With his weight, he could lean on sections and break it down. Precious couldn't weigh more than five to ten pounds.

She went into the kitchen and started taking out fish and veggies for dinner. She wanted to try out a new recipe that she might include on the opening menu, but not until she tried several versions herself. She hit speaker on her cell and called Felicia while she worked.

"What's up? Did you ditch the goat?"

She rinsed off the peppers and small summer squash. Turning off the water, she sighed. "Actually no. I've called someone but until he or she calls me back, I guess I'm hosting a sleep over. The sign said they milked at five. Maybe someone will call me then."

"How do you know it's even Old Man Moss's goat? It could be wild."

Angie stared out the kitchen window at the small black baby wandering through her back yard. "No, I met Precious on Sunday. It's the same goat. I just wonder where her mom is?"

"Maybe she got out too?" Felicia rustled papers. "Anyway I believe I've hired three main servers, one backup, and a bartender. You have all the kitchen staff hired, right?"

"I'm missing a sous chef still. Weren't you looking into that with the college?" Angie peeled a carrot, still watching the goat. This felt right. This felt comfortable.

She watched as Precious ran up to the side of the yard and vaulted right over the short fence. "Crap, hold on…"

Angie ran outside and scooped up Precious who was now checking out Mabel and eating the chicken's feed. The goat turned toward her and bleated. "You are supposed to stay in the yard."

She glanced around. The barn hadn't had a main door for years, there was no way to keep the goat closed up there. She saw Dom's chain. She'd have to shorten one of his collars but if she could get one small enough to stay on Precious, it might work.

Angie took the goat into the kitchen and closed all the doors before sitting her down on the floor. Dom whined. "It's okay, she'll only be in here for a while."

"Are you talking to me? I can barely hear you." Felicia's voice came over the speaker.

Angie stood near the phone, digging through what Nona had called the junk drawer. And then she found it. One of the cat collars. Nona's last cat had died a few weeks before she had. Angie thought it had known her master was leaving this plane of existence. "Sorry, I have an escape artist here. Can I call you later?"

"Sure. I'll follow up with the college and call you tonight." Felicia paused. "Take a picture of the new addition."

"I'm not keeping her," Angie called out, but then she realized Felicia had already ended the call.

She got the cat collar on the goat, then took her back out to the yard and hooked her up to the clothes line. Nona had set up a tether for her indoor cat that ran the back side of the yard. Angie moved the water dish, then went into the barn and got a large cup of the feed she gave Mabel. Then she climbed the porch to the back door.

Precious tried to follow and tested her lead. When she realized she couldn't go any further, she bleated out her frustration.

Angie paused at the door watching the baby struggle, then give up and lie down, still munching on grass. Satisfied that the goat was going to stay put, at least for a while, Angie went back to her kitchen and made dinner. Actually, she made three dinners. Each one with a little different mixture of vegetables and a different sear on the fish. She took pictures of each, finished making notes on the preparation, then sat down to judge the three.

She heard a car's tires in the gravel of her driveway just as she picked up her fork.

Standing, she went to the door to see who was visiting. If it was Felicia, she could help choose the version that would go on the menu. If any.

Angie recognized the wagon immediately. Ian McNeal got out of the front seat and went to the back, pulling out a burlap bag of some sort of feed. He came up to the porch and dropped it off near her front door. "I can put this in the garage if you'd like."

"Until I find out what is in the bag, right there is fine. What are you doing here?" She eyed him suspiciously.

Instead of answering, he walked over to the gate and called to Precious. "Hey pretty girl. How do you like your new digs? Smart idea on the leash. That girl's a Houdini."

"You know Precious? Can you take her back to the farm?" Hope swelled in Angie's throat. Not that she didn't like the little thing, she just didn't have time.

Ian turned and leaned on the gate, watching her. "We found her mother dead this morning. We thought the coyote had taken Precious to the hills for dinner. Until I got your message, that is."

"The poor little thing, she must have been scared and ran away." Angie glanced over at the orphaned goat. She pushed the tears away. "Wait, you said you got my message? You're running Moss Farm?"

"I'm managing the dairy until the next of kin can be informed and get someone here. Allen, he asked me to step in." He pointed to the bag of feed. "That should get you through at least a couple months. When the new owner comes in, I'll tell him that you're fostering Precious."

Angie's hands landed on her hips. "Who said I was fostering her? I have a life. I have a restaurant to open. I don't have time…"

"Being seen as part of the community and willing to help out when needed will go a long way towards paving good relationships with the farmers you'll want as suppliers. I think your finding Precious might have just saved you a lot of headache." He pulled out his cell and snapped a picture of the baby goat.

"What are you doing now?" Angie leaned on the side of the porch watching him. She knew she'd lost this battle. And if Ian was right and it made her look good in the supplier's eyes, well, she could deal with one little goat. Dom on the other hand was going to pout for days.

He held up the phone and grinned. "Introducing you to the group. I'll send out that email to the members tonight with a request to email you with any hints on how to raise a baby goat. It will be a good introduction to the guys. Come by the market on Saturday and I'll introduce you around."

"All I had to do to get in your good graces was take in an orphaned goat?" Angie couldn't believe this was the same man who'd basically tried to banish her from the market less than a week ago.

"I may have been overly negative at our first meeting. You seem like you're not a flake. That's the right term, isn't it? Besides, Allen told me about your grandmother. Apparently, you do have roots in the community." He turned to go, but then stopped. "One more question. Where did you find her? I'll send some guys out to check the fences if we can pinpoint where she got out."

"I was walking Dom down at Celebration Park. We took the Red Hawk trail and she was coming down as ..." She paused wondering if she should mention Reana's weird behavior. She decided it wasn't relevant to the story so she skipped that part. "We were going up," she concluded.

Ian walked toward her and leaned his arms on the porch railing. "That's strange. The Red Hawk trail is on the far side of the farm from the barn. I wonder if she followed someone or another animal toward the trail. Did she look hurt at all?"

Angie had checked Precious out for injuries when she put her in the back of the car. "I don't think so. Do you think I should take her to the vet and get her checked out?"

He turned back toward the yard where Precious was standing still, then jumping straight up, then standing still again and repeating the process. "Unless you start seeing her acting lethargic or looks like she's in pain, she looks fine now."

"Okay then. How much of this food do I give her and when?"

Ian went through feeding instructions with her. It seemed simple enough. She could feed Precious twice a day, along with Mabel. Keep her bowl full of fresh water. And check the line to make sure she didn't tangle herself in the leash. "You're probably going to need a stronger collar soon, just get her a large dog collar down at the hardware store. Or if you're in Boise, you could go to the pet store. I'll come out and do her shots next week."

"How long do you think it's going to take to find one of Mr. Moss's relatives?" Angie followed him to his car as he made to go.

"Who knows? Allen's trying to go through the house to see if he can find an address book, but apparently Gerald was a bit of a hoarder. There are Ding Dong boxes stacked everywhere, filled with receipts and more." Ian climbed into the car. "I appreciate you taking her in. I won't forget this, I promise."

And with that, he drove away. When Angie went back to the kitchen her dinner and the two alternates were cold. She grabbed a plate and put it into the microwave to heat as she watched Precious dancing in the early evening light. What where the odds she just got one more pet to add to her small family?

But you'll be in good with the community. Ian's words came back to her. Well, at least he was warming to her. What was the saying, no good deed goes unpunished? She sat down to make notes on the dishes and to eat, hoping her gut wasn't right this time.

After dinner, she called Felicia back and they spent the rest of the night going over the plans for next week's family meal. Which would be only part of the family unless she got a sous chef before the staff training day. When Angie fell into bed, exhausted, she expected sleep to come easily. Instead, she kept thinking about goats and coyotes and Old Man Moss talking about the people who wanted his farm.

She sat up. Why had Reana been so insistent that she'd been seen on Saturday at the farm? Angie grabbed her phone and typed in a few notes into her text program. She had a few questions for the fashionable real estate expert. And this time, she was going to get honest answers.

Sleep finally came, but when she woke the next morning, she felt groggy. Heading downstairs to start coffee, she glanced out the window. Precious was staring back at her from the end of her leash in the backyard. She glanced longingly at the slowly dripping pot and gave in. "I'm coming."

She'd taken the bag of feed out to the barn after Ian had left. Slipping on her crocs, she made her way to the barn, and proceeded to get food for both Mabel and Precious. Dom was at her heels. After dumping out the grain for both, she turned on the water faucet near the fence and took the hose over to refill the goat's water. While she was there, she refreshed the bird bath that sat outside the fence. Wasn't she becoming the gentlewoman farmer? Glancing at her herb garden, she sprayed the plants quickly, then turned off the water. She'd come back later and set the irrigation water she got weekly from the ditch that ran the back of the property. Her time started at nine and people got touchy if you took your share too early.

She found Dom exploring back behind the barn. Far enough away from the goat that he couldn't see the offending creature in his yard. Angie called him back. She needed to get working on the final menu and determine what she needed to find Saturday at the farmers' market to demo the dishes for the new crew. And she needed coffee.

Dom came bounding towards her, only giving Precious one quick look to make sure she was still confined in the yard, before following Angie into the house. The coffee was done so she poured a cup and stood at the counter, sipping until she felt more awake. "And I gave up a perfectly good apartment for this life."

Dom circled on his bed and flopped into it as if to say, *but what about me*?

She had to admit, even with the addition of a goat to worry about and feed, she liked this life better. No one banged on the wall when she played music. No one came knocking at her door at two in the morning because they had the wrong floor. And she owned the place. Or she had owned it before she took out the loan to open the restaurant. She pushed the thought away with one of her Nona's favorite sayings: "Scared money never wins."

A knock came to her door. Surprised since she hadn't heard a car pull up, she swung the door open to see Mrs. Potter on her porch, watching Precious in the back yard. Angie held the screen door open wide. "Good morning. Do you want some coffee?"

"That would be lovely." Mrs. Potter slowly made her way into the kitchen and sank into one of the chairs at the table with a sigh. "That walk shouldn't be so hard. I can't tell you the number of times I came over here to have coffee with your grandmother. Then I'd go home and clean my house. Today, I'm probably going to have to take a nap."

Angie poured coffee then got some shortbread cookies she'd baked to have with the strawberry jam that burned yesterday during the sheriff's visit. She joined her neighbor at the table. "I'm glad you decided to make the trip."

"You have a new pet." Mrs. Potter picked up a cookie with her tanned and wrinkled hand and waved it at Angie. "I hope you're not thinking of building a goat herd. They're unpredictable creatures. I don't know anyone who had more than one who liked taking care of them. Well, except Moss. Of course, he'd rather be with animals that matched his own personality. The old goat, himself."

Angie hid her smile behind her coffee cup. "So what happened between the two of you?"

"Besides Sophia?" She shook her head. "Nothing, but I don't like to talk about her. It's all so painful."

"Did you and Nona grow up with Mr. Moss?" Angie knew that her grandmother had gone to school with Mrs. Potter. Then her husband had bought the farm next door when Nona and Grandpa took over the farm from her parents who went back to Scandinavia. She'd heard this story many times when the women were sitting around drinking wine and reminiscing. Nona's attachment to the land and the community was one reason Angie had decided to come home. To continue the tradition.

"He went to school with us. Always the troublemaker." A faraway look crossed over Mrs. Potter's face. "Everyone thought he was dangerous and exciting. And the man was handsome, I'll give him that. But I knew he was trouble. When he started hanging out with Sophia, I tried to talk her out of going with him. She was just a kid. So full of life, so happy. They were like night and day."

Angie took a cookie and waited. Sometimes stories came out even when you didn't want to talk.

"Margaret and I graduated the same year as Moss. He went off to the army and I married Mr. Potter. Of course, Margaret beat me to the altar by a full month. Your Nona, she was a competitive sort." Mrs. Potter smiled at the memory. "We started our lives. Sophia was still in school. She didn't tell me they were pen pals. I found his letters to her afterwards. Then a week after she graduated, she disappeared."

When Mrs. Potter didn't continue, Angie picked up the thread. "Disappeared? How?"

Before she could answer, a knock came to the back door. Before Angie could even stand, Erica Potter stuck her head inside.

"There you are, Grandma." Relief filled the young woman's face as she strolled into the kitchen. "I've been at the house for ten minutes looking all over for you. You have a doctor appointment in Boise this morning. We've got to go."

Mrs. Potter turned and started out of her chair. "That's on Tuesday. Today's just…" She paused, trying to remember the day of the week. "I went to bridge yesterday with Delores and that would make today Tuesday." She sighed.

"Yep, all day. You have a few minutes to get changed, but we really have to get a move on." Erica looked down at the table. "Shortbread, my favorite. Can I have a few for the road?"

"Sure, let me get you a bag." Angie started to stand but Erica waved her off.

"Two's enough. If I have more than that, I won't be able to stop. Sugar is the devil." She patted her hips. "And goes right to my hips. I'll have to run tonight just after the two."

"Sorry to leave you," Mrs. Potter patted Angie's shoulder. "We'll talk later. Just know that karma has a way of cleaning all slates."

Angie watched as Erica put an arm around her grandmother and helped her out of the house. She thought of Nona's last years and kicked herself for not being here with her. She should have stayed in Boise; that way she would be available to help out. Instead, Nona had hired a local girl who'd lived with her as a companion and a nurse's aide. Her name had been Tina and she'd been lovely. She'd moved on to another live-in job right after Nona passed, but she'd been kind to Angie at the funeral.

*Can't change the past.* Nona's voice sounded in her head. But something about the story Mrs. Potter had been telling made her wonder if the past had caught up with Gerald Moss on that rocky hiking trail. Something had.

She glanced at her clock. She needed to get a move on if she was going to get to the realtor's office close to opening. She wanted to talk to Reana and see what exactly she'd been doing out on that trail in heels the day before. And why she didn't want people to know she'd been out at the farm on Sunday.

*This isn't your problem.*

The words echoed in her mind, bringing her up short for a minute. Then she shook them away. She looked at the framed picture of her grandmother and her that she'd hung over the table. Nona would want her to help her friend. "It may not be my problem, but I'm going to find out what happened to the man. He deserves someone on his side."

# CHAPTER 7

Like she suspected, Reana Whiting was sitting at her desk promptly at ten when Angie came through the door. She'd told Angie when the best time to reach her in the office when they were looking for buildings for the restaurant. She looked up with a big smile when she heard the door open, and that smile wavered just a bit when Angie walked through the door.

"What's up? I'm sure you're not in the market for another property." Reana didn't stand, but motioned Angie into one of her visitor chairs. She took her hand off the modem and focused on her visitor.

"You're right. I can't even think about doing something else until The County Seat is up and running. Some chef owners jump into two or more properties at the same time. I'm not that brave." Angie settled into the chair, hoping she sounded casual.

"I'd say you were smart. What's the stats on new businesses? How many go out of business in the first year, eighty percent? Believe me, I've thought of branching out on my own, but I have the best of both worlds. I run my own listings and rent a spot out of the agency here. They bring in the big franchise name and I get the benefit." She leaned back in her chair. "But you didn't come to discuss the pros and cons of small business development. What's on your mind?"

Angie decided to be blunt. "Why were you out on the trail yesterday? I know you weren't hiking, not in those shoes."

A coy look came over Reana's face. "You're a curious one, aren't you? You know what they say about curiosity and cats. Maybe the same could be said for chefs."

"Look, I'm just wondering why you were there?"

Reana started playing with her pen. "You're right, I didn't plan on ruining a perfectly good pair of Jimmy Choos on a dirt hiking trail. And when that goat attacked me, she ripped a piece of fabric from my skirt. That suit was vintage Chanel. If I could find the little monster, I'd tan her hide and make me a new purse. Goat purses, it could be the new fashion trend. At least out here."

"I don't think Precious attacked you. I think she was lost and looking for someone to take her home." Angie didn't mention the goat was safe at her house. Who knew if Reana's revenge plans were only talk. "Anyway, why were you up there?"

Reana looked around. "I gave Gerald my personal cell phone on Sunday when I was there. He told me he was thinking about selling, finally, and I didn't want him talking to anyone else. I was surprised to find you sitting with him all chummy drinking coffee when I came to visit. He never has guests. I got worried that you were trying to run a deal without me."

"Wait, you thought I wanted to buy the farm?" Angie shook her head. "What would I want with a goat dairy?"

"Who knows what you foodie types want? Besides, you came from California. Those guys are always here buying up property cheap and building things we don't need." Reana rubbed her face. "Okay, so I overreacted. I left him my phone and when I found out he'd died, well, I went looking to see if I could find it on the trail where he fell."

"That was where he fell? Why would he be out there, that's the very edge of the farm?" Angie wondered if Sheriff Brown had considered this as odd as she did.

"Maybe he was chasing that stupid goat?" Reana shrugged. "All I know is now I'm out a phone and it was one of those nice iPhones too. And I'm going to have to wait until the next of kin shows up and start the relationship building all over again."

"Maybe the phone is in the house. Have you asked the sheriff?" She could almost buy Reana's story. Her cell phone had been pricey but the carrier she used pretended like it was just another payment. Until something happened to the first one.

Her computer alarm chimed and Reana turned to look at the display. "Sorry, I have to go. I'm in charge of the open house out at the new subdivision. Hopefully we'll get some qualified buyers looking today. Last weekend, I sat out there alone all Saturday with no bites. That's one of the reasons I was so excited to get Gerald's call about selling. It's a hard business."

As Angie left the realty office, she glanced down Main Street to her building. Workers were out front painting and installing signage. She might as well pop in and see how things were going. Besides, she needed to make sure her kitchen box had been unpacked. She'd brought all the stuff they'd used at el pescado but she knew she needed to go shopping for a few odds and ends this week. She'd get her list done today and head out tomorrow for the supply store in Boise. Maybe she and Felicia could stop for lunch too and make a day of it, if her friend didn't have other plans.

She found Felicia in the bar area, boxes of wine and other liqueurs stacked around her. "Your friend Rob did us right. He sent over enough supply for a month or two. And he hooked me up with a beer distributor who works with several local microbrews. We're all set. Now I just have to get it unpacked. Do you want to help?"

"I thought I'd run through the kitchen and make a list of what else we'll need. Then I can come help you finish up." She leaned on the dark wood bar they'd rescued from the Mexican restaurant that had been in the location before. She glanced around the freshly painted dining room. "It's starting to feel like home here."

Felicia handed her a bottle of water from the bar fridge. Cracking her own open, she hopped up on the counter and took a swig. "I like it. I think I like it better than our first venture. This feels more authentic. More like a place where you sit down for dinner and talk. The other place always felt stuffy to me. Like everyone was showing up to show off. This feels like home." She echoed Angie's words. "Why are you in town? I thought you were menu planning today."

She told her friend about the visit from Mrs. Potter and the one with Reana she'd just finished. "I don't know why this is bugging me so much, but I think there's more to Mr. Moss's death than just an accident. He shouldn't have even been near that part of the ridge. Not at night."

"What does your friend the sheriff say?"

"He's not my friend, and honestly, he didn't say much. Mostly he just asked me questions on why I was even out there. Luckily Ian was there to back up what I told him."

Felicia narrowed her eyes. "I wonder…"

"What?" Angie finished off her water bottle and threw it in the recycling can they had in the middle of the area.

"Doesn't it seem odd to you that he didn't just tell the sheriff that when he agreed to come out to the farm to interview you? It seems like that would have just been a phone call, especially if his good friend Ian had already told him why you were there." Felicia shrugged. "All I know about police procedure is what I see on television. So I could be wrong. It's just a little weird."

As Angie unpacked the last of the boxes from the kitchen, making lists of what she needed and another column with what she wanted if there was enough money, she thought about Felicia's statement. It *was* odd that Ian had come out to the farm with the sheriff. Of course, his response that the guy wasn't good with people kind of made sense, but wasn't that an elected position here in town? He would have to talk to people sometime.

By one, she'd gotten all the boxes out of the kitchen area and all of the pans and utensils unpacked. She'd moved a few of the boxes into the dining room since they held linens and she'd been surprised at the amount of dinnerware they had collected over the five years.

"We may not need to buy new dishes." Angie carried a plate into the dining room, then stopped when she saw Felicia wasn't alone. Kirk Hanley leaned against the bar, the stereotypical version of a cowboy, chatting up her friend. They turned to look at Angie when she entered. "Sorry, I didn't realize you had company."

"This is Kirk. I met him at the Cherry Festival last weekend." Felicia put a hand on his chambray shirt. "Kirk, this is my friend, Angie."

"We've already met. How's the pup of yours doing?" Kirk stood and took a step away from the bar and distanced himself from Felicia as well.

Angie could see the confusion in her friend's face as she watched the man. "Dom's great. I've got an appointment next week to bring him in for his booster shots." She turned to Felicia. "Kirk actually owns some property out by the farm. Dom and I ran into him while we were walking."

"Oh," Felicia took a breath. "I didn't know you were a vet."

"A guy's got to have some secrets." He tipped his hat. "Ladies, I'll see you around." Then he walked out of the restaurant.

They watched him leave, then Angie came out of the doorway and sat the dish on the bar. "That was awkward."

"You're telling me. Before you came in he was all flirty. I thought he was going to ask me out but then he turned to ice as soon as he saw you." Felicia stared out the window. "Did he ask you out when you met?"

"No. I've only talked to him that one time. Maybe he took something I said wrong." Angie rubbed a spot off the plate's surface. "I'm definitely not interested in the guy. Besides, I'm not ready to date yet. Todd and I just broke up."

"You and Todd were over years ago. I think you missed the memo." Felicia watched out the plate glass windows onto the street. "How old do you think he is?"

"I'll check the year he graduated veterinarian school when I take Dom in next week." Angie picked up the plate. "I think we should use these until we grow out of the set. We have a lot of pieces. We might just have to fill in some holes."

"I doubt we can find somewhere that sells replacements, but we could get lucky." Felicia turned the plate around to look at the watermark at the bottom. "I'll do some research and get you numbers."

"That will work. Do you want to go to Boise with me tomorrow? I'm visiting the restaurant supply house and getting some new pans and odds and ends." Angie pointed to the plate. "Bring that and what you think we need additionally for front of house. I'd like to make this our last shopping trip except for food before we open."

Felicia checked her phone. "Works for me as long as we go after eleven. The plumbing inspector is supposed to be here at eight and I'm not sure how long he'll take. The office said to expect at least two hours."

"Eleven will be fine. We can start at Canyon Creek for lunch. I've been dying to eat there since we moved here." Angie glanced at her watch. "I better get home and check on Dom and Precious."

"Did you bring me pictures?" Felicia stepped closer.

"I'm not keeping her, so no, I don't have pictures." Angie pulled her tote over her head and settled it on her hip, stuffing her notebook inside as she did. "Ian says her mother was killed by coyotes. I hope I don't have any sniffing around the farm."

"I think you would have heard them." Her friend walked with her to the door. "You've seen a lot of Ian lately."

"Don't go there. I told you, I'm not interested in dating." She opened the door to the empty sidewalk. "The sign looks amazing."

"Thanks. They did a great job." Felicia stared up at the old west themed wooden sign proclaiming The County Seat in carved and stained letters. "Don't let me forget to get an open hours sign tomorrow. Now that we have a name, people are going to start showing up like flies, wanting to be fed."

"I hope that's true." She waved at her friend and started toward the parking lot where she'd left her crossover.

"Hey, Angie?" Felicia called after her.

She stopped just before she went around the corner. "What?"

"You told me you weren't interested, but I wonder if you've told him you're not?" Felicia waved and turned back into the restaurant. "See you tomorrow."

Angie stood frozen to the ground. She hadn't mentioned this to Ian because, well, she didn't know if she was interested in him as more than just the farmers' market guy. Okay, so that was a bald-faced lie, but she really hadn't thought of him that way. Or she had, but she hadn't thought of the two of them together. Not really.

The thought haunted her all the way home. When she arrived at her house, Ian's little wagon sat near the barn. She got out and looked around, finally finding him sitting in the yard with Precious on his lap. Standing by the gate, she stared at him. "What are you doing here?"

"Waiting for you. I need to talk to you about your goat cheese order." He pointed to the door. "You might want to let your dog out first. He's been going crazy since I pulled up."

"He probably heard the car and thought we had a prowler." Angie went and unlocked the back door, stepping to the side so Dom wouldn't knock her over in his rush to get outside to slay the dragon he expected.

When he got to the fence, he froze, staring at Ian and the goat. Finally, he lifted his leg and relieved himself on the post, turned his back on the offending site and went back to Angie where he flopped next to her leg and leaned in. Point made.

Angie reached down and scratched his head. "Why don't you come in for some coffee or a cold drink? I made a cherry crumble last night too, if you're interested."

"That would be lovely. Do you have any hot tea? I can't seem to break my habit and drink that coffee you all are so in love with. You should see the odd looks I get when I'm dining with some of members of the coalition." He moved Precious off his lap and stood brushing the dirt and grass off his jeans. The goat bleated once, but then went to get a drink of water.

"She likes you." Angie commented. "You should take her home with you."

"I live in an apartment over my office in town. I don't think they'd appreciate me walking a goat around the streets of River Vista." He held the door open for her.

"I'm sure they've seen odder things." Angie smiled at the image. "I would have thought you would have a small, organic farm, being a true believer and all."

"Do I hear a touch of sarcasm in your voice?" He sat at the table and gave his attention to Dom. "Be careful, I haven't sent out that email to the members yet."

"Idle threats don't bother me." She put a kettle on for his tea and plated up some crumble. "I think I have some vanilla bean ice cream if you want me to heat this up for you."

"You are a charmer, at least with your food, aren't you? That would be great if it's not a bother." He stood. "Can I use your facilities to wash up?"

"Sure. First door on your left." She focused on dishing up the dessert, then formulated a way to get her questions answered without looking like she was grilling him. Maybe it might even just seem like conversation. All of their encounters so far had been strange and stilted, why should this one be any different?

The kettle started to whistle and she poured two cups of water and put them on the table along with a basket filled with an assortment of teas. She grabbed the honey pot and quickly sliced a lemon. She got out a small pitcher for milk, but she'd wait until he got back to ask his preference. She'd just finished scooping the ice cream on the cobbler when he returned to the kitchen.

"Thanks for letting me wash up. Between Precious and Dom, I was feeling a little gamey. I have to go set up the milking in a bit and then the crew's working on the soft cheese for the week so I wanted to get your order in now." He pulled out a notebook and sat back down at the table. Glancing at the basket, he put the notebook and pen down riffled through until he found a tea bag he wanted. He held it up like a trophy. "You really are a surprise. I haven't had this brand since I left England before college."

"I had it on a vacation, liked the taste and ordered a few boxes for home." She watched as he unwrapped the tea bag. "Do you want milk?"

"What?" He looked a little dazed. "Actually, I've stopped taking milk in my tea. It makes it a little more acceptable in local circles."

"I won't tell." When he didn't look up, she shrugged and sat next to him, grabbing an English breakfast tea and drizzling honey into the hot water. "So you're from England?"

"My mom and I lived there for most of my childhood. I was a youthful indiscretion and rather than marry the guy, Mom took off for England. I felt like an outsider there, but when I moved back to the States, it was worse." He sipped his tea, then stared at the cup. "You sure you didn't doctor the tea? I don't think I've told anyone that story for a long time."

"No truth serum here. Did your mom move back with you?" She let a lemon slice float on the top, then let the drink steep and picked up a fork. The cherry cobbler was perfect. The cherries, just a little tart to set off the ice cream. If she'd just drizzled some dark chocolate over the top, the dessert would be ready for the menu.

"You look like you're enjoying that a little too much." Ignoring her question, he smiled at her and the implication behind his words caused her face to heat.

"So, when will I get the cheese if they're making it tonight?" She tried to change the subject. Heat filled her body like she was about to spontaneously combust. She just hoped her face wasn't as red as it felt. Thankfully, he followed her cue.

"Monday, if that works. I can have someone run it over here as soon as we get clearance from the commission. They're coming in to inspect just to make sure we haven't changed anything in the last couple of weeks. I am beginning to understand why Gerald was so upset with Mildred. That woman can be a tiger." He picked up his fork and took a large bite of the crumble. "If everything you make tastes like this, I'm going to be a regular customer for The County Seat."

"We aim to please." She tilted her head down so he wouldn't see her smile. She liked feeding people. She liked good food. There was nothing unusual about a man with bright green eyes sitting at her table eating dessert. Just because he looked like he could have walked off the cover of one of those time travel books Felicia loved so much, didn't mean she had feelings for the guy.

Of course, there could be worse things for her to be thinking about right now.

# CHAPTER 8

By the time Ian left, dusk was beginning to settle around the farm house. He'd helped her clean up their dishes after several cups of tea, had gone outside with her to feed Precious and Mabel, all the time talking about the farmers' market, his vision for the area, and why he believed in developing communities.

They had sat on the porch for a long time talking about the effect community gardens had on the health of the poor. His facts were remarkably solid but Angie knew in the River Vista area, the guy would be called a flaming liberal, except for the fact he'd helped out so many people that he'd gained their trust. Which was one reason he'd been asked to manage Moss Farm until an heir was identified.

She watched him pull out of her driveway, heading the little car toward the farm to finalize the milking and check on the cheese making. "I wonder when he sleeps?"

Dom looked up at her, apparently surprised that she was already talking about bedtime. He nuzzled her hand.

"I know. You and I are the only two that haven't eaten dinner yet." She walked toward the porch, Dom padding softly by her side. He was growing taller and bigger every day. Or at least it seemed that way. In the kitchen, after she'd fed Dom, she glanced through her fridge and pulled out a steak. She grabbed some fingerling potatoes, a red onion, and a couple of green chilis she'd picked up at a roadside stand a few days ago. Steak and roasted potatoes could be a menu addition but she needed another element. Her gaze fell on the turnips that Mrs. Potter had given her from her garden and decided to make a puree.

The dish formulated in her head, she went to cooking.

As she was taking pictures and finishing her notes for the recipe binder, her phone rang. Glancing at the display, she put the call on speaker. "Hey Felicia. What's going on?"

"I wanted to tell you that I was right about Kirk wanting to ask me out. I ran into him at the grocery store just now and he asked me to dinner." Felicia's words bubbled out of the phone.

"So where are you going?"

A clank came over the phone. "What do you mean? I'm right here."

"No, where are you going to dinner?" Sometimes her friend could be cast as the ditzy blonde, but typically, it was when her mind was otherwise occupied.

"Oh, I didn't say yes. I'm not sure I'm interested." Felicia grumbled something Angie couldn't hear. "This stove in the apartment needs to be replaced. One of the burners isn't working at all."

"You could use the kitchen downstairs until we open." Angie sat her pen down. "Or we could go looking for a new stove tomorrow when we're in town. I thought you were interested in the guy."

"I like the second option better. I don't want to be hanging around the restaurant when I'm not working. It will feel, well, like work." Felicia sighed. "And I was interested until that thing today. If you can scare him off like that, I don't know if I want to bother. I wonder why you scare him so bad."

"Who says I do?" Angie sliced the steak, looking at the cut to check the level of doneness and made another note before she popped it in her mouth.

"He does. He says you're intimidating. And he's just shy."

Angie choked on the bite of meat she'd just taken. When she got control of herself, she focused back on the phone. "I'm intimidating? To who? Small children?"

Felicia laughed. "I knew you'd get a kick out of what he said. But it bothers me. You only met this guy once, right?"

"We had maybe a five-minute conversation out on the road last week. He didn't seem scared of me then." Angie gestured to Dom to go lie on his bed as he was too focused on the steak dinner.

"That's what bothers me. I think he's lying, but I'm not sure what about. I don't think the guy is intimidated by anyone and certainly not shy."

That had been the impression Angie had of the local vet too. Friendly, confident, and easy to get along with. This other guy they'd met today was secretive and seemed to be scared of something. But what? "Hey, did he say anything else besides asking you out and telling you what an ogre I was?"

"One thing. He made it sound like his crops were coming in soon and he'd have a lot of money to burn." Felicia laughed. "Like that makes any difference to me. I'm not looking for a sugar daddy. I think that's another reason I'm not sure I want to go out with him. He's cute but seems locked in this patriarchal paradigm. Can you imagine me taking orders from anyone?"

They said their goodbyes and Angie went back to her dinner. She hadn't eaten a quiet meal without an interruption for a couple nights. It was beginning to annoy her.

Dom had looked up hopefully when she set the phone down.

"No begging, it doesn't become a dog of your stature." Angie laughed as he plopped his head down and covered his eyes with his front paws. Apparently Dom agreed with her assessment.

Cleaning up the kitchen, she put her menu book on the table by her purse. She'd like to try one more out before meeting up with Felicia tomorrow. Then they could finalize the menu plan and get to work on the kitchen staff training and the family meal for the team. One more step, one more sleep, and she was one more day closer to opening her own restaurant. With a little help from her friends.

* * * *

The next morning, she heard Precious bleating before she left her bed. "No need for an alarm clock around here," she grumbled to Dom who was trying to hurry her to let him out as well. "I live in a freaking zoo."

After taking care of the animals and two cups of coffee, Angie headed straight to the attic. She'd thought about the conversation with Mrs. Potter a lot as she'd lain in bed, not sleeping. Nona had put a lot of her old memory boxes upstairs. If there were any relics left over from their high school years, it would be in the attic. She got a step stool out and pulled down the attic ladder from its storage space. Carefully, she made her way up the stairs while Dom sat watching her. When she disappeared into the darkness, she heard his whine and a short bark. She poked her head out of the hole and he had one foot on the ladder, looking up at her.

"No. Go lay down. I'll be out in a few minutes." She waited for him to follow her directions before she turned on the flashlight and started hunting for the right box. The problem was Nona had saved a lot of stuff. Eventually, she'd need to get up here and clean out these boxes before the attic floor gave out and they came crashing down onto the second floor.

It took her a few minutes, but she figured out Nona's system. Her and her parents' boxes were near the south corner. In the north was her father's childhood stuff, and on the east and west were Nona's and Angie's grandfather's. He'd died before she was born, but Nona had held him close and talked about him to her only grandchild. She started opening Nona's boxes and with each box, another set of years past. Nona as a grandmother, as a young mother, and a new bride.

Finally, she found the high school box. RV 1940 was written on the box in black marker. The year Nona had graduated. She sat on the floor, angled the flashlight between two boxes, and opened the lid. A graduation gown and cap sat on the top of the box. Black with gold tassels. Then some textbooks from what looked like a home ec class and an English class. Then notebooks and papers. Finally she found four slim yearbooks that resembled magazines rather than the hardback books she'd gotten in high school. She repacked everything into the box except the graduation outfit leaving that on top of the box pile. She scooted her way to the opening and the ladder. She glanced down. Dom lay at the bottom of the ladder, looking up. When he saw her, he sat up and barked, his body wiggling with joy that she hadn't been killed while out of his sight. The dog worried too much.

"I'm coming. Geez, you would have thought I'd been gone for hours." She glanced at her watch. She'd been searching the attic for over an hour. She needed to get in the shower and get ready to go pick up Felicia. Strolling down her grandmother's memory lane would have to wait until tonight. She made her way down the stairs, put the ladder away and closed the entrance. Then she headed downstairs and set the box on the kitchen table. She grabbed a cup of coffee and headed back upstairs to shower.

Thirty minutes later, she was on the road to get Felicia. If she didn't get behind some tractor on the road or Mrs. Potter's friend, Delores, driving to town, she might be close to being on time.

Felicia piled into the car, dressed in a floral sundress that really needed one of those sweeping floppy hats to match it. Instead, she wore a too long gauze scarf. She glanced over at Angie who wore clean jean shorts and a purple tank. "Oh, I figured we were dressing up since we were going to lunch."

"Since when have we been part of the ladies who lunch crowd?" Angie put the car into gear. "Let's get moving. Our reservation's for eleven and the chef has offered to show us the kitchen before we eat."

"Seriously? That's so cool." Felicia unwrapped the scarf from her neck and stuffed it in her purse. She pulled her hair down from the upsweep, and fluffed it in the mirror. "There, I look almost casual."

"You always look amazing. I'm not quite sure why we're still friends, I'm that jealous of you." Angie pulled the car onto an empty Main Street and headed out of town toward the highway.

"Whatever. You can outshine anyone when you try." Felicia glanced out the window. "So I heard that Ian came calling last night."

"He didn't come calling. He came to get our goat cheese order." Angie snuck a glance at her friend. "Wait, who did you hear that from?"

"I shouldn't reveal my source…" Felicia let the silence hang for at least thirty seconds, then broke. "Okay, so Erica was at the store getting some supplies for her grandmother. She said he was there for over an hour. Are you denying it?"

"No. We had some cobbler and some tea. And then he talked to me about Precious, and the best way to raise a goat." She turned down the radio. "I'm still a little worried about her being out in the yard all the time. He says I should fence off some of the barn if I'm planning on keeping her."

"Are you planning on keeping her? I thought when the new owner of the farm comes, you were giving her back." Felicia studied her nails as she waited for Angie's answer.

"I don't know yet. And no, it has nothing to do with Ian. I just met the guy, I don't know what I'm thinking yet. So stop looking at your manicure like you're totally uninterested in my answer." She pulled the car onto the freeway. "Let's do something productive rather than talk about cute guys in our lives. I hated that conversation in high school, it hasn't become more fun over the years. Grab my bag and get out the notebook. I think I have our first weekend's menu planned out. Or maybe we'll run it the full month. What do you think?"

"I don't know yet. I haven't had time to look at what you set up." Felicia repeated Angie's response. She reached into the back and grabbed Angie's tote. One of the yearbooks tumbled out with the notebook. "What's this?"

"Nona's yearbook. I wanted to go through it and see if there are any clues about Mrs. Potter's sister."

"Like what? A caption under Gerald Moss's picture voting him most likely to kill someone?" Felicia tucked the yearbook back into the tote and opened the notebook to the last page. She listed off the items, putting question marks with a pen where she paused, then grinned at Angie.

She'd been so quiet looking at the menu, Angie thought maybe they'd been on different pages when they'd talked food. This menu was totally sustainable in the local area. When she saw the reaction from Felicia, she blew out a breath. "You think it will work then?"

"I think it will be the bomb. I've gotten calls from The Statesman and The Free Press wanting information about what we plan to be serving. The way you did the menu, with descriptions of the food, it's thoughtful and gives the producers a shout out too." Felicia turned back toward the page. "We'll have to get a graphic designer to implement the look, but this is strong."

"I love it. I started playing with the idea last night after dinner." She nodded to the page. "Do you think I need to add to some of the sections?"

"Depends. If it's just for opening night, then no. We have enough choices, but if we run the same menu for a month, we need to add a few more items." Felicia chewed on the end of the pen. "If we only change out dishes monthly, it will save on printing costs."

"Maybe we should do a special one for opening weekend, then expand it for the rest of the month?" Angie took the Franklin exchange exit and headed toward the fairgrounds. "Oooh, we could give away the menu for opening night. Like a memento only for people who come the first weekend."

"I like it. We could fold it up with their bill and put a gold sticker on the fold so it looks special."

Angie pointed to the page. "Write this stuff down. It's great." She turned into a parking lot with the restaurant next to the Boise River. "We're here. Let's go see what they're doing for the local foodies."

As they walked up to the door, a couple got out of a black BMW that pulled in at the same time. The woman driving chatted animatedly to the man who climbed out the other side. As Angie opened the restaurant door, she saw the man's face. Ian McNeal.

The hostess greeted them before Ian and his dining companion could get inside the building. "You must be Angie and Felicia. Sydney's expecting you. Come on back to the kitchen first, then we'll get you settled at the chef's table."

They followed the woman through the dining room where a large stone fireplace separated the main dining from the bar area. The set up was upscale country and reminded Angie of the restaurants around the ski resorts she used to visit in Colorado. She glanced back as the kitchen door swung shut. Ian and his date were standing in the archway near the hostess table, waiting.

Felicia angled closer and whispered. "Why are you looking behind us? Did you see someone?"

"Maybe." Angie didn't know why she wasn't being up front, but right now, she didn't even know if Ian was on a real date. And again, why should it matter. They weren't dating. Why would it matter if he saw someone? This is why she didn't open her heart to people. She got burned. Sometimes it was her own lack of boundaries that hurt her, but sometimes, men lied. Maybe this was one of those times.

"I'm so honored you came to Canyon Creek." Sydney Cook stood a full five feet two, if that. Her hair was a bright pink and peeked out from her chef's cap. "I'm looking forward to visiting The County Seat. I called last week, but you're already full up for opening night, so I have the first reservation I could get."

"We'd love to squeeze you in for opening night." Angie glanced at Felicia who shook her head. "But my front of house expert tells me it's impossible."

Sydney patted Felicia's arm. "People like you rule the world. I'd be lost without my manager, Heidi. She's the woman who brought you into the kitchen. If she says no, it's no. I've learned from experience she's always right."

Felicia poked Angie in the ribs. "I wish this one was just as reasonable."

"It takes time. Heidi and I have worked together for over fifteen years now." Sydney started the tour of the kitchen. By the time they were done and sitting at the chef's table, two glasses of wine and an assortment of appetizers were waiting for them.

Angie spread her napkin on her lap and grinned at the plates. Looking up at Sydney, she shook her head in amazement. "You really shouldn't have. We were just expecting lunch."

"I believe we should be open and supportive of each other. Welcome to the community. We're excited to share this great area with you." Sydney turned toward her sous chef who had walked up as they were talking. The two conversed for a few minutes, then she turned back to the table. "I'm being called away, I'm afraid. Don't worry about ordering, we'll be bringing you entrees in a few minutes and be sure to save room for dessert. I have a huckleberry cobbler on the menu with black pepper ice cream that's to die for."

By the time they left the restaurant, it was already after two. Sitting in the car, Angie shook her head. "That was so good. When I left town, the only upscale places were downtown in the larger hotels. Now, there's a lot of places that are comparable to what we're doing."

"Except for the farm-to-fork concept. We're the first in the area to embrace that. Don't worry, we'll be fine." Felicia checked her list on her phone. "Restaurant supply or appliance store first?"

"Let's get your stove ordered, then go to the restaurant supply place. It's next to the Ice Cream Palace and I wanted to stop there for a treat." Angie pulled the car out of the parking lot and headed toward the part of town where the mall sat.

"I can't believe you're still hungry."

Angie felt her phone buzz with a text. As they were at a stoplight, she read the display. "I'm not hungry yet, but since Sheriff Brown wants me to stop by the police station at my earliest convenience, at least I can have one last meal before they lock me up."

"Seriously? What can he want now? It's not like you killed the guy." Felicia was checking the map app on her phone. "I think there's an appliance store on the left once you get on Fairview."

"Let's go check it out." The light had changed so Angie headed toward the next stop. Something else was going on with the death of Gerald Moss. There was no way it had been an accident or the sheriff would have moved on to other things. Even in a small town, sheriffs are too busy to worry an investigation that wasn't there.

She just hoped she wasn't on the top of the suspect list just because of her trip out to Moss Farm on Sunday.

# CHAPTER 9

"Sheriff Brown's been expecting you." The young deputy glanced at the clock. It was almost five. Angie had hoped the Sheriff would have been gone by the time she got back to town, but no such luck. "He's with someone right now, but I'll let him know you're finally here."

"The message didn't say when I was supposed…" Angie's words trailed off as she watched the deputy leave the front without stopping to hear what she said. Apparently, she was wrong and he was right, no matter what. She glanced around the small, dark waiting room and settled on a 1960s-era plastic chair. The magazine selections looked almost as old as the chair, but she picked up a *Country Estates* copy that was dog eared but seemed to have fewer coffee stains on the front cover than the other choices.

The deputy came back and sat at his desk. He didn't say anything to her, just went back to typing something into the computer. She returned her gaze to the magazine and found an article on redesigning your kitchen. The hints and suggestions weren't bad and before long, she found herself lost in the article, "Not Your Grandmother's Kitchen." Several of the ideas she'd wished she'd thought of a few months ago when she remodeled Nona's kitchen. A shadow fell over the magazine page and she turned her gaze upward.

Sheriff Brown and Ian McNeal stood in front of her.

"Seriously, you have to stop stalking me. It's getting a bit creepy." She stood and pointed at Ian.

"What are you talking about?" Ian's eyes went wide. "I just stopped in last night to see about the cheese order."

"And you were at Canyon Creek today with your date." She said it before she could think about what her noticing him really meant. She brushed off her discomfort and added, "And now you're here."

"Sheriff Brown asked me to come in and answer some additional questions." Ian shot back. "Now that he knows Gerald…"

Sheriff Brown put a hand on Ian's shoulder. "I think you need to go. I'll inform Ms. Turner about the change in circumstance."

Ian nodded, then beelined to the door.

Sheriff Brown watched him leave. "You know you get under his skin right? I've never seen him so worked up about a gal."

"He tells me you are related." When the Sheriff didn't answer, Angie swallowed hard. She was trying hard to ignore his words. "Why did you want to see me?"

"Let's go into my office. I need to get off my feet. I can't believe how bad my ankles are swelling and it's not even deep summer." He headed toward the back of the building, obviously expecting Angie to follow.

She walked past the reception desk where the young officer glared at her like it was her fault the sheriff's ankles were swelling. People were weird here. First Kirk freaked out about her, and now this guy. She absently ran a hand down her hair. Maybe it was sticking out or something. When they reached his office, he indicated that she should sit in a leather visitor chair. The office was nice, wood desk, good chairs, and what looked like a small kitchenette at the back.

"Can I get you a cup of coffee? I just made up a fresh pot. Mrs. Brown's going to tan my hide when I get home and confess, but honestly, I needed the pick me up." He held up the pot.

"Sure." Angie knew better than to try to rush this. Small towns had their own pace. And the sheriff didn't care that she had a ton of work to do when she finally got home, mostly finalizing the menu for opening night and creating a shopping list. With the trial run in less than a week, she needed to make sure everything was ready for her kitchen staff, including recipes and correct ingredients.

He handed her a cup before sitting down heavily with his own behind his desk.

She took a sip mostly to be polite, then her eyes widened. She took a second sip. "It's good."

"I guess you didn't think you could get a good cup out here in the boonies, huh?" He pushed a card toward her. "My wife's nephew owns a coffee shop in Meridian. He makes his own blends. You might want to talk to him about buying some for your diner. He'll give you a good deal."

"I'll check it out." She tucked the card into her tote. She'd text Felicia the information later. This was how business ran here. One referral at a time. "Ian said there was a problem with Gerald's death?"

"No problem really. I just have to ask you a few more questions since it's highly unlikely he just fell from the ridge. From the coroner's preliminary report, it looks like he was restrained and then pushed." He pulled out a file. "Instead of just being an unattended death, we've got a murder on our hands. So tell me, when did you go to Moss Farm?"

"Sunday morning around six thirty. I met him at the farmers' market the day before and Mrs. Potter, my neighbor," she paused making sure the sheriff knew who she was talking about, "well, she said I needed to get to know Mr. Moss so he'd be more agreeable to selling me his goat cheese. I guess he can be a bit of a curmudgeon at times."

"If that's a fancy word for butt, yes, Gerald Moss was that. I can't tell you how many times I got called out to the place because some kids came too close to his property. He liked his privacy." He shuffled some papers. "Last time we talked, you said Reana Whiting arrived at the farm just as you were leaving. You know who Reana is right? I mean, you'd recognize her by sight, correct?"

"I should. She sold me the building where I'm opening my restaurant." Angie knew where this was going. "Besides, we talked a little as I was leaving. It's not like I caught a glimpse of her from far away. Reana arrived somewhere around 8:00 a.m. because I checked the clock on my dashboard when I left to see what time it was."

"Did you have another appointment?"

"No, I wanted to spend the day developing menu items for the opening. It takes time to get everything just right." She paused. "And I wanted to make jam the next day, but you know how that turned out."

"Too bad about that. Sorry we interrupted you so early." He put his glasses on and peered at a sheet of paper. "You're absolutely sure on the date."

"I am. Mostly because I had just met Mr. Moss the day before. Ian can verify that. He saw me at the market and we talked."

"Yep, he mentioned that, but when I asked if you could have known Gerald prior to that date, he was a little hesitant. He said your dog tried to get between him and Gerald due to a heated discussion." He leaned back in his chair. "Does your dog go on protection mode for everyone?"

"Actually, he doesn't like raised voices. But he stepped in between me and Ian. Not Ian and Mr. Moss." She let her back straighten and looked him directly in the eye. "I'll make this clear. The first time I met Gerald Moss was Saturday at the farmers' market. No matter what Reana says. Besides, he couldn't have been at his place meeting with all of us on Saturday, the market opens at nine."

"If Reana's story is the truthful one, he would have just enough time to leave the farm to get to the market and still be within your timeline." He threw down a pen. "I was hoping you'd give me something stronger."

"I'm not lying." Angie was starting to worry about where this whole line of questioning was going. "Wait, what about the milkers? They were still there when I pulled up. And I bought the Ding Dongs for the meeting on Saturday. I probably still have a receipt in my purse for them."

"I'm interviewing the milkers tomorrow morning. Maybe one of them saw you, but typically, they leave from the back gate. It's closer to town." Sheriff Brown leaned forward. "It's not that I don't believe you, I just have conflicting stories and I have to know what's behind them."

"Then go figure out why Reana it is lying." She wondered if she should tell him Reana's story about the phone. Now, it seemed like more likely it was just a story. Instead, she pointedly looked at her watch. "Are we done? I have a dog at home who probably needs to be let out."

"Sure." He stood. "I need to get home anyway. The missus doesn't like me late for dinner. Of course, that's happened too often to count with this job. You'd think she'd get used to it over thirty years."

He walked her out of the building, then stood watching as she made her way back to the restaurant where she'd parked. She thought about Reana's insistence that she had been there on Saturday and wondered why, even for a real estate contract, the date would make any difference at all.

\* \* \* \*

Thursday morning the fencing guys were there just after she'd gotten everyone fed and had sat down with a cup of coffee. When she'd called the company early in the month, they'd put her on some sort of standby list. For in between big jobs. The good news is they would be in and out of her place today. She walked the crew manager over to the barn where she'd laid out a more permanent area for Precious.

"No problem, we can probably get that done today too, but I'll have to run into town for more materials." The man tapped on the barn posts. "This old thing is in great shape. That's what happens when you purchase quality materials to work with."

He promised to give her a quick estimate of the additional costs, but Angie's mind was made up. She was keeping the stupid goat. As she walked by the back yard where Precious was watching all the excitement, the goat saw her and bleated a greeting.

"She knows her mama." One of the men joked. "Baby goats bond quickly with humans when they are isolated from the herd."

"You know a lot about goats?" Angie paused next to the guy who was laying out boards for the new fence.

"Grew up on a farm. Everyone has a goat at one time or the other. It's your first large animal project for 4-H." He grinned at her. "I named mine Thor. He would follow me anywhere on the farm. When I left for the army, my mom kept him around for years, mostly for the company I think. My dad had passed a few years prior and she downsized most of the animal herd."

"Except Thor." Angie loved the story. It was something her Nona would have done. Kept the pet she'd loved as Angie went out into the world. That way, when she'd come home, they'd still be there, waiting.

A car pulled into the drive way. Felicia waved at her from the front seat. Angie excused herself and walked toward the car. "You here for breakfast?"

"Actually no, but since you mentioned it. Yum. I haven't eaten yet. What are you making?' Felicia got out of the car and looked around. "You remodeling again?"

"Fence day. By the end of the day, Dom will be able to use a doggy door in the mud room and go outside to his private back yard retreat any time he wants too."

"Isn't that going to be a problem with the goat being there? He's kind of a chicken when it comes to her." Felicia followed Angie into the kitchen and dropped her bag on the table before heading to the coffee pot to pour a cup.

"Precious is getting her own space in the barn." Angie held her hand up. "No judging. And I don't want to talk about what a softy I am. What do you want for breakfast? I can do an egg and avocado toast real quick with some cherry cobbler for dessert."

"Sounds wonderful." Felicia went back to the table and dug through her purse. "And I come bearing gifts. This arrived in my inbox sometime last night. I think I have your new sous chef."

Angie took the printed resume and laid it on the counter, reading as she cooked the eggs and toasted thick slices of the focaccia bread in the oven. "He looks perfect. What's the catch?"

"He does this Basque Festival every July he's already committed to, so he'll need a week off next month."

"That's all? No prison record, no warrants, no personal life issues?" Angie glanced at Felicia. "Did you call references?"

"First thing this morning. Everyone said he was a quiet, hard worker. But..."

Angie finished plating the dish and took the two plates to the table. "But what? Come on, spill. A guy with these types of credentials should be working as an executive chef by now. Why is he interested in a sous chef position?"

"According to the references, he has a bit of a temper and, I quote, a problem with authority." Felicia dug into her meal. "You need someone soon."

Angie considered her options. Take a chance at having no one, or hire a known hothead. "Maybe he'll be different with a female boss." She mentally flipped a coin. "Hire him. If I don't think he'll work out we'll keep looking."

"I'll call him after breakfast. So what did Sheriff Brown want yesterday?"

"Mr. Moss was murdered, at least based on the coroner's preliminary report. Now, he's questioning my relationship with the guy."

"What relationship? You met him, what, twice? And now you're stuck with taking care of his baby goat?" She held up a fork. "Don't tell me they think you're involved somehow?"

"I don't get that feeling, but there might be a problem, especially since Reana is contradicting my statement." Angie went on to tell Felicia what had happened, except the encounter with Ian and what the sheriff had said about her getting in the guy's head. Her friend had too much matchmaker in her to divulge that nugget. If she didn't watch out, Angie would be married off to the guy with Felicia's maneuvering. When she got to the end, she finished her breakfast and got out the crumble and ice cream. "Want yours heated?"

"Please." Felicia took her own empty plate to the sink after giving Dom a crust of bread. "We might have to figure out who killed Old Man Moss ourselves just to save you from going to prison. The good news is it's right between Boise and here. Out in the desert."

"I think that's the male facility. I wouldn't be going there." She set the dessert dishes on the table and ladled out the last of the black pepper ice cream. She'd been eating way too much, mostly because of the stress of opening, now she had to save herself from a murder rap? She would definitely have to make brownies next week. Just to survive. She grabbed a notebook and a pen from her supply. "I feel like no one is standing up for him. Mrs. Potter hated the guy. The Sheriff doesn't seem to want it to be a murder. And all the cheese guys are glad the goat man is gone.

He needs someone in his corner. Nona would have helped. So who do we know would want to kill Mr. Moss?"

They brainstormed a few names. Angie lifted eyebrows at Felicia's mention of Ian, but wrote his name down anyway. "I think the only thing he's gotten out of his death is more work."

"Yeah, but some guys crave power. Even in a baby pool like River Vista. I know, it's a long shot, but aren't we brainstorming? And you know the rule..."

"Nothing is ever too stupid." Angie finished her sentence. They'd been brainstorming for most of their friendship. 100 ways to make a chef salad. Or one Sunday, as many ways to make a Bloody Mary that they could think of. She still remembered the hangover that next morning since they'd tested out more than a few of the drinks. Angie glanced over at her friend who had finished her cobbler and was now stroking Dom's ear. The dog was in heaven. She was lucky to have such a good friend. Sometimes, things just worked out.

"We have Reana. And the missing nephew. What about him?" Angie wrote down a question mark after the word.

"We're still brainstorming. No evaluations yet. Who was Reana planning on selling to? That could be the killer. He got tired of waiting."

"But she claims Mr. Moss was considering selling. Oh, and the lady at the cheese commission. Mildred? Mr. Moss said she was out to close him down." She glanced at the list.

"There's another line of maybes you haven't written down yet." Felicia held out her hand for the pen and wrote Mrs. Potter and Erica on the list.

"That's silly." Angie challenged her friend but Felicia held fast to the pen.

"It's the brainstorming rules, you have to put down everything, even if it's silly or stupid because it might spark another idea."

"Okay, they can stay, but are we done for now?" Angie glanced through the list. Most of the names were just thoughts about people who might be angry at Moss. Except for Mrs. Potter, who had come out and said she was glad he was dead.

"I can't think of anyone else."

"Good, you go call and hire the new sous chef and I'll get Nona's yearbooks. Maybe we can scratch off Mrs. Potter and Erica before lunch."

# CHAPTER 10

By lunch time, all they had was more questions. Felicia glanced at her watch. "We're not very good at this investigation thing. Anyway, I've got to go. The electrical inspection is at two. Are you going to have the menu done by Monday? The printers said they need a few days to get it typeset and run."

"I guess since I haven't found any smoking guns in these old yearbooks, I should get back to work on the menu. I'll have something you can look at Sunday night. Maybe you should just come over for dinner and I'll run the dishes by you then." Angie stacked the yearbooks in a pile with the notebook she'd been making their brainstorming notes in. "Did you see what Mrs. Potter's sister listed for clubs? She was in dance, drama, and some sort of speech club. And Mrs. Potter was president of the Future Homemakers of America. Totally different kids."

"My sister and I were that way. She's a big shot in the army now and I'm in the restaurant business. It's just what floats your boat." Felicia keyed something into her phone. "What time do you want me here on Sunday?"

Angie thought about her plan. "Early. We'll do a dry run for all the dishes. So come hungry."

"I can do that." She stared out the screen door toward the Potter farm house across the street. "Do you really think Moss could have killed her sister? I didn't see anything bad in any of those yearbooks. He looked like a nice kid."

Angie went to the sink and rinsed her coffee cup. She needed to slow down on the caffeine or she'd never sleep tonight. "I'll admit, it seems odd, but she was so serious." She joined Felicia at the door. "I don't know, and the two people who do know are now dead. It could be a coincidence."

"Maybe you should go over and see if she'll tell you anything else." Felicia started to leave, then turned and held out a hand. "Stop. Don't even think about this. Until we know she's not a murderer, you should stay out of that house. Don't they call those women too stupid to live when they go down into the basement to check out a noise?"

"I won't be stupid." Angie smiled at her friend. "Besides, do you really think either Mrs. Potter or Erica could really kill someone?"

"It's always the quiet ones when they interview the neighbors. Just once I'd like the nosy neighbor to say something like, I knew it. I knew it. They were always carrying chainsaws into the house and boxes of poison. I told my wife, just wait. Those people will be in jail sooner than later."

Angie shivered. "I don't know if I'd want to know or not. Knowing makes it all the creepier, at least in my mind." She motioned Dom to stay inside and followed Felicia outside to her car. "You sure I can't make some lunch up for you before you leave?"

"Nah, I'm stopping at the River Vista Drive-In. I've been craving one of their triple decker hamburgers." When she saw the look on Angie's face, she laughed. "Don't worry, I'm getting a small fry to go along with that."

"So only half your arteries will be clogged after the meal. That's being kind to your heart." Angie waved her friend off and then went over to check on the fence progress. Dom's new outdoor patio was all fenced in and the dog door installed in the mudroom door. The crew manager came over and nodded toward the house.

"That's the biggest door they had. I'm not sure what you're going to do when he's full grown, but I've seen dogs who should be too tall bend down to get out. Now if he gets too wide, you may have another issue."

"I really wasn't planning on getting a St. Bernard. But when I saw the litter, I knew I was done for." Angie smiled at the memory. She put her hand on the gate and jiggled it. It felt solid under her weight.

"He's not pushing that over. We dropped an extra five inches of cement into the post holes. Just our way of helping keep him inside the fence instead of running out in the road. Too many dogs get hit out here." He opened the gate and crossing the yard took Precious off her lead. "Let me show you the princess's new digs."

"You're done already?" Angie followed him to the barn. Precious watched her over the guy's shoulder. The goat thought she was a lap dog.

"Yep. Your barn has good bones, I told you that." He directed his men to start loading up the tools in the truck. "We finished a good two hours before we'd planned so you should be getting a nice cut on your bill."

She watched as he put Precious in a stall and shut the gate. He or someone in his crew had already set up her indoor pen with straw and put food and water into the containers that they'd found in the barn. Precious looked around, and then jumped. "She likes it."

"You do know how to take care of your pets." He leaned on the gate, watching her. "She's a character. I think you'll enjoy having her around."

Angie nodded wondering again, what she'd gotten herself into. Mabel scratched in the dirt next to her and watched the interloper into her domain. "If I get to keep her."

"So she's from Old Man Moss's tribe?" He grinned at the confusion that must have been on Angie's face. "Tribe is what he always called the herd. I looked it up on Google one day. Surprisingly, a group of goats is called a tribe, along with a herd."

"Yeah, she was lost so I tried to take her back to the tribe," Angie tried on the word, smiling as she watched Precious find the food dish and start on her lunch. "Instead, I got a temporary house guest."

"I'm not sure it's so temporary. From what I've heard, no one's come forward yet as a long-lost relative and the guy didn't leave a will." He looked around and dropped his voice. "I probably shouldn't be saying anything, but did you know he was murdered?"

"I've heard that rumor."

He shook his head. "Not a rumor at all. My wife's sister works at the county coroner's office and she said Old Man Moss was pushed off the cliff. Right there in his back yard. Too crazy, don't you think? And someone at church said the cheese commission was about to shut him down so he was selling the farm."

"I didn't hear that." Angie leaned closer. "Why would they shut him down? Health conditions at the plant?"

"Hell, no. He kept that milking facility and the cheese factory clean as a whistle." He picked a piece of straw off his flannel shirt. "Everyone knows the dairy farmers have too much power here in the area. If they think someone's encroaching on their income, any one of them would have pushed Moss over the cliff rather than try to work something out. I'm not kidding."

A horn blared from the driveway.

"I've got to get going." He nodded toward his crew. "We've got a porch to build over on one of the new houses in River Vista. That homeowner's going to be pleased as punch that we're early. They were hoping to get their job finished up by next week. I guess they're having some party."

Angie followed him out to the driveway and watched as the men drove away. Funny how much information he'd given her in just a few minutes. She wondered if that was the secret to small town life. Learning what to talk about so people didn't find out all your deepest secrets. She went back into the house and while she made herself a sandwich, she looked up the office address of the cheese commission. It was time for her to go see what this Mildred had to say about Gerald Moss. Besides, she was a possible user of the product. She had a right to determine if it was safe for serving and cooking with at the restaurant.

That was her story and she was going to stick to it.

After showing Dom the back yard and his new entry into the house, she took off for town. The menu would hold until this evening when she would finalize it for Felicia. Besides, she thought better if she had a little time to let things marinate. Thinking about her partner, Angie glanced at the clock. Ten to two. The electrical inspector should be at The County Seat anytime. She had just enough time to get to Meridian, find this office building, and talk to Mildred before five. She paused at the driveway. She could take the long way and go through town, maybe stopping and talking to Reana, or, she could drive to the freeway and take the faster route.

She chose fast. She popped in a Fleetwood Mac CD and sang all the way. The parking lot in front of the little white building was filled so she parked across the street at the bank and walked over. Opening the door to the office, she realized they must have been having a meeting that had just broken up. Men stood around the office lobby, drinking coffee and talking. Angie made her way through the crowd to a woman sitting at a small desk, a telephone at her ear. She was frowning at the crowd as she tried to listen to the caller. Finally, she put a hand over the headset. "Hey, quiet down. I'm on the phone."

The voices turned to murmurs. Then she saw Angie standing by her desk. "Hold on a second. Let me finish with this guy."

Angie flipped through the pamphlets on the desk apparently for visitors. SIGNING UP TO BE A CHEESE COMMISSION MEMBER. And one last copy of, GOVERNMENT GRANTS AND SUBSIDIES. WHAT YOU NEED TO KNOW. She grabbed a copy of both, shoving them into her purse while the woman finished her conversation.

Finally, she hung up the phone. "What can I help you with? You missed the monthly meeting if that's what you're here for. Starts promptly at noon. These guys love catered meetings."

"Actually, I was wondering if I could talk to Mildred for a minute." Angie put on her best smile that she hoped didn't make her look like a serial killer.

The woman glanced down at the phone on her desk. Another line was lit, then as she talked, it winked out. "She's on the phone. Oh, wait a minute, she's off now. So go on in. Third door to your left."

"Thanks." That had been easier than she'd expected. Angie quickly moved around the men whose conversation had increased in volume as soon as the receptionist had hung up the phone. The hallway was well lit, with framed posters of cheese. And two of friendly cows. There were no framed posters of goats. A photo of a large group of men with one woman in a dark blue suit and a flowered scarf had a small plaque under it. 2016 CHEESE COMMISSION BOARD. From what she saw in the promotional pictures in the hallway, Gerald Moss's death must have made Mildred's life ten times easier. A man swung a door open and stormed past Angie.

When she looked inside the office, a woman sat at her desk, her head in her hands. Angie counted the doors again. Yep, third door on the left, this must be Mildred. She knocked on the open door and the woman looked up at her.

Angie covered her mouth to hold in the gasp. It was the same woman that had been at lunch with Ian the other day. Was this Mildred? And who was the man who just stormed out, making the woman tear up? Curious.

"Can I help you?" Mildred composed herself and ran a finger under her eyelids to remove any stray tear that might have fallen. Now the woman was all professional.

Angie stepped in the room, her hand outstretched. "Hi, I'm Angie Turner. I'm opening The County Seat in River Vista and had a few questions about Moss Farm."

The woman eyed her suspiciously. "Gerald Moss is recently deceased, but I'm sure you know that. Why do you want to know about his farm?"

"Actually, I wanted to know about the cheese. I'm planning on using some in my opening night menu and I wanted to see what kind of reports you had on the facility. Is he rated?" Angie sat down in the visitor chair without being asked and pulled out her notebook. If her pretend visit reason was to look plausible, she needed to act the part. She held up a pen and looked at Mildred waiting for an answer.

"We don't really have a rating system, not for the goat cheese. It's a newly regulated item. Ten years ago, we didn't know there would be any kind of cheese besides good old-fashioned milk from cows. Now, you got all sorts of crazy things out there and I've got to manage it all." She stood and took a cup over to her coffee pot. "Sorry, I'm whining. Let's start over. I'm Mildred Platt and I wrangle the cheese producers in the area. Those that are part of the commission, that is."

"Was Gerald Moss part of the commission?" Angie took the cup Mildred handed her and took a sip. Not bad.

Mildred waited until she sat down again to answer. "No, no he wasn't. He thought we just wanted to mess up his business. To run him out of town basically."

"Seriously? That's some major paranoia."

Mildred glanced toward the doorway like she could still see the man who'd left just before Angie had arrived. "That's the thing. Now that Gerald's dead, I'm not sure it was all just in his head."

"What do you mean?" Angie leaned forward waiting to hear the woman's theory, but then the door swung open again.

"Mildred, you need to come out here. Simpson is heckling Martin again. This time I think they actually may come to blows." The harried receptionist stood at the doorway, waiving toward the outer area.

"Sorry, I need to go. Set up an appointment for tomorrow and we can talk about your options for cheese now that Gerald's out of the picture." Mildred stood and started walking toward the doorway.

"But they're keeping the dairy farm open, aren't they?" Angie followed her out of the office.

"That's not what I heard yesterday." She caught up with her receptionist. "Ian doesn't think the business will be able to finish out the month and still pay their employees. I guess Gerald was hanging on by a thread."

Angie stopped in her tracks and watched Mildred force herself between two burly men. There was no way she was going to follow her into that, even if she did want to know more about Mildred's discussion with Ian. That must have been what the lunch was about. He was reporting the state of Moss Farm. Or maybe he was looking for financial help to keep it open? Either way, Angie couldn't see this woman killing off a man who hadn't even been part of the commission. But the two men puffing their chests out in the middle of the lobby, now they were a different story. She paused at the receptionist desk and the woman held out a card.

"Come back at one tomorrow. She's at the farmer's market in the morning and a lunch with her women's church group but she always works Saturday afternoon in the office. I'll make sure you get a good half hour."

Angie took the card and used it to point at the two men Mildred was talking out of taking a swing at each other. "Who's that?"

"Carl Simpson owns the largest dairy farm in Meridian. He's been the big dog here for as long as I've worked for the commission." The woman sat and turned her chair sideways to have a better view of the disturbance. She pulled a bag of pretzels out of her drawer and offered one to Angie. "The other guy is new in town, but thinks he knows everything. It ticks the guys off to have a know it all in the group. This time, Martin Lowe might have just pushed the wrong button. Carl's been antsy since he heard about Old Man Moss's death."

"Do you know why?"

The woman shrugged. "He's conceited enough that he might think someone is trying to kill off all the milk suppliers in the area. He doesn't like it when anyone gets attention he thinks should be his."

Angie wondered if antsy was the right descriptor. Maybe this Carl was jumpy because he was expecting the cops to show up at his door at any minute. Because he'd killed Gerald Moss and his conscience wouldn't let him forget it. She tapped the card on the desk. "Thanks for this. I'll see you tomorrow."

"You aren't staying for the show?" The receptionist pointed to the men who were ignoring Mildred's attempt to calm them down. The two men were taller than Mildred and were literally yelling over the woman's head.

Angie shook her head. Listening to people yell at each other made her head hurt. "I'll let you catch me up tomorrow. I've got things to get done today."

"Your loss." The woman turned her attention back to the men.

Angie had what she needed. An appointment to grill Mildred and find out what she knew about Gerald Moss's death. And she had fallen into a large pool of suspects to give to Sheriff Brown that didn't include herself or her elderly neighbor.

# CHAPTER 11

After checking in by phone with Felicia to make sure the inspection had gone well, Angie headed home. Dom may not need out, but she didn't want him to have any issues his first afternoon with his own personal door.

Besides, she had a menu to finalize.

She parked the car near her back door and hurried inside. Dom was asleep on his bed in the kitchen. Angie started cooking and didn't stop until ten when she sat down at the table and outlined the final menu. She shot the list to Felicia's email, even though she knew her friend was probably on some date or checking out the night life in one of the surrounding towns. For River Vista being so small, it was centrally located between larger towns that brought in people from all over the valley to celebrate the start of the weekend.

Dom had gone in and out several times, without disturbing her. But when she looked at her watch, she realized she hadn't fed Mabel or Precious. "Crap."

She grabbed a flashlight and headed outside, Dom on her heels. Mabel was in the barn near the food, pecking at grains that had spilled earlier. She scooped a cup and dumped it in front of the chicken. "I'm sorry dinner's late tonight."

The hen looked up at her in a disapproving stare, then started pecking at the feed. Angie took the other cup and filled it with the goat food. She made her way to Precious's stall and dumped the food in her bowl. The water trough had an automated feed that kept the level even. Nona had put the system in years ago and when the construction guys had set up the new pen, they'd also checked out the water pump and deemed it good enough to keep the little goat hydrated.

Precious was asleep in the straw. When she saw the light, she came running to the gate, ignoring the food Angie had put in her dish. No, the goat wanted to be petted. Angie knelt on the straw floor and reached her hand through the gate slats. Precious's hair was soft and her lips nibbled on Angie's hand. "You're such a love. What am I going to do with you?"

The goat bleated and Angie rubbed between the nubs that would soon be horns. Ian said he'd come over and dehorn the baby soon. Angie didn't want to think about the process even though he'd said it would be painless.

Dom stood from where he'd been watching Angie and the goat. He stepped between Angie and the open barn door and growled.

Angie grabbed her flashlight and got to her feet. "What do you hear boy?"

She listened for a car door or any sign that someone had arrived at the farmhouse. But all she heard was the summer crickets. She checked on the goat's gate, just to make sure it was closed, then, shining the light down to her feet, made her way to the barn door. She clicked off the light before she arrived, then stood in the darkness. letting her eyes adjust to the night. A slight breeze ran through the driveway, kicking up dirt but she didn't see any movement, human or animal. Dom growled again, but this time, it was less certain, as if he didn't know what he was seeing or sensing. She paused a minute longer, really focusing on the dark corners and hidey holes in the yard. Nothing.

She glanced back at Precious and wondered if she should lock her up in the barn at night, just in case the coyotes who took her mom came looking for the one who got away. Did they come this far down into farm country? She'd have to ask Mrs. Potter tomorrow. Just to be safe, she pulled the barn door closed on Mabel and Precious. Tomorrow she'd look at the other entrances and exits and make sure they were secure. Tonight, this would have to do.

As she flicked back on her flashlight and made her way to the house, she decided to take a quick trip into town first thing in the morning. Depending on the broadcast range, she thought she had just the fix for her concern.

The next morning when she went to feed the goat and chicken, everything seemed fine. She scanned the dirt for paw prints, but didn't see anything in the dust outside the barn. Of course, she couldn't even see her own foot prints from last night, which meant the breeze she'd felt had kicked up to a good-sized wind.

She finished breakfast and headed into town. On the way home, she got a phone call from Felicia. She picked it up using the car's Bluetooth feature. "Hey."

"Hey yourself. Where are you? I thought you'd be at the farmer's market as soon as it opened."

She turned the car at the next intersection and headed into town instead of home. "I forgot it was Saturday. I just ran into town for something. I'll be there in," she glanced at the clock, "Ten minutes?"

"I'm already here. Do you want me to pick up what we need for Wednesday?"

Angie could hear the voices surrounding her friend and judged the crowd to be pretty heavy already. "You have the menu. Start shopping. Keep your phone handy, I'll meet up with you as soon as I park."

She pushed down on the accelerator, taking a chance on exceeding the speed limit by a few miles per hour. It wasn't being pulled over that kept her vigilant on the drive, there weren't many traffic cops out in the rural side of town where she found herself. No, she was on the lookout for the random loose dog, goat or, worse, cow, in the middle of the road. If she hit a cow or a horse, she'd kill the animal as well as total her car. And, probably, send herself into the hospital with a few broken bones. When she was a kid, her best friend Holli Blackwell's mom had been driving home from Saturday shopping and had clipped a Black Angus bull that came out of a corner in her blind spot. She'd rolled the car and without a seatbelt to secure her, she had been thrown out of the car and killed. Since that time, Angie had always worn a seatbelt, even if she was just going down the street.

Thinking of Mrs. Blackwell, Angie dropped her speed back down to the legal limit. She'd get there in plenty of time and besides, Felicia knew what to look for. She could count on her friend.

She finally found a parking spot two blocks away from the old high school gym. Throwing her wallet and phone into her large tote with a strap so long she could cross it over her body, she locked the car and powerwalked to the market. She dialed Felicia's number. When she picked up, she just started talking. "I'm here, where are you?"

"The trout farm stand. You should see how lovely these fish are." Felicia answered.

"Which end of the market, north or south?" Angie knew they didn't always set people up in the same spot. She wondered if Moss Farm would have a booth today, especially after Mildred's statement that the place was underwater in debt.

"North side, almost at the end." Felicia paused. "I see you coming. Do you see me?"

Angie looked up and saw her friend waving wildly. In true Felicia style, she wore a sky-blue sundress that looked like the ones Angie had longed for in high school. Lacy and feminine, it made her friend look young and better, friendly. Since they were making connections for the restaurant today, it was a perfect outfit. She looked down at her own cutoff jeans shorts and a blue tank top. It was clean, but she looked more like she should be working the farm not opening an upscale restaurant. Oh, well. Like Nona always said, the wrapper isn't as important as what was inside. "I'll be right there."

She tucked the phone into her jeans pocket and crossed the street to the market.

Felicia pulled her close and smiled at the young man who was standing on the other side of the stand. "This is Angie, she's the head chef for The County Seat. Angie, this is Jacob. He and his family have owned the trout farm for over twenty years."

"I was telling your friend that we have natural hot springs on the property. That way, we can keep the temperature perfect for spawning and raising the fingerlings." Jacob must have read Angie's confusion. "That's what we call baby fish, fingerlings."

"I was picturing potatoes." Angie admitted. She stroked the skin of a large trout on display. The eyes were clear and bright. This fish had just been harvested within the last few hours. She lifted it up and took a whiff. Fresh and clean. "We'll take half a dozen for today, but can we special order and pick up on Thursdays when we open?"

"I already set that up." Felicia held out a card while Jacob slipped six trout into a bag and quickly weighed them. As he wrapped the weighed bag in paper wrappings, Felicia handed her credit card to the woman who was manning the cash register. "One supplier down, a ton to go."

"I'm hoping one of the farms can do most of our vegetable orders, but I know we'll have to find different fruit and herb suppliers." Angie glanced down the already crowded aisle and spotted Ian talking with a young man who appeared to be stocking cheese curds on ice. "I'll be right back."

Ian smiled at her, then his smile faded and he stepped back around the counter. "Are you still mad at me?"

"I wasn't mad at you." She pushed her hair out of her eyes. "Okay, so maybe I was a little gruff when I saw you at the police station. But I've been questioned twice already and before I moved home, I don't think I ever even talked to a cop."

"Not even a speeding ticket?" The young man dropped two bags of cheese into the ice and stared at her. "Man, my folks would love you. I'm on number four and if I get another one, I lose my ride."

"Thom, why don't you go get that last cooler out of the truck." Ian looked pointedly at the kid. "I'll watch the booth until you get back."

"I was planning on it. Man, you don't have to get huffy. I was just making conversation with the pretty lady." Thom walked around them and headed north out of the market aisle.

She glanced after him, then focused on Ian. "I'm surprised you opened the booth. I thought Moss Farm was bankrupt?"

"Now where did you hear that rumor?" He studied her. "You must have been talking to Mildred. She has never learned when to keep her mouth shut."

"So is it true?" Angie lowered her voice. "She made it seem like I'd be buying my cheese for the restaurant somewhere else soon."

"I was hoping she'd see her way into granting us a short-term loan. But there are just too many variables. Unless an heir is found sooner than later, I'll have to go to the court to be made executor. And that might be outside our window to save the place." Ian stepped closer. "I'd rather that not be made public if you don't mind."

"I don't know anyone to gossip to." She felt her lips curve. "Except you, of course. Anyway, I came by to let you know I hired a construction crew to set up Precious in the barn. So if you stop by to de-horn her and I'm not home, you'll find her in there and not in the back yard."

"I'd forgotten I'd agreed to do that. I'll pop over tomorrow if that's okay." He glanced around the market. "I'll be here until late and then I'm heading over to Moss Farm to supervise the milking. They like having someone there in charge. It makes them move faster."

"Stop by around one and I'll cook dinner. Nona had a fried chicken recipe that I haven't made in a while."

"That would be nice." A silence fell between them.

Angie felt the electricity flowing between them. "I'll make dinner to pay you back for taking care of Precious, I mean."

"That's what I thought." He glanced around breaking the gaze between them and Angie's heart rate slowed just a bit. "I need to get busy. I'll drop off your cheese order on Wednesday morning?"

"I'll be at the restaurant by six. You can just come in the back door anytime after that."

He nodded. "I'm an early riser myself."

As he walked away, Felicia came up to Angie's side. "He's hot."

"He's a business contact." Angie kept watching him walk away. She had to admit, he looked as good leaving as coming.

"Whatever. But wipe that drool off your face. I want you to meet the owner of Southside Farms."

By the end of the afternoon, Angie had all the ingredients for Wednesday's dry run along with verbal agreements for ongoing suppliers from several of the local farms. Keeping the menu local and seasonal was going to be more work and more coordination than el pescado had been, but it was going to be worth it. Angie dreamed of even having a cooking class on weekend mornings maybe once a month. She put the idea aside. Get the restaurant up and running and maybe in the fall she'd start the classes.

"What are you thinking about?" Felicia asked as they carried their totes stuffed with goodies down Main Street toward the restaurant. "Ian?"

"No. I was not thinking about Ian. If you really want to know, I was thinking about how fun it would be to hold cooking classes at the restaurant one or two mornings a month." Thank God she hadn't been thinking about Ian, she wouldn't have had time to make up a plausible lie. Besides, Felicia seemed to know what she was thinking no matter what was going on.

"It's a great idea. We can do one during the week for the bored stay at home group and one on Saturday for the high-pressure career gal." Felicia kept talking about the idea, bringing in more and more ideas as they walked.

A movement from one of the buildings across the street caught Angie's eye. A man stood in the window of the upstairs apartment, looking down on them. When their eyes met, he moved out of view from the window. Kirk Hanley had told her that he lived in the apartment above his veterinarian clinic. Why was he watching them? Or was he watching Felicia?

"What's wrong?" Felicia glanced across the street. "Did you miss Dom's appointment?"

Angie shook her head, not wanting to worry her friend. "No, it's Monday. I was just thinking about my schedule."

Felicia held the door open for her. "Are you sure? You seem a little off."

"I'm fine. Just nervous for opening night. Let's get these put away and make sure we're ready for training day. I'd like it to run smoothly for once."

Felicia flipped on lights. "It's a good thing if the bad stuff happens on training day. That way we have time to fix the bugs before opening night the next week."

Angie knew she was right, but for some reason, she had a bad feeling about next week. Not about opening, but something else was bothering her. And until she put her finger on the problem, she wasn't going to rest easy, not with people watching them and the strange reaction Dom had last night at the farm.

As they unpacked, Angie told Felicia about what had happened when she went out to feed the animals. When she was finished, she asked one question. "Do you think coyotes would come in that far? I know they run the river area, but that's mostly wildlife reserves and a state park."

"I don't know. Maybe you should ask Mrs. Potter if she had trouble before. She'd be the best source," her voice trailed off. "But we're not talking to Mrs. Potter until we figure out if she killed Old Man Moss. Geez, sometimes it's hard to keep all the players straight."

"Well, the good news is there hasn't been a murder in River Vista for years so once the sheriff catches this one, we should be good for twenty or thirty years before the next one happens." Angie folded her tote looking around her new kitchen with what could only be expressed as joy.

"Totally. Too bad it had to happen now, especially since we're the new kids in town and everyone is watching us, thinking we are bringing our serial killer ways up from California with us."

Angie's laughter echoed in the room. "I think they're more upset we moved here from California than the possibility of us being serial killers. I guess there's been a mass exodus from the Golden State to Idaho for several years."

"Probably because of the cheap real estate." Felicia shrugged. "We came in with cash and a secured business loan. I bet a lot of people come with cash from selling their California homes and can buy almost anything."

Angie leaned on the expediter table and focused on her friend. "Like a piece of land with a killer view that's currently home to a goat dairy? Could the answer be that easy?"

"Doesn't seem like anything is easy here. Hey, I got you something but I left it out in the car. I'll be right back." Felicia headed to the back door. When she opened it, Angie saw the note tacked to the door with what looked like a Bowie knife.

"Stop. Go call 911."

Felicia turned toward her. "What are you talking about?"

"Just step away from the door." Angie stepped toward the door trying to make out the words. Someone had taped a picture of a large black cat on the page, wrote one word under it, then shoved a knife through the kitty's heart.

"What does it say?" Felicia's words caught in her throat.

Angie grabbed her cell and took a picture before dialing 911. "Curiosity killed the cat."

# CHAPTER 12

After the Sheriff had left with the note and the knife tucked away in plastic bags and a promise to have an officer walk by more often, Felicia walked Angie to her car. The chatter about plans she had for the restaurant had dried up.

"Maybe someone thinks they're funny." Felicia leaned on the car as Angie opened the back and put in the bag with the items she'd bought for home, including another supply of cherries. She would make jam before the supply of cherries went away for the year.

"I don't know. But I don't like it. Maybe we should think about a security system."

"Whoa, what's this for?" Felicia peeked into the bag labeled Babies, Babies, Babies. "What on earth did you buy there?" She pulled out the lone box. "A baby monitor? Why?"

"You're going to laugh." Angie sat on the back of her open hatchback.

"I might not." Felicia sat next to her, and shrugged. "But I probably will. Besides, I could use a good laugh. That stupid note has me in a funk. Spill, are you stockpiling because your biological clock is ticking?"

"No." Angie laughed and took the box from her. "Why would you even say that?"

"Because Ian's a hottie," they both said together then the two friends burst into laughter. "So if it's not the biological thing going on, why do you have a baby monitor? Do you have a shower to go to I don't know about?" Felicia glanced at her phone when it went off, indicating she had a text.

"You can take that if you need to."

"Nah, I'm just meeting a few people for open bowling tonight in Meridian. You should come." Felicia slipped the phone in her pocket.

"I'm making jam." Angie stood and put the box back into the sack.

Felicia jumped up and closed the hatchback. "So why do you have a baby monitor?"

"I'm putting it in the barn to keep an ear out for Precious and Mabel." Angie added the hen to the list so it wouldn't look too crazy that she was worried about a baby goat.

Felicia burst out laughing. "That's so sweet."

"You mean, that's so lame." Angie walked around and opened the driver's door. "Have fun bowling. Do you want me to drop you back off at the restaurant?"

Felicia came over and stood next to her. "I think I can walk two blocks by myself. Besides, like you said, the serial killer has already taken his once in twenty-year victim."

"You may not want to count on my theories for your safety. Besides, that note wasn't just a joke. You know it." Angie started the car and after saying goodbye to her friend. She wanted to head home to make jam. Again. Hopefully this time she wouldn't be interrupted by Ian and his bestie, Sheriff Brown. But she still had a meeting with Mildred before she could start the process.

But Angie ended up sitting in the plastic reception chair until almost two.

"I don't know what happened. She must have run late at the women's group. I've called her several times, but her phone keeps going to voice mail." The receptionist stood by Angie's chair. "I'm sorry, but I'm going to have to reschedule your appointment. I'm locking the doors at two."

Angie tucked her phone into her purse. "Sure, when can I come back?"

"What about Wednesday? Same time?" The woman walked back to her desk to write down the new appointment in her paper calendar.

Angie shook her head. "Sorry. Wednesday's totally booked. What about Monday?"

"We're closed on Mondays and Tuesdays Mildred saves for dairy visits so she's out in the field that day. I could get you in at ten on Thursday if that will work?"

"Sounds great." As she walked out the door, Angie wondered if Mildred just didn't want to talk to her or if she had forgotten about the appointment. Mildred didn't seem the type to flake out on commission business, so maybe she had realized Angie's true mission was to get information about Gerald Moss and his relationship to the commission.

* * * *

The jam sat cooling on the counter and Angie was sitting at the table going over her recipes one more time. A knock came at the door and she looked up and saw Erica Potter standing at the door.

"Erica, come on in. What's going on?"

The young woman came in and gave Dom a hug before sitting down at the table with Angie. "I just came to let you know I'm heading to Boise overnight. We're going to a concert, then an after party so I'm staying at a friend's house. Granny says she'll be fine, but just in case you see something weird, I wanted you to know she's alone."

"No worries. Do you want me to take her dinner?" Angie grabbed the iced tea out of the fridge and offered Erica some.

She shook her head. "No, I'm good. And we just ate so Granny should be good until I get back. She only eats toast for breakfast anyway. And she'll be in bed in a couple of hours. I just worry."

"Well, don't tonight. If I see anything weird, I'll deal with it. And I'll call her in a couple of hours and make sure she's okay." Angie nodded to the jam. "I could drop off some cherry jam for her toast in the morning."

"Thanks, I'd appreciate it." Erica stood and gave Angie a quick hug. "You're a good neighbor."

As she watched the girl make her way back across the road, Angie shook her head. "I'm so not a good neighbor, especially since I'm thinking that girl or her grandmother could have killed a man."

Dom stood by her side, watching. Glancing at the clock, she realized it was time to feed Precious and Mabel. As she and Dom left the kitchen for the front porch, he didn't even glance over toward the road. Instead he bee lined to the barn and waited for her at the open door.

"You're getting the hang of the routine?" She rubbed his soft fur behind his ears as he wagged his tail. She found Mabel already perched on the gate of an empty stall. When Angie threw out some corn, she opened one eye to check on her morning snack and then closed it again. Precious was tucked into the same spot where Angie had found her yesterday. The goat came running when she saw Angie and Dom. This time, Dom let Precious sniff his nose before stepping away. "If I didn't know better, I'd say you two were starting to be friends."

Angie fed the goat, turned on the baby monitor she had set up on a shelf near her pen, and then went outside and closed the door. On really hot summer nights, she might have to leave this open, but she would have tested out the baby monitor by then. Precious was part of her life, she needed to just accept it. Unless the new owner of Moss Farm was a total jerk and insisted she return the goat.

That night she fell asleep with the songs of crickets serenading her from the barn.

A knock on the door early the next morning had Angie scrambling to grab a robe and hurry downstairs. She expected to see Mrs. Potter at her door. Instead, Ian stood there, a bag of donuts in his hand. Self-conscious, she ran her hands over her hair to minimize the bed head.

He smiled. "Sorry I'm early. I've been called to Moss Farm this afternoon to do inventory for the court appointed estate executive. I've already taken care of Precious."

"What?" Angie's brain wasn't connected yet. She looked at the kitchen wall clock. Ten after five. Way too early for a Sunday. Especially since she'd gotten to bed about one last night after finalizing all her recipes.

"You aren't much of a morning person, are you?" He opened the door and shoved the bag into her hand. "I've got to run. I wanted to honor our agreement to de-horn your goat this morning. Too much longer and it would have been more difficult."

Angie could smell the yeast and sugar from the donuts. "Thanks."

"You are most welcome. Go back to bed." He turned and headed to his car. Angie watched him leave, then a thought struck her. She should have offered him coffee at least. "He probably brought donuts to share, not for me to eat alone."

Dom woofed and watched the car drive away.

"You want out since we're up anyway?" She looked down at him and got a full-fledged grin in response.

While she was up, she went into the barn to feed. Precious had red-colored goop on her nubs and a full bowl of food. "Ian must have fed you already."

The goat bleated in affirmation, not seeming to mind the de-horner solution she wore. Mabel scratched at the corn near the door. Angie reached up to turn off the baby monitor, but it was already shut off. Ian must know her little secret. She wondered what kind of mileage he'd get out of that piece of gossip.

"Looks like I didn't have to get up at all." She whistled to Dom who was checking out the pasture area. He came running back and followed her into the house where she ignored the donuts and went back upstairs to get another couple of hours.

When she woke a second time, it was the ringing phone that brought her out of a perfectly crazy dream that had her and Ian in a relationship rather than just friends. Angie brushed a hand over her lips, still feeling the kiss between the two of them as her dream had ended. Grabbing the phone, she blurted, "What?"

A minute of silence fell and Angie wondered if they had gotten disconnected. Then a small frail voice asked, "Angie, is that you?" She sat up in bed. "Mrs. Potter?"

"Sorry. Did I wake you dear?" Mrs. Potter signed. "I've been up for hours and was just wondering what that man was doing over at your house this morning. It was very early for a social call and he went into your barn. Things are okay over there, right?"

"Everything's fine here. How about with you? Are you doing all right with Erica staying overnight with friends?" Angie glanced at her alarm clock. Six fifteen. At least she'd gotten another hour of sleep. Her eyes felt like sandpaper against the morning light.

"Oh, well, then I'll let you go. I was just worried."

Angie rubbed her eyes willing the tiredness to go away. "You don't have to, I'm awake now."

"No, I shouldn't have called so early. I'm an early bird these days and I guess I expect everyone else to have the same hours that I keep." Mrs. Potter laughed at herself. "Erica will be home by noon and we're going into the buffet for lunch. I might miss out on church today, but I'll be able to get all the gossip at lunch."

"I can come over and visit in a few minutes." Angie crossed the worn wooden floor to the window and looked out on the morning.

"Don't bother, I'm actually a little sleepy so I'm laying back down. Now that I know you're all right, I think I can get a couple more hours in before Erica comes back."

*Glad you can.* But instead of verbalizing her actual thought, Angie found the energy to be positive and wished her neighbor a good day. Then she plopped back down on the bed, her phone still in her hand.

Considering her options, she groaned and pulled herself back up and headed for a shower. Now that she didn't have Ian coming for lunch, she could take a nap. Or, she mused, she could take lunch to him. What a great way to get access to Moss Farm and look for clues along with pumping Ian for answers to her many questions.

By eleven, Nona's fried chicken was packed in her picnic basket along with red potato salad and a jar of iced tea. She threw in a checked table cloth. If she remembered correctly, there was a picnic table set near the edge of the yard at Moss Farm. She tucked a bag of cookies into basket and then put Dom into the back seat.

As she backed up to turn around in the driveway, she saw Dom staring at her. "This is definitely not a date. So stop looking at me that way."

She turned up the music and started singing along. Life was good. Even when she was stressed about opening night and the little matter of the murder down the road, she felt more comfortable in her own skin than she had in a long time. This must be what being home feels like, she thought.

When she got to the farm, Ian's car and a black Suburban sat near the barn. Staying in the car after she parked, she dialed his number.

"Good afternoon. Sorry I woke you so early this morning." Ian's voice sounded muffled.

"No problem. Hey, I promised you lunch, so I brought it over." Now Angie was second guessing her plan. This felt like a date even to her. "But if you're too busy, I can just leave."

"You brought me lunch?"

"Nona's fried chicken, potato salad, and some cookies for dessert. If your friend wants to join us, I brought more than enough." She felt like she was rambling. "Or like I said, I can just leave."

"No. Don't leave. That sounds wonderful. All I've had all day was two of those donuts I brought you, and man does not live by donut alone. No matter what kind of sweet tooth they have." He paused and Angie could hear someone talking in the background. "Go get set up on the picnic table and we'll be out in five to ten minutes. We're just finishing up the production house inventory."

"Sure thing. Oh, and I brought Dom. Just so you won't be surprised."

Ian laughed. "I would have been surprised if you'd brought that bloody goat. Dom, I expect to see with you most of the time. We'll be right out."

Angie tucked her phone into her back pocket and let Dom out. Then she grabbed the tablecloth and the basket. She'd just finished setting up the table for three when Dom barked behind her. Turning, Angie expected to see Ian and the court-appointed person coming toward them. Instead, the area between the barn and the table was empty.

"What are you looking at?" She bent down to Dom's level, letting her gaze follow his. She tightened her grip on his collar when she saw movement. But instead of the coyote she feared she'd see out this way, she saw a woman running toward the back of the property. Where the trail she'd been on last week must intersect with Moss Farm.

The woman turned and glanced over her shoulder and Angie recognized her. Mildred had been in the house and was now running away. She moved toward the table, keeping hold of Dom. Things were getting weird. Why would Mildred be out here, especially since she claimed Gerald Moss hadn't been part of the cheese commission? And if she was part of the court group doing inventory, why was she trying to be sneaky about leaving?

When Ian and a young man came out of the barn, Dom wagged his tail furiously. Ian hurried over and introduced his helper. "Angie Turner, this is Will Bergin. He's clerking for one of the district judges this year and is working part time this summer as a court representative for the probate department."

"Nice to meet you, Will." Angie held out a hand and the young man dressed in a white shirt and tie shook it vigorously.

"Thanks for bringing us food. I'm on per diem, but it rarely covers more than one meal. The court division is pretty cheap with their temp staff." He sniffed the air. "That chicken smells amazing. I haven't had good chicken since I left Alabama and Mama sent me off with my last Sunday dinner for a while."

"Well, I hope I come close to your mother's cooking." Angie glanced toward the barn. "Just the two of you? Who else is here?"

"No one. The milkers left at seven and since then, it's just been the two of us." Ian sat down at the table and poured iced tea for all of them. "Well, us and the goats. But they're all out on the pasture by now."

Angie unpacked the basket and handed Will the chicken. Obviously, they hadn't known Mildred was sneaking around the house. What had she been looking for? "Are you done with the house then?"

"Haven't even started. I think this is going to be a two-day job." Will took a leg and a wing and sat it on his plate, handing the rest to Ian. "The guy had a lot of junk to go through."

Ian took the chicken and then Angie unpacked the salad. "Well, I can't promise to bring lunch tomorrow, but I could leave the leftovers if you want to keep them in Mr. Moss's kitchen."

"Well, isn't that a great idea. Nothing better than leftovers." Ian smiled at her. "What a lovely thought."

Angie felt a stab of guilt since the only reason she'd suggested it was so she would have a reason to get into the house.

This investigating was hard work. And she had to be a little deceitful to get what she needed. But it wasn't quite lying, now, was it?

# CHAPTER 13

"I've got to call my girlfriend." Will rubbed his stomach. "Thank you so much for the eats ma'am. Ian, I'll be in the barn in twenty minutes to start back up, will that work?"

"I'll help Angie pack this up and be there as soon as I'm done." Ian watched as Will took off for the ridge, as he pulled out a cell phone. "That girl has him on a short leash. He's called her four times this morning alone. I hate to see what's going to happen when he's actually in court for hours and can't touch base."

"Young love. They'll get to the point they don't want to talk to each other. It's sweet that he misses her so much." She opened the Tupperware with the cookies. "Shortbread?"

"My favorite. Of course, any homemade cookie is my weakness. When I moved into town, the church ladies took turns visiting me with their creations." He took a bite. "But I have to say, yours are better."

"I'm a professional. Like buying from a store, but not prepared in a factory." She took a cookie and leaned back in her chair. "So why do you do this?"

"What?" He filled her tea glass and then his own before grabbing another cookie.

"Help people. You can't be making much from running the farmers' market. And this, this is just above and beyond." She watched him as he considered his answer.

"Probably the same reason you came back to this little town. I like helping people. Gerald Moss was a pain in the rear. But he made great goat cheese. He cared for his animals like they were family. And he didn't deserve to lose his life this way." He smiled at her. "He would have liked you. I mean, I think he did already, but if he knew how you were taking care of Precious, he would have loved you."

"You turned off the baby monitor." She didn't frame it as a question, just a statement.

"Yes, I did. I was impressed with your ingenuity. Can I ask what you're worried about?"

Angie shifted uncomfortably in her seat. "Dom was growling at something when we were out feeding late on Friday. I remembered what you said about coyotes, and well, I was concerned."

"I don't think there's a pack that far from the river. Are you sure it wasn't a two-legged intruder? You're pretty far from town." He glanced toward the ridge and shrugged. "Although you aren't that far from the canyon. Gerald was always complaining that the coyotes were getting too brazen out here. He said it was a good thing he'd never sell for those fancy condos because the damn dogs would carry off a baby before the clueless parents would know it was gone."

Angie pressed her lips together, trying not to smile. "I think he was thinking about the dingoes in Australia."

"He seemed to think a dog is a dog." He pointed toward Dom. "Your dog could carry off a small woman with no issue."

She rubbed Dom's head as he leaned against her leg. "When he's full grown, maybe. Right now, he'd be pushed to carry Mabel anywhere."

"Mabel, is that your neighbor?" Ian closed his eyes, looking like he needed to clock a few more hours of sleep in his schedule. "I haven't met her yet."

She laughed in spite of herself. The way this conversation was going, she'd never get any dirt on Gerald Moss or the reasons he was killed. "Mabel's my hen. Actually, she was my Nona's hen. She rules the place, and is kind enough to let me live there as long as I keep feeding her."

"Oh. You Americans choose such interesting names for your animals. Where I grew up, dogs were called Spot and chickens didn't even have names." He shook his head like he could will away the fatigue and took another cookie. "Why are you so interested in Gerald?"

The bluntness of his question shocked her. "Why do you say that?"

He watched a hawk soar over the canyon ridge, playing with the wind gusts. "I hear things. Allen isn't an idiot. He doesn't need help solving the murder, if that's what you're thinking."

"I'm not thinking that. But sometimes I worry that my friend Felicia and I are the newcomers in the area and everyone knows I came up here on Sunday to talk to Gerald."

"Or Saturday."

"What?" Now it was her turn to be confused.

"Some rumors say you were here on Saturday."

"You mean Reana. She says I was here on Saturday. Which you know better because the first time I met Gerald Moss was on Saturday at the farmers' market."

"But that's not true, is it?"

Angie sat forward, feeling the fire in her veins. "I wouldn't say it if it wasn't true."

He watched her for a while. "Angie, you came out here with your grandmother when you were a little girl. Before you lost your parents. He told me how pretty and happy you were back then. That your eyes sparkled with joy when you saw the goats. And that the loss of your parents made that light drop out of your eyes."

"I didn't come here. I would have remembered." Would she really have remembered? She'd taken a lot of the memories from before the crash and locked them away. Why couldn't this be one of them? She took a deep breath. "I didn't remember him at all. How insensitive could I be?"

"If you don't remember, you can't be held responsible. He remembered. And it gave him joy that the little girl who'd had so much pain in the past had found her true path. Her calling. That's all any of us can wish for our children. That they find their path." He reached out and grabbed her hand. "He knew and that's all that mattered."

"Maybe that's why I can't get his murder out of my head. Why I feel like it's up to me to find out who killed him and why. I knew him." Angie blew out a long breath. "So do you believe me that I was here Sunday?"

"I do. But I have no clue why Reana would be so adamant it was Saturday." He looked at her. "Do you?"

"She told me he was going to sell the property. That she was getting an exclusive agency to sell the entire farm. She wanted to keep it under wraps until she had his John Hancock on the paperwork." Angie shrugged. "I don't understand real estate contracts and why it would matter."

"Especially now that Gerald is dead. Keeping it a secret doesn't make any sense at all." Ian rubbed his chin, playing with the little bit of beard shadow that was coming on his face. "I can see keeping him under wraps so someone didn't come by and steal the listing. Now that he's dead, there has to be another reason she doesn't want to admit she was here on Sunday."

"Exactly." Angie looked around the empty yard. She spotted Will down the fence, out of earshot. "So I want to look around the house and see if I can find any clues."

"And that's why you're leaving tomorrow's lunch in Gerald's fridge? You realize he was a bachelor and that thing might have a few science experiments growing in the back."

"I'll clean it out and throw away any gross stuff. I'm thinking it's more likely it will be empty or filled with cheese or Ding Dongs." She focused on Ian's face. "Are you going to tell me not to go snooping?"

"I have no right to tell you to do anything. Besides, I was kidding about the fridge." Ian's eyes sparkled. "I will tell you that our besotted Will doesn't miss much, so I wouldn't take too long in there. The boy has a keen eye for details."

"Thanks." She glanced over to where Will had completed his call and was walking back toward them. "I'll call you later tonight and I'll tell you if I found anything."

"Now I'm part of the investigating team too? Don't I feel like your Nancy Drew."

Angie smiled. "I think I'm Nancy Drew. You're Ned or better yet, Frank Hardy. He was the cute one, right?"

"Again, you realize I didn't grow up in the states and I have no clue what you're talking about." Ian stood and stretched. "Anyway, today, I'm too tired to think of a British equivalent for your teenage sleuthing models."

"So you do know who I'm talking about."

He gave her a grin as he walked away. "I wasn't born yesterday."

As he met up with Will and led the young man away to the barn, Angie packed up the basket, setting the food on top so she could easily transfer the containers into the refrigerator. There was no crime scene tape on the front door. As she entered, she hoped Sheriff Brown had already had investigators go through the house. She didn't have gloves but at least she'd be able to explain away any prints they might find in the kitchen. Now, if she left some in the guy's bedroom, those would be harder to explain.

Giggling at the look she imagined Sheriff Brown would give her as they talked, she headed to the kitchen to drop off the basket, then she'd quickly go through the house and see what she could find. It shouldn't take her long since she had no idea what she was looking for or if she'd know it when she found it.

The kitchen was surprisingly clean. She set the basket down by the fridge and peeked inside. It was completely empty, except for the half-gone loaf of focaccia bread she'd given to Mr. Moss. She brushed it with her fingers, feeling the man's loss and her own of not being able to get to know him. Nona had liked the guy, he had to have some redeeming qualities.

Angie decided that Ian must have come and cleaned out the perishables. The man seemed to think of anything, including all the details of life. She smiled, thinking of the way he'd turned off her baby monitor in the barn so that he wouldn't disturb her as he took care of Precious.

Leaving the kitchen, she headed into the living room. Shelves of bookcases lined the three walls that weren't taken up with a large rock fireplace. An old leather couch and a recliner faced the fireplace. And peeking out from under the couch was a spot of pink. Angie bent over and pulled out a floral scarf. She blinked, trying to remember where she'd seen one just like it. Then it came to her: Mildred's office. She'd been wearing this same scarf. She picked it up and put it in her pocket. Focusing back on the room, she didn't see a television. Had the guy been that far off the grid? She picked up the book on the table next to the chair. It was a well-read copy of *Treasure Island*. The surprises just kept coming.

She sat the book back down and headed to the end of the room where an old roll-top desk sat with a desktop computer on the top. No television, but a computer. She powered it up but didn't get farther than the sign on screen. Gerald Moss had password protected his documents. She glanced around for a small notebook, the ones you keep important facts you don't want to forget, like passwords, but came up empty handed. Nona had gotten a computer a few years before her death and she kept all her passwords close by. She'd joked with Angie that if she didn't, she'd be locked out of her games forever. He had to have kept his somewhere.

She turned off the computer after searching through the desk drawers and finding nothing except tax records and receipts for the dairy. She couldn't waste too much time here, or Will would be suspicious. She left the living room and headed into the hallway. The tiny house had two bedrooms. One looked like a storage closet, filled with boxes. She opened up one of the boxes and found women's clothing. From the look of them, they were decades old and well worn. "These must be from his wife." A wave of sadness came over her as she looked at the boxes from his marriage. Memories locked away, but he was unable to part with the items, even years after she passed on. She shut the door and went into the other bedroom. This room was neat and tidy too. The bed had a worn but clean quilt on top, probably from his marriage. Again, there was one book on the bedside table, Michael Crichton's *Pirate Latitudes*. The man had had a serious affection for pirate books.

She glanced through the table and found a journal and a pen. The handwriting was scratchy, but from the last notation, he had written in it nightly, recording the events of the day. She flipped through a few pages.

Records of goat births and deaths, money earned at the farmers' market selling cheese, visitors to the farm, and a list of his employees and their weekly pay. A record of his life. On a shelf, under the drawer, a stack of identical journals sat.

Angie grabbed two of the newest journals and carried them to the kitchen. She'd put the food away and leave the cabin with her find, for now. They might not have all the answers, but the journals would at least give her some idea of what was going through the guy's mind in the last days of his life.

She put the food containers in the fridge along with the half gone iced tea containers. Then she tucked the journal into her basket under the table cloth. Pausing before she left the cabin, she took out her phone and went through all the rooms, taking several pictures of everything, including the bathroom and the medicine cabinet. She might not have access to the actual cabin again, but she could study the photos more closely when she got home.

Glancing around the living room, her eyes fell on the computer. There were answers there, she could feel it. She just couldn't get past the sign on screen. No use worrying about something you can't fix, her Nona always said.

Dom sat on the porch, looking in through the screen door. She'd left the front door open and told him to stay, but she hadn't thought he would. If he had wandered, the goats were down on the ridge pasture and out of his eyesight so she had assumed he wouldn't go far.

Too late, she remembered Mildred and wondered what she'd been looking for in the cabin. Could it have only been the scarf? Turning around, she debated going back in, but saw Will and Ian heading her way. She plastered on a smile and left the cabin calling out to the guys. "Good news, the fridge was clean. Tomorrow's lunch will be waiting for you."

Ian took her basket from her and walked her to the car. "I wouldn't have sent you in there if I hadn't cleaned it out last week."

She let Dom in the backseat as Ian put the basket in the hatchback. "I figured that was you. What, do you like to see me cringe?"

Will was on the porch now, apparently waiting for Ian. She leaned against the car and lowered her voice. "He's watching us."

Ian chuckled and put his hand on her arm. Chills filled her body. "You're right. He thinks we make a good couple. So let's pretend for a minute that we are. Did you find anything?"

"I'm not sure. The computer is password protected. Have you got any idea what his password was?"

"Not a clue." Ian smiled like they were talking about future dates and not a dead man's belongings. "Anything else?"

"Did you find a cell phone? Reana said she left one with him." She looked at the rustic cabin without even a television. "Could he even use a cell phone?"

"Maybe she pre-programmed her number in the phone. But no, Allen's guys didn't find a cell here in the cabin, nor in the barn. You would have thought he would have been carrying it, but he wasn't."

"Or Reana was lying about the phone." Angie shrugged. "Not like that hasn't happened before."

"Anything else we should talk about?"

She wondered how much she could really trust him and shook her head. If she found something in the journal, she'd mention it then. "He must have loved his wife. He still had all her things."

"I know. He talked about her a lot when we sat and watched the sun set over the ridge. It must be nice having such good memories." Now Ian was looking into her eyes and the shiver went all the way from where his hand caressed her hair to her toes. "Nothing else?"

She decided to change the subject. "You're good at this fake relationship thing."

He smiled and stepped away. "Who said I was faking?"

She stood there a minute, dumbfounded at his words. When she got her emotions under control, she faked a smile and climbing into the car, rolling down her window. She waved and called out her goodbyes to the men and slowly eased down the driveway. When they were on the road, she glanced in the rearview mirror at Dom. The dog was watching her.

"Okay, maybe you were right. It was a date."

Dom seemed to grin, then lay down on the seat and closed his eyes. He was taking advantage of the short car ride to nap before he had to take up his role as the house watchdog again. Rough life, Angie thought as she navigated the country roads home. No worries and no dead man's journals to read and interpret.

She had a lot of work to do when she got home and none of it dealt with the restaurant she was opening in less than two weeks.

# CHAPTER 14

Angie made a pot of coffee as soon as she got home and took the journals into her own living room and reading spot. Hours later, when her stomach growled, she stopped to make a quick dinner and feed her circus. Dom looked up from his spot near the wood stove and followed her into the kitchen, expecting food.

Thirty minutes later, she was back to reading the journals. She'd found what she assumed was Precious's birthdate and wrote it down for future reference. Did people celebrate goats' birthdays? She knew Dom's birthday too and the dates were just weeks apart.

She needed to get the restaurant going, she had way too much time on her hands if she was thinking about things like this.

She went back to the journals and worked until Dom nudged her leg. Glancing at the clock, she realized it was past midnight. She put her notebook down and put a bookmark in the journal she'd been reading. The man had kept notes about everything. Even when Reana had come by to offer him money for the land. Date, what she offered and what she'd said the new owners were going to do with the land. And surprisingly, Mildred's name showed up in the journal a few times a month. The woman must have been closer to Gerald than she wanted people to know. Or she was really persistent about Moss Farm joining her cheese commission as a member. One more thing to talk to her about on Thursday, if the woman showed up this time.

Angie stood, stretched and headed upstairs to her bedroom. Tomorrow was a busy day with Dom's visit to the vet clinic—and her discussion with Kirk Hanley about his strange behavior. She started to think about how she was going to ask why the guy was being such a weirdo when sleep took over and she fell into a dreamless slumber.

Her alarm woke her the next morning and by the time she'd eaten breakfast and gotten her chores done, it was only eight. Dom's appointment was at ten so she had some time.

She grabbed her last loaf of homemade bread and cut it in half. Wrapping it up in cellophane, she put it and a jar of the cherry jam in a bag. Then, after closing the door on Dom so he wouldn't try to break through the screen door and follow her, she walked across the street to Mrs. Potter's house.

She knocked at the kitchen door and waited. Erica swung open the door and Angie could smell the bacon frying on the stove. "Hey neighbor, come on in. We were just getting breakfast on the table. Have you eaten?"

"I did about an hour ago. I wouldn't mind some coffee though. I wanted to stop by and give you this." She handed the bag to the young woman.

Glancing inside, Erica pulled out the jar of jam. "Totally cool. I had jam on the shopping list. And fresh bread. I think I'll make Granny a slice right now."

"You'll make me a slice of what?" Mrs. Potter came into the kitchen using her walker. "Oh, Angie, dear. I didn't know you were here. Come in and sit down."

Angie waited for Mrs. Potter to get settled at the table, then joined her. Erica brought them both a cup of coffee, sitting a tiny creamer pitcher in front of her grandmother. "Sugar?" She asked and looked at Angie.

Angie shook her head. "Black's fine."

"Well, my dear, what brings you over besides trying to fatten up an old woman?" Mrs. Potter sipped her now light brown coffee.

"No small talk today, huh?" Angie grinned. "Actually, I do have a question. And I don't want you to get upset."

"No worries. There are few things in this world that get my heart racing anymore. Including that cute man who keeps showing up at your door." Mrs. Potter curved her lips into a sly smile. "Don't think I don't notice when you have gentlemen callers. Your Nona was my best friend. I told her I'd keep an eye out for her."

"Ian and I are…" Angie paused wondering how to actually end that statement, especially after yesterday's picnic. Her face burned at the thought of their conversation by the car. "We're friends. For now, that's all."

"If you say so dear." Mrs. Potter patted her hand. "Now that I've got you blushing, what did you want to ask me?"

Angie sipped her coffee, stalling for time. Finally, when both Erica and Mrs. Potter were staring at her, she asked the question. "Why do you think Gerald Moss killed your sister? I mean, I can't find anything about her murder in the local paper archives and I would think a murder would have shown up at least as a sideline."

"I never meant to say he killed her. But the man was responsible for Sophia's death, as much as he would have been if he was the one to put a knife to her throat." She looked at Erica who was standing by the stove. "Grandchild, come over and sit with us. I'm only telling this story once and you have a right to know about your great aunt too."

Erica turned off the stove and lifted the bacon onto a paper towel-covered plate. She put the plate in the oven and turned it onto a low heat. Then she filled her own cup of coffee and sat down. "You said your sister died in New York City. That she was mugged on the street."

"And that's true. But I never told anyone why she was there." Mrs. Potter shook her head. "Not even Mama and Papa knew how Sophia got there. Papa would have killed him if he'd known."

Confused, Angie glanced at Erica who looked as lost as she felt. "Maybe if you start at the beginning."

"Of course, that's always the best way." Mrs. Potter stirred her coffee for the third time. "We were seniors when Sophia started high school. She wasn't just pretty, she was like Erica, stunning. All the boys were trying to get me to introduce them to her, but Papa had a strict no dating until you turned sixteen rule. You can't stop love though, and she fell hard for Gerald Moss."

Angie thought about the room filled with his deceased wife's items and realized the man was a romantic.

"They started sneaking out. Seeing each other after school, after her drama club meetings, where ever they could spare a second. She turned sixteen the summer between freshman and sophomore years and Gerald started courting her officially. My parents, they were skeptical, but since Sophia was determined, they let Gerald into our lives. I had met Mr. Potter by then and we were planning our wedding. Sophia's junior year, I was a new bride and didn't have time to listen to my sister's crazy dreams about making it big in the theatre." Mrs. Potter paused and took a sip of coffee. "I always wonder if I'd been a better sister back then, if things would have been different."

"You can't change the past." Angie said before she realized she was going to say anything.

Mrs. Potter smiled, her thin lips disappearing completely. "Margaret always said the same thing when I'd bring up Sophia."

"Go on Granny, what happened?" Erica was entranced with the story, Angie could see it on her face.

"After the fall production, she'd gotten a letter from a theatre in the city. She had an audition for a really small part. I guess her drama teacher knew someone in the business. So she took off to try to make it big." Mrs. Potter shook her head. "We found out later that he'd paid for her bus ticket there and back. She was only supposed to be gone a few days, but when she got to the city, she was attacked. They sent her body home on the train."

"Did they catch her killer?" Angie swallowed hard. She hadn't expected this.

Mrs. Potter nodded. "Some guy she'd given a dollar to as soon as she got off the bus. He'd followed her and dragged her into an alley. He wanted the rest of the money he'd seen in her purse. He swore in court he was high and didn't know what he was doing. But he was still convicted."

"Gerald must have felt responsible." Angie shook her head. "He loved her and supported her dream only to have it kill her."

"He did. He sobbed at the funeral, but then I made a scene and told him he might as well have killed Sophia. I was hurting too, but looking back on it, it wasn't my place to put more guilt on him." Mrs. Potter shook her head. "We never talked again. He married a few years later to a woman who'd gone to Nampa High. And we both went on with our lives."

"Oh Granny, I'm so sorry." Erica patted her grandmother's wrinkled hand.

Angie saw Mrs. Potter squeeze Erica's hand quickly, then she lifted her cup and took a sip of her coffee. "What's done is done. Just make sure you don't hold on to something all your life. Forgiveness can't be given once the door is shut forever. I wish I'd told him I was sorry for what I'd said."

"It wasn't your fault." Erica protested. "She was your sister…"

"Get me some more coffee dear and let's put this aside. An old woman can only live in the past for so long before it starts to swallow her alive." She stared into her cup like it held the answers to long held slights. A smile gently curved her lips. "Gerald Moss was always a ladies' man. He could charm a snake out of its den."

"I'm sure he loved your sister." Angie wasn't sure how to keep the conversation going and more importantly, if she really wanted to know the answers. "What else did you know about Mr. Moss? Any rumors lately? Was he dating anyone now?"

"Gerald? At his age?" Mrs. Potter giggled. "I think he might have wanted someone around to keep him from being lonely, but dear, the man was in his eighties. Of course, you never know, right?"

"I didn't mean," Angie felt her face burning. "I'm not sure what I'm asking. I just don't understand why someone would murder him."

"Sometimes things just happen." Mrs. Potter spread jam on the toast Erica had just set in front of her. "Of course, there were rumors that Moss Farm held a treasure, but I'm sure that was probably just gossip."

"Treasure?" Angie perked up. Could someone have been hoping to get rich off Old Man Moss's land in an unexpected way?

"Like I said, silly gossip. The kind of thing kids make up when they're bored."

After a few more tries, Angie gave up. If Mrs. Potter knew anything more about Gerald Moss or the so-called treasure on his land, it had been lost years ago. She promised to come by if anything came to mind and with that promise Angie headed home.

She checked the time. Dom had his appointment at ten. She could head into town early and check in with Felicia, but instead, she sat down at the table and made notes about what Mrs. Potter had said.

She didn't have a next step. Maybe there was an online investigation course. She grinned at the thought. Maybe it would have a cheat sheet on who to talk to when an old man is pushed off a cliff.

At a standstill, she put Gerald's murder out of her mind and took out the file on Wednesday's training schedule. This made sense. This she could work with and plan and actually complete something. Before she knew it, it was time to leave for Dom's appointment.

She loaded him into the car and drove into town. Fifteen minutes early, she was surprised to find the door to the vet clinic locked. Peering in the window, she didn't see anyone at the desk. The sign on the door said they opened at ten, so she sat with Dom on the bench outside the building.

Angie dug out her phone and dialed Felicia. When the call was answered, she asked. "Hey. What are you doing?"

"Eating breakfast. I didn't get in until late. Did you know there's a cave out in the middle of the freaking desert here?"

Angie stroked Dom's head as she talked. "Of course, it's where the kids went to party when I was in high school. Like the cops couldn't find them."

"I think they still use it for that. There were a lot of beer cans around and a few unmentionables. But the cave is amazing. Mike said there is an underground river farther in." Felicia yawned. "We didn't get back into town until two. I'm beat."

"Well, just make sure everything's ready for Wednesday. I'd like this dry run to go without a hitch." Angie watched a woman walk from around the back of the building where there must have been employee parking and toward her. "I think the clinic is opening. I've got to go."

"Wait, you're outside on the street and you call me instead of knocking at my door?"

Angie could see Felicia peeking out from the apartment window across the street. She waved at her friend. "I didn't know if you were awake."

"You were afraid I wasn't alone," Felicia countered. "Geez Angie, I'm not a total idiot."

"I didn't say that. I just think you deserve privacy too. Hey, after Dom's appointment, I'll come over and update you on the Mrs. Potter story. It's a doozy."

"Wait, what? You found out about Moss and her sister? You could have led with that." Felicia leaned on the window frame and watched her.

Even across the street, Angie could tell her friend was put out. "Sorry, gotta go. I'll talk to you soon."

She hung up the phone before she could get the lecture on not sharing information and stood when the woman came up to the door and unlocked it. "Good morning."

The woman smiled down at Dom. "I take it you have an appointment this morning? I didn't see Kirk's truck in the back, but maybe he ran to the store. Come on in, you can wait inside. I'll give him a call."

"Great." Angie wanted to get out of Felicia's sight just in case she came down to grill her about Mrs. Potter. One thing at a time and right now her dog needed his booster shots. Well, that was her story and she wasn't backing down.

She found a place to sit near a pile of old magazines. Dom sat at her feet, a small whine coming from the back of his throat. "You must smell the other animals that have been here."

"They all get a little freaky coming in." The woman was on the phone, but apparently, no one had answered yet. Her nametag only had her first name on the badge, Gloria, and was crooked on her shirt. "We try covering up the smells with cleaning solutions, but they all still know there were animals here before them. They have much better senses than we do."

"No one's here now," Angie gave Dom a reassuring hug. He was shaking. She looked at the receptionist. "We'll be in and out of here soon, right?"

Gloria held up a finger and then spoke into the phone. "Your ten o'clock is here. Where are you?"

Angie watched as Gloria's face hardened. "You should have left earlier, even if you were on a roll. I'm not sure how long I'm going to keep covering for you."

Angie's gaze met Gloria's but instead of a reassuring nod, she turned around, still listening to the conversation on the other side of the line. "I'll tell her. Just get here soon."

Angie heard the receiver slam down, but Gloria didn't turn. When she did, Angie saw her cheeks were wet. She stopped petting Dom. "Is something wrong?"

Gloria shook her head. "Sorry, ongoing fight. You would think the guy either would stop making Monday morning appointments or learn to leave Jackpot earlier."

"Jackpot? The town in Nevada?" Now Angie was confused. "That's about three hours away, right? Should we come back?"

"He's about ten minutes away. If you want, I can make some coffee. I'm thinking he'll be wanting some anyway." She waited for Angie's answer. When she didn't get a response, Gloria put on a fake smile. "Don't worry, he'll be here soon. And we'll get Dom's boosters done and you guys out of here in no time."

"Coffee would be great." The professional had taken over again, Angie thought as she watched the woman disappear into the back. But she had been mad at her boss. Or maybe frustrated was the better word. Angie wondered about their relationship and then about her vet, who apparently liked spending weekends in the closest gambling town to River Vista. The man was looking more like a total loser. First, he was weird with Felicia, then watching them through his window, and now, Angie learned about his apparent gambling habit. Yes, small towns held their own secrets. She decided she'd find a vet in Meridian for Dom's next checkup. Just as a precaution.

When fifteen minutes had passed, without seeing anyone at the desk or her promised coffee, Angie decided to leave. She walked to the reception desk and called out, "Hello? Is anyone back there?"

Gloria appeared in the doorway and frowned. "Crap, I forgot your coffee." She disappeared again before Angie could stop her.

"Seriously, I don't need coffee." She called after her hoping the woman would come back so Angie could explain how she needed to leave.

Instead, Kirk Hanley strode through the doorway. "Hey Angie, Dom. Come on back. Let's get this guy weighed and see how he's doing."

Dom wiggled at the sight of Kirk. Angie gave in. As long as Dom was happy, she'd deal with an appointment running a little late. She'd solve the problem by scheduling his next appointment with a new doc. Dom liked everyone, but it was better to switch vets early if she was going to do it. She followed Kirk into the back of the office and after getting Dom weighed, went into an exam room.

"This shouldn't take long. I'm sorry I'm running a little late." Kirk smiled at her as he lifted Dom up onto the exam table. "He's looking really good. You feeding him a premium dog food?"

"I still have him on the puppy food the breeder suggested. Do you think I should change up to adult food?" Angie saw the flip flops and jeans under the white lab coat Kirk wore. Of course, that could have been his usual office attire, but she doubted it.

"He needs the higher nutritional value of the puppy formula for at least six months. A year is preferable, but I'm thinking he's pretty expensive to feed, right?" Kirk smiled at her and for a minute, she forgot all the weird encounters she'd had with the guy. He was a lady killer, especially one on one. The guy was smooth.

"I want him to have what he needs so I'll keep him on the puppy food." Angie watched as he checked out Dom's health. After giving him the shots, he sat Dom on the floor where he immediately ran back to Angie.

Kirk leaned against the counter. "I think he's doing great. I don't need to see him again until his annual, unless you're concerned about something."

Angie stood. "Sounds great." She could make the decision later on changing to a different vet. After she'd learned more about Kirk. After all, if he wasn't going to be dependable, he probably wouldn't be in business in a year anyway.

She headed directly across the street and up the side stairs to Felicia's apartment. When she knocked, Felicia swung open the door and leaned down to greet Dom. "That took longer than I expected. Is he alright?"

Angie followed her into the apartment. "Dom is, but Kirk is a complete mess. He was in Jackpot this weekend so he was late for the appointment. And from his receptionist's reaction, this wasn't the first time."

"It's not illegal to go play the tables in Jackpot." Felicia held a cup of coffee out for Angie. "Now, being late for his business appointment, that's more problematic. I kind of did some research on our doctor friend after that incident at the restaurant."

"And what did you find?"

Felicia sat at the kitchen table and motioned for Angie to join her. "Dom's doctor is a bit of a flake. He's dating the woman who works for him. All of the old guys at the diner have switched over to another vet clinic for their farms. And he's missed so many appointments, most of his practice is just emergency treatments or new patients, like Dom."

"Until he doesn't show up for an appointment and loses those too."
Angie shook her head. "Too bad. He seems really nice, but reliability is
something that once you break trust, it's hard to get back."

"Everyone's betting his clinic will close this year. He just doesn't have
enough repeat customers to keep it going." Felicia glanced out the window.
"I guess the vet who retired and sold Kirk his business is thinking about
trying to get it back."

"He must be upset with the way it's being run." Angie sipped her coffee,
with one hand resting on Dom's head as he leaned into her.

"Upset? From the rumors, he's ready to kill the guy."

# CHAPTER 15

Tuesday flew by in a flurry of activity. Angie came into town and cooked every dish to make sure her recipes were spot on. Felicia set up the sample table for the dining room as well as finishing touches on the décor and setting up the bar area.

As they sat, eating the dishes she had cooked, Angie looked around the dining room. "It's never as perfect as this moment feels."

Felicia paused mid bite, the fork hovering over her plate. "What do you mean?"

"Today. The County Seat is this perfect idea in our heads. It's what could be. Tomorrow, when we add staff and train them, we leave behind the ideal and it becomes a reality. Maybe not perfect all the time, sometimes we'll fail, but sometimes, it will be better than we could have imagined." Angie sighed. "Don't get me wrong, I'm excited about the opening, but right now it's our idea, all shiny and perfect. Soon, it's going to be reality. And reality is hard and dirty and tough."

"Aren't you Debbie Downer today?" Felicia sat her fork down and focused on Angie. "It's going to be great. You're going to be great. And we're going to make a success out of this place, even if it kills us."

"Tell me you haven't gotten any more cryptic messages."

"I haven't gotten any more messages, cryptic or not." Felicia held up her hand in a salute. "Scout's honor."

"Were you ever a scout?" Angie studied her friend.

"Until they stopped doing cooking demos and wanted to take us camping, most definitely. I loved talking about cooking and baking. But sleeping on the ground in a tent? Not for me." She glanced at her watch. "Do you have plans the rest of the day?"

Angie rolled her shoulders. "I'm going in to clean up the kitchen then heading home. Precious and Mabel are probably wondering when they'll get fed again. I'll see you at seven tomorrow?"

"Bright and shiny. I've got our new staff arriving at eight and I told them to expect to be here a full day." She stood and picked up Angie's plate. "Go home. I'll clean up here. Living upstairs, I have the shorter commute."

"You're the best." Angie grabbed her tote and headed out the front where she'd parked the car. She beeped it open and glanced over at the vet clinic. It was almost six and the place looked like it had been closed for days. She believed in supporting local businesses, but only when they believed in themselves. She thought Kirk might just be a full-time farmer in the near future—until he lost that property as well.

The evening was warm and after taking care of the feeding, she sat on the porch with a cup of tea. Coffee this late in the day would have kept her up, and she knew she was going to have enough problems sleeping tonight as it was. Of course, this wasn't even opening night and she was antsy. What would she be like next Thursday before their Friday open?

The light was perfect and so she picked up a mystery novel she'd bought on her last trip to the bookstore and started reading. The combination of the book, the tea, and the evening did its magic and soon, she was yawning and ready for bed.

"Tomorrow is coming no matter what," she said to Dom as they made their way upstairs. "I might as well be positive about it."

\* \* \* \*

She woke early, took care of the animals, then sat and planned her day. Again. When she was done, it was still just after five thirty. She didn't have to leave for town for another hour. She picked up the novel, but instead of drawing her in, like it did last night, she found herself reading the same page, over and over. She set it down, went upstairs and grabbed laundry. No use being idle if she couldn't enjoy herself.

By six fifteen, the laundry was in the dryer, she'd cleaned out the dishwasher, inventoried her fridge and pantry for any shopping items, and vacuumed the entire downstairs. If she stayed here any longer, she'd have to resort to cleaning the bathrooms and then she'd feel like she had to take another shower after her efforts. She checked Dom's water and food, again.

Satisfied there wasn't anything she was missing, she drove into River Vista. Parking in the back, she got her keys to the building out just in case Felicia wasn't downstairs yet. She shouldn't have bothered.

Felicia met her at the back door. "I heard you drive up." She pulled her into a quick hug. "Can you believe it's almost opening day? Come in, I made us breakfast."

Angie followed her friend into the kitchen the smell of baked cinnamon, sugar, and yeast leading her to where a pan of cinnamon rolls sat on the counter, cooling.

"And I squeezed fresh orange juice. Do you know how many oranges it takes to make a glass of juice? Way too many." Felicia took out a bottle of champagne and popped the cork. "I know we can't drink all of this, but I thought mimosas were in order. The County Seat is going to be amazing."

Angie grinned at her friend's excitement. While she was all about the numbers and the details, Felicia was great with the energy and the idealism. "We are going to make this work, aren't we?"

"Darn right we are. You sound surprised. Give yourself and us a little credit. We are the smart girls after all." Felica handed her a glass flute with the drink. "To The County Seat and to us. May we always be as good of friends as we are today."

"Or better." Angie clinked her glass and then took a sip of the orange juice mixture. "I suppose you'll want a celebration on opening night too?"

"Of course, but that will be everyone. We'll gather in here, pour the champagne and then toast to our new adventure and our new family." Felicia grinned. "I might just make this an every week occurrence. You have to celebrate the little victories too."

Angie grabbed a couple of plates. "Let's see how your rolls turned out."

"Don't be knocking my baking skills. I did excel in that class if you remember." She grabbed a spatula and served out two large, thick gooey rolls.

As they sat and ate, Felicia went over the schedule. "I'll be done with training and setup no later than two. So plan on serving and going over the menu no later than two thirty. We'll have them fast friends by the time they leave this afternoon."

"I don't care if they're friends, I just want them to have the skills and knowledge to do the job." Angie broke off a piece of the roll and dipped it in the warm glaze. "Tell me about who you hired?"

Felicia took out a notebook and skimmed over her front of the house staff, but Angie noticed, she highlighted their past experience and references. No matter what kind of 'let's get in a circle around the campfire and sing' mantra Felicia talked, she hired strong, capable people. She always had.

Angie grabbed her own notebook and her paper calendar when Felicia started talking about the kitchen staff. "Two prep cooks, a sous chef, and a dishwasher, right? That should do us until we're open for more days. I'd rather they get the hours they want before we add on staff."

"I did. And our dishwasher is actually a student at the culinary arts department over at the college. She's just looking for part time now while she's going to school. But I thought if everything goes right, we might be able to intern her here next fall."

"Nice thinking ahead here. I'd like to be hooked up with the school. You never know when you're going to need someone quick. If we teach them ourselves, we'll have exactly what we need." Angie held her pen out. "What's her name?"

Felicia went through Angie's staff, this time slowing down and talking about personalities. Finally, she got to the sous chef hire. "He's the guy who already needs a full week off in July."

"Remind me why again. Vacation scheduled?" Angie didn't look up from her notes.

Felicia laughed. "No. Estebe volunteers at the local Basque Festival each year and he won't be available to work any hours that week."

Angie made a note on the calendar. She needed to get a digital calendar started on her computer so she could keep track of these things. "Okay then, I think we're good for today. I've got some things to deal with in the office. Did you find a local bookkeeper to deal with the payroll and accounts payable?"

"All set up. Tasha's coming in Thursday to get the computer set up with her software and she'll walk me through it, just in case. She's a stay-at-home mom with a really cute two-year-old girl that she's bringing in too. You should be here to meet her."

"I have a meeting with Mildred tomorrow. What time is she supposed to be here?"

"All afternoon. So come when you can." Felicia checked off an item on her list. "And that's it. Are we going to have Wednesday meetings each week to talk and make sure everything's on track like we did at the last place?"

"It worked there. We should keep what worked." Angie held up the half full glass to cheer her friend. "The County Seat is in business. May it live long and prosper."

"Quoting *Star Trek*? That's a good omen. That show will never die." Felicia clinked her glass. "Thank you for being my friend. I would hate to imagine what I'd be doing if we weren't in business together."

"You'd probably be running a restaurant for one of the celebrity chefs in Vegas and making bank." Angie closed her notebook and grabbed her tote.

"That's so sweet of you to say. I have nightmares that I'd be managing a Denny's in Nebraska." Felicia drained her glass.

"Nebraska's not that bad. A little flat, but I hear the people are nice." Angie grinned. "I'll be in the office. Let me know when my staff arrives and we can start cooking."

Angie went through the kitchen to the back hallway. This area had staff bathrooms, a large storage room, and an office. Two desks, one generic workstation, and a couple of file cabinets were set around the room. Angie's desk had a view of the end of Main Street and the town park and water tower sat. The other workstations had no window at all. Felicia had decorated the room with an old sign from el pescado they'd taken down after serving their last meal in the building. A framed picture of the staff taken the next day when they had said their goodbyes was hung next to it.

Feeling nostalgic, Angie went over and stared at the group of people she'd come to call family. She would have brought each and every one of them north to work at The County Seat, but no one had taken her up on the offer. They'd had lives in the San Francisco area. Families, and some already had new jobs. Still, she'd made it clear the offer was always on the table. You developed bonds with the people you worked in the trenches day in and day out. Those were the people you trusted. Angie said a short prayer that Felicia had hired strong for The County Seat. They didn't need kitchen divas to deal with.

She sat at the desk, powered up her computer and set up the systems she needed to manage the new restaurant. She had just finished keying in her plan for open days through the end of the year when Felicia popped her head in the door. "Everyone's here and waiting in the kitchen for you. They are so cute. It's like first day of school."

Angie rolled her eyes. Hopefully she wouldn't have to play the hard-as-nails teacher with this group. She just wanted people to act like adults. Fun adults, yes, but responsible ones. She grabbed a chef coat off her coat rack and slipped it on. Then she went out to tame the lions she called her staff.

One man and two women stood in a circle chatting. That was a good sign, she thought. She glanced at the lone wolf back behind the warming counter, checking out the equipment. She'd lay bets that the one guy not making friends was her assistant, Estebe. She put on a smile and went up to the circle.

The chatter subsided as they saw her approach. Angie pushed her hair behind her ears, wondering what had them staring so hard at her. "Hey guys, welcome to The County Seat. I'm Angie Turner and I'm the head chef. You already met my partner, Felicia. If I'm not here to ask, she's in charge."

"Except in the kitchen." The tall, dark and scowly man came around the cook area and stood. "I'm the assistant chef in the kitchen. You can call me Estebe."

Angie took a deep breath, deciding not to challenge the guy's first power play. This was going to be a challenging problem. She could feel it. "Well, yes, if it's a food issue, and I'm not here, ask Estebe. But don't feel like Felicia isn't a good reference too. She's an excellent pastry chef and has the same training that I do." She let the implication hang in the air. "Now that you've started introductions, let's continue. Tell me where you worked before and for fun, what's your favorite food. Estebe, why don't you start?"

He narrowed his eyes but leaned on the counter and after a big sigh, complied. "I'm Estebe Blackstone. Before you ask, it's a Basque version of your 'Stephen.' I graduated from the local college ten years ago and have been working in my parent's restaurant ever since. They are thinking of retiring and closing in the next few years, so I came here."

Apparently he was done talking but Angie wasn't going to let him off the hook that easy. "And your favorite food? Some kind of Basque secret family recipe?"

He smiled at her. A real smile that made her heart stop. The guy was too good looking. Movie star good looking. "My guilty pleasure is the deep-fried chicken burritos at Taco Time."

Chuckles came from the rest of the room and right then, the tension that had been surrounding the group disappeared. The young blonde rubbed her stomach. "Those things are the bomb. Especially after clubbing or a long shift. I'll go next." She smiled shyly at the group. "I'm Hope. Yes, that's my real name, so no wise cracks. My mom named all of the girls from Bible verses. Anyway, I'm still in school. I have one more year, but I'm your dishwasher until I master the art of the soufflé. My favorite food is my mom's homemade vanilla ice cream. She has one of those crank-by-hand makers that we pull out every 4th of July. It's to die for."

Nancy and Matt rounded out the team and they both agreed that the burgers from this one lunch place in Boise were the best food they'd ever had. Of course, the place was only open for a few hours and when they were done serving, people were turned away. Angie had to wonder if the exclusivity of the place had something to do with the rave reviews they'd given the burgers.

"Great. Now that you know each other, let me go through the dishes we'll be serving today for family meal and for opening night. We'll add on to the menu the next week and keep that menu, hopefully, for a month. But there may be alterations if something goes out of season or we find something particularly nice we want to highlight. So that should keep you on your toes."

"Better than cooking at the breakfast place where I came from. Corporate food wants the same plate every time, like we were robots or something." Matt grumbled. "I like cooking new things, trying new recipes."

"That doesn't mean we won't have quality standards. I don't want someone complaining their meal was great one night and so-so the next time they ordered. We're a small business. Quality food is part of the experience." When Angie looked at the group, they were all solemn and nodding. "Let's get cooking. Our salad course is going to feature the Bing cherries from a local Emmett farm and Moss Farm goat cheese."

"That's so sad about what happened to Old Man Moss. We took my sister's FFA class out there last year and toured the place." Nancy smiled at the memory. "The goats were so sweet."

"I'm going over to talk to the cheese commission about alternate local sources for goat cheese, just in case the farm doesn't survive after this all shakes out." Angie wrote the first recipe on the white board she'd set up on the far wall for kitchen staff meetings. "We may only be using this product for a little while."

"The cheese commission doesn't care about goat dairies." Estebe interrupted. "All they want to push is their all-American cow milk. I'm surprised they let him survive this long."

"They're not that bad." Nancy shrugged. "It just takes time for people to accept something new."

"I was there when that woman came by to bully him into closing down. My uncle was picking up some of the goats for his herd and she was screaming all kinds of threats at him. Her and one of her dairy goons." He glanced at Angie. "I'm sorry, I don't typically indulge in gossip, but Gerald Moss was a kind man. He didn't deserve to die this way."

Matt slipped his phone back into his pocket. Angie had noticed he'd been playing on the thing since the discussion started. "What do you mean? I thought it was an accident."

Estebe had all their attention now. "Gerald Moss was murdered."

# CHAPTER 16

Angie tried to calm the murmurs from the group. She had wondered how long the sheriff's suspicions would stay a secret, but she should have known. Nothing was ever a secret in a small town. "Look, what happened to Mr. Moss is upsetting, but one way to honor him is to use the product he gave us in a way that highlights the ingredients. And we have five people in the other room that are expecting a family meal at the end of the day."

"We should cook." Estebe pointed to the board. "Explain your preparation steps."

Yep, the guy had control issues but this wasn't the time or the place to show him or the others who was boss. And it wasn't the first time she'd had to work with an egomaniacal chef. For some reason, the type seemed to gravitate toward the career choice.

Angie went through the menu, then set up stations for teams of two. "I want you all to make the same dish, and then we'll compare. Get a feel for the kitchen. Hopefully, you'll be spending a lot of time in here."

Hope raised her hand. "Should I go help set up the dining room?"

All eyes turned toward Hope. Angie felt her brows narrow. "Why? Don't you want to cook?"

Awareness came over her face. "But I'm just the dishwasher."

"You're a part of this kitchen team." Angie glanced at the other three who were nodding. "When we open you'll probably have a different role, but today, we don't need a dishwasher, we need a chef."

"Besides, what happens if we get busy and we need your hands to finish out a meal?" Estebe stepped closer. "You need to know how to prepare a dish just like the rest of us. Do you want to work with me today?"

Hope shot a glance at Angie. "If that's all right?"

"Sounds good to me." Angie turned to Matt and Nancy. "You guys are the other team. Let's cook."

"I was hoping for a girls-against-guys pairing." Nancy held up her hand for a high five from Hope. "But I'll sacrifice one for the team."

Matt rolled his shoulders. "Woman, once you work with me, you'll never want to partner with anyone again."

Angie watched as her team came together. Two hours and they were already starting to bond. This was what she'd hoped. Felicia had some mad hiring skills. She prayed the front of the house was working out as well as her kitchen had. At least for the day. She watched as Estebe talked Hope through a tricky knife cut. The guy could be a problem, especially if they butted heads over an issue. But Angie didn't have an ego to appease. She only wanted what was best for The County Seat. And today, it looked like that was happening.

By the end of shift, they had gone through the recipes twice and Angie felt comfortable that the food would not only pass muster opening night, but it would be as amazing as she'd planned. They'd made up all the dishes family style for the final round and she was ready to serve.

Felicia popped her head in the kitchen and took a deep breath. "It smells amazing, guys. We're ready when you are."

They carried the food out to a table that had already been sat for the staff. Felicia made her introductions and then Angie introduced the kitchen team. She sat at the head of the table. "Hope, do you want to explain the first course?"

The woman turned beet red, but with an encouraging nod from each member of her team, she stood and walked the rest of the group through the preparation and ingredients. Angie noticed all of Felicia's crew had mini notebooks and were scribbling as Hope talked. Yep, this was going to be a great team.

Felicia leaned toward her and whispered. "That was nice, including her with the team."

Angie dished up salad and then passed the bowl to her friend. "That's the point, I don't have to include her, she is part of the team."

As the dinner progressed, each of the kitchen staff took a turn explaining a dish. She called on Estebe last, for the dessert round. She swore one of the waitstaff sighed when Estebe started talking about melted chocolate that went over the creamy cheesecake. No matter how big his ego was in the kitchen, his presence and looks were always going to give him the advantage with at least the opposite sex.

As they finished up the meal, Hope raised her hand. "So we're opening not this Friday but next? What time do you need us here?"

"I'd like to have the kitchen team," Angie paused and smiled at the girl, "Including you, Hope, here by noon. We'll have lots of prep to set up for the first day. Then we'll be open for dinner only on Friday. On Saturday and Sunday, we'll open at two to grab some of the late lunchers. On those days, we'll keep the noon start time to begin with. I want you guys to get as many hours as possible until we go to our full opening schedule. Your weekends or days off will be Mondays and Tuesdays starting next month. Plan your outside-of-work appointments for those days."

Hope nodded. "I'll let the school know. They said they'd work around my schedule. Right now, we're off for the summer, but I'll be slammed in the fall to fit in the last few classes."

"You can do it. You were meant to be working in the kitchen." Estebe turned his smile on his cooking partner and Hope's face turned beet red.

"Are there other questions about the schedule?" Angie looked at Felicia when no one spoke. "What about you, have anything you want to say to our new team?"

"Thank you all for today and for the hours we'll be putting in starting next Friday. We can't make The County Seat into the restaurant we imagined without your hard work." Felicia stood and held out her water glass. "To the opening staff of The County Seat. May you find you love working here with us as much as we love having you here."

The group stood and held out their own glasses.

After the table had been cleared and the kitchen cleaned, the staff left. Angie and Felica sat at the table in the kitchen and updated each other on the day's events.

"I love my group." Felicia picked at a bowl of cherries that Angie had placed on the table. "They're all so energetic and fun. How did the kitchen team get along? Judging by the food, you have some great cooks in that group."

"They'll be fine. Probably better than fine." Angie decided to hold off telling her partner about her fears on Estebe. Maybe they would come to an agreement around the power issue sooner than later. "Anyway, I'm beat and it's time to feed the circus."

"You mean zoo." Felicia smiled.

"My circus, my monkeys." Angie rolled her shoulders. "And I'm taking a long hot bath, then pretending to read as I drop into sleep."

"Drive safe." Felicia glanced upstairs. "This is one time I'm glad I live so close. I'm not sure I would stay awake driving."

"No worries. I'll take some coffee with me." Angie went over to fill her travel mug with the last of the coffee. "Anything you need me for tomorrow?"

"Nope. I think I'm sleeping in until noon then having a spa day. Want to join me?"

Angie grabbed her keys and her tote. "Sorry, I've got some appointments. Besides, every time I get my nails done, the polish looks like crap in a day or two. I'll go the day before opening. I promise."

"Then I'll make us an appointment and put it on your calendar." Felicia yawned and walked over to follow Angie to the door. "We did good today. Opening night is going to run like clockwork."

As she drove home, Angie hoped her friend was right and she hadn't jinxed the whole thing with her optimistic foretelling. But even though she knew she was beat, she couldn't think of anything that would go wrong. Which usually meant everything would go wrong. She fed the animals, letting Precious nuzzle her in the goat's version of a hug for few minutes. Then she turned on the baby monitor and headed into the house. She was done.

* * * *

By six, she'd finished her new morning routine which included spending some time talking with Precious. She worried the goat might be lonely, especially while she was gone at the restaurant all day. Sipping coffee on the porch, she did some research on her phone on the lifestyles of goats. Not the rich and famous, but still. She heard the crunch of tires on her rock driveway and looked up to see the Sheriff's car rolling slowing toward her. When he climbed out, she held up a cup. "Coffee?"

"That would be nice, but I won't be here long. So make it a short cup." He walked over to the porch and sat in one of the two white rocking chairs she'd bought Nona a few years ago. When she returned and held out the cup, he leaned back and took a sip. Smacking his lips, he grinned. "If you cook as good as this coffee, you'll be married off in no time."

"Thanks for the compliment, but that's not why I love cooking." Curling her feet up underneath her, she sipped her own coffee. Dom hadn't moved from his spot on the porch, but he was watching the newcomer closely. "What can I do for you this morning, Sheriff?"

He sat the cup down on the wooden table next to him. "I'm just seeing what you're doing, Ms. Turner."

Angie blinked. Not how are you doing, but what? "I'm drinking coffee at the moment. Then I'm going into town to talk to Mildred at the cheese commission. Why?"

"I wasn't asking what you were doing today, but that brings up even more questions. Why are you visiting with Mildred?" His dark eyes bored into her like he was looking for the lie.

"She said she could get me replacement vendors if Moss Farm goes out of business. I'll be talking to a lot of farmers and suppliers in the area. Do I need to clear each one with you?"

"No. Unless you're talking to them about Gerald Moss's death." He pulled out his notebook and scanned a few pages. "I've been interviewing people the last couple of days and found you've talked to several of them already about their relationships to Mr. Moss. This morning, when I was clearing up some past issues with Mrs. Potter, she also mentioned you had asked her about her sister Sophie and Mr. Moss."

"I'm curious. Is that a crime?" She lifted her coffee cup to have something to do with her hands.

"Not a crime, but suspicious. You realize investigating murder is a dangerous thing. You don't want to be going around gathering evidence and have the killer get antsy about what you know." He sipped his coffee and watched her.

"I just want to find out what happened to the guy. I'm the new factor in town. I'm sure people think I'm involved somehow."

"Now, Angie, just because you got into a little trouble in high school doesn't mean the town's against you." He rocked and glanced toward the barn. "You got a nice little spread here. You should focus on your restaurant and this place. It will be safer for all of us."

"I didn't get in trouble. All I did was sit in the car. I didn't know he was going to try to rob the store. Besides, Kenny didn't even get out of the store before he was caught. I thought we were on a date." She'd explained this to everyone for what seemed like days during the Junior Year Troubles. "I thought I'd put this behind me."

"You know people like to gossip. Don't worry, that's the story I heard when I checked you and your friend out a few months ago when you moved into town." He smiled at her shocked face. "I'm not a country bumpkin. I actually do know how to investigate."

"I didn't say you didn't." She closed her eyes. "I'll try to stay out of your way and stop asking questions."

He drained the cup. "I'm not sure you can. You always were curious, even as a kid. All I'm asking is you be careful and if you hear something you think might be important, call me."

Angie could feel the smile playing with her lips. "Call you? That's all you wanted?"

"What, you thought I was going to do the whole obstruction of justice thing and throw you in jail?" He shook his head. "Ms. Turner, I've been married over thirty years. I've learned the quickest way to get a headstrong woman to do something is to forbid her from doing it. You remind me of my wife. A lot."

"Is that a compliment?"

Sheriff Brown laughed, a deep hearty sound that somehow made Angie feel safe and included. "Definitely. Now that I have you settled, I just hope treasure hunters don't start flocking to Moss Farm before we can locate the next of kin. I probably should think about having the court hire full time security for the area. I better be getting back into town and give the judge a call."

"Wait, what treasure? I didn't see anything worth money out there, other than the view that is." Angie leaned forward. "Is it pirate treasure?"

"We're a little far from the ocean for pirate treasure." He smoothed his shirt. "There's been a local legend that the Moss family farm was the location of a great treasure. It's been handed down for years, one generation to the next. Nothing substantial, but rumors that maybe an outlaw buried his gold, thinking he'd come back some day. Stuff like that."

"So wishful thinking. Mrs. Potter also mentioned something about a treasure, I guess I was just wondering." Angie shook her head. "Nona told me about all the treasure hunters that went after that D. B. Cooper guy when he jumped from the plane. Even though there was no indication he survived the fall."

"Yeah, like that. I just don't want folks thinking they have a free pass to go digging up Gerald's lawn. Even if he isn't around to chase them off. Now remember, you call me if you think you figured out something. You promised."

"Hey, can I ask you something?"

Sheriff Brown paused on the edge of the deck, his hand on the pole. "Of course."

"Ian said you and he were related. Is that true?" Angie saw the surprise form on the man's face.

"He told you that? Hmmm, this must be more serious than I thought." He studied her thoughtfully. "I guess if he's told you, I can confirm what he said."

"Are you his dad or something?"

The sheriff barked out a laugh. "No, I'm not his dad. His mother was my sister. The folks disowned her once she took off, but I started looking for her and Ian as soon as I was able." He smiled at her and put his hat back on. "The kid's got a kind heart. My sister did one thing right in her life."

She watched him amble off the porch and down the driveway toward his cruiser. She called after him. "I think Gerald's death has something to do with the cheese."

He paused as he was getting into his car. "So do I, but I've been wrong before. Thanks for the coffee."

As he drove away, she reflected on their conversation. Was she putting herself in harm's way for no good reason? Then she thought of the way Gerald Moss had smiled when Precious had danced in front of them that Sunday morning. The guy hadn't deserved to die. And if she could help find his killer, she wanted to do it.

She went back into the house and got ready for her day. Ten minutes before her appointment, she was still sitting in the parking lot in front of the building, wondering how to ask the biggest question she had. Why had Mildred been in Gerald Moss's house this weekend?

Angie glanced at the clock again and gave up. She'd figure out something.

The same woman sat at the reception desk when Angie stepped into the now quiet room. No mass of people mingled around the lobby, just the woman clicking on her keyboard. She looked up when the bell over the door rang. "I'm so glad you're a little early. Mildred has an appointment right after yours so she'll be running out of here in a few minutes."

Angie followed the woman back into the same hallway. "I appreciate you getting me into her busy schedule."

"It's always crazy around here. The life of a lobbying group." The woman knocked on Mildred's door, then swung it open. "Mildred, your appointment is here."

When Angie stepped into the room, Mildred went white. But to her credit, she held it together for her assistant. "Thanks, Heather. Shut the door, will you?"

Angie walked over to the chair Mildred indicated and sat, pulling her notebook out on her lap along with a pen. "Thanks for seeing me today."

"I don't have much time." The woman's eyes bored into Angie, like she was trying to determine how much she knew.

Angie decided to go with the obvious. She pulled out the scarf and sat it on Mildred's desk. The woman blanched white.

Reacting quickly, Mildred picked up the scarf and rolled it up, putting it into her desk drawer when it was done.

"Do you have anything to say about that?" Angie pointed to the empty place where the scarf had been.

"I guess I'd forgotten." Now that the scarf was tucked away, she seemed stronger, more in control. "But I'm curious, how did you know it was mine?"

Angie pointed to the door to the hallway. "You wore it for your pictures."

The other woman gazed at the door, like she could see the offending picture through the wall. "My, my, you are observant. So what else do you think you know?"

"What?" Confused, Angie dropped her pen. When she bent down to grab it, Mildred spoke again.

"I know you saw me at Gerald's the other day. It's not what you think." Her voice was calm and even.

Angie decided to turn the question. "What is it that you think I know?"

"I was seeing Gerald on a personal matter." She stared Angie in the eyes, not breaking the gaze. "A very personal matter that if it was revealed to my members here at the commission, my loyalty might be brought into question."

Angie frowned, trying to decipher the meaning behind the words or the true message the woman was telling her. Then she got it. She felt the surprise widen her eyes and a short squeak escaped her lips.

"You didn't guess that," Mildred sank back into her chair and took out a photo of the two of them from her desk drawer. "You thought I had something to do with his death."

"You were in love with him?" Angie stated it as a question, but she already knew the answer, just looking at the woman across the desk.

Now Mildred shrugged. "What is love? At our age, comfort and companionship is more important than love. We enjoyed each other's company. I realized a few days ago that I'd left my favorite scarf over at the house. I didn't want to just leave it there. If the Sheriff had found it, I'd be telling him this story, and not you."

This was not what she'd expected at all. To hear Gerald tell it, Mildred was the enemy. And he had been sleeping with her? Hiding in plain sight. The plan had been brilliant. No one would have suspected a relationship. Shaking off the visuals that came with the idea, she decided to get right to the point. "So if you didn't kill Gerald, who do you think did?"

"If I was to point a finger at anyone, it would be Carl. Carl Simpson. He's been angry about the goat cheese production for years. He blames Gerald for cutting his prices but really, the guy just has really bad business sense. If there's a decision to be made, Carl will pick the wrong one. That's why he was fighting with Martin on Friday. Martin called him on something he said in the meeting." Mildred wiped her eyes with a tissue. "I miss Gerald so much. It's going to be hard to get over losing him."

"Why did you keep your relationship a secret?"

"Old habits, I guess." Mildred grabbed another tissue. "Cattle folk don't mingle with goat folk. It's just the way it is. And the board would have seen it as a conflict of interest."

"But you think Carl might have a reason to kill Mr. Moss?" Angie wasn't following the woman's logic.

"He blamed Gerald for everything. If Carl thought getting Gerald out of the way would increase his profits, he would have done anything to get the goat dairy to shut down." Mildred sank back into her chair. "Believe me, there wasn't anyone in town who hated Gerald as much as Carl did."

# CHAPTER 17

Angie got directions to the Simpson Dairy from Mildred. But she didn't need them. When she walked out into the lobby, Carl Simpson stood in front of Heather's desk, arguing with the red-faced receptionist. He pounded the desk. "I pay your salary."

"No, Mr. Simpson, you don't. And you can't bully your way into an appointment with Mildred. I've already told you she's with someone and then she has to leave for another appointment." She caught Angie's gaze and shrugged. "I'll be glad to make you an appointment for tomorrow."

He turned to follow Heather's gaze. "You done with her? I need to get in there."

"Sorry, she left a few minutes ago. I've been on a call. She was nice enough to let me use her office." Angie hoped Mildred wouldn't walk out and prove her a liar. But she figured the woman had heard the ruckus and was hiding under her desk, hoping for the man to go away. "But I need to ask you a few questions, if you don't mind."

Now, his eyes left the hallway where he had been focused on any sign of his target. "Who are you?"

Angie stepped forward and held out her hand. "Angie Turner. I'm opening The County Seat next week. I don't know if you've heard of us, we'll be a farm-to-table restaurant, so I need to set up arrangements with local producers."

She could see the wheels turning in his mind. And from what she saw, she figured she would be paying premium prices to do business with Simpson Dairy. "I had heard something about your little venture. Are you sure River Vista's big enough to support a fine dining restaurant?"

"We'll be fine, I'm sure. Now, can you tell me about your relationship to Gerald Moss?" Angie decided to attack directly.

"Why do you care?" Carl shrugged, no emotion showing on his face. "The man was a fraud. I wouldn't doubt if he actually used store-bought milk for his cheese products. Goat milk just doesn't have the fat content needed to develop a good cheese curd."

"You would say you were rivals?"

"No way. I don't have a problem selling my cheese. In fact, I've got too much demand on my product. Why would I worry about a little podunk dairy that doesn't even use real milk?" He sat half on the desk.

Angie saw Heather's grimace and figured the woman would be Lysoling the desk as soon as soon as she got the man out of her office. Angie fought the grin that wanted to curve her lips. "So did you kill him?"

"You're joking right?" Carl rolled his shoulders. "I wasn't even in town the night the old man went over the cliff. I took a date up to Sun Valley for a show and we didn't get back into town until Tuesday morning. When I found out the old goat was dead, it was a good day."

"Who would want to kill him?" Angie figured the guy was talking, she might as well play all her cards.

"Probably that realtor. I heard he was playing her and was actually about to sign a sales contract with another realtor. Some guy out of Boise who specialized in developments. Women are useless when it comes to business decisions. Gerald and I did agree on that fact." Carl stood and focused on Heather. "Get me an appointment for tomorrow and call me on my cell. I've got better things to do than waste my time here."

Angie and Heather watched as he left the office, then through the window as he climbed into his jacked up black Dodge Ram. The truck looked like he'd just taken it off the showroom floor.

"What a jerk." Angie let her smile crease her lips. "I can't believe you didn't deck him."

"I've had a lot of experience working with that guy. He's being truthful at least on where he was when Mr. Moss died. I know the girl he took to Sun Valley. She said the weekend was awful and she had never been so happy to be home as she was on Tuesday. He won't be getting another date." The woman started moving things so she could wipe down the area where the offending butt had touched her desk. "How did things go with Mildred? Is she really gone?"

Angie glanced back toward the door that was inching open. "It's safe to come out. He's gone."

Heather whistled. "You're lucky he believed you. I've had him storm past me and check the office, even when she's really not here."

"I have a trustworthy face." Angie said her goodbyes and went out sit in her car. She pulled out her notebook and made notes from the two conversations she had. Glancing at her watch, she decided to stop by the restaurant and check in with Felicia.

She dialed her friend who answered with a sleepy, "Hello?"

"Don't tell me I woke you." Angie laughed. "I'm on my way into town. You need anything?"

"I'm not at the apartment. I stayed over at Connie's last night. We went into Boise and must have hit every bar downtown. Everyone was having Ladies' Night specials which is just a code for we need more people in the bar mid-week." Felicia paused. "It was fun, then. By the time we ran out of bars, I was tore up so Connie let me crash in her guest room. Did you need something?"

"No, I'll talk to you tomorrow. Don't forget we have to do ordering at the farmer's market on Saturday morning. I think we should be able to get everything we need there." After getting Felicia's assurance she'd be there, Angie turned at the next side street that went through to Southside Blvd and headed home.

When she pulled into the driveway, she was just getting out of the car when she heard Erica calling her. She waved her over, then went to the porch to let Dom out. The dog may have his own exit, but when she came home, he still wanted to be with her. She sat on the rocker and gave him loves while Erica walked the rest of the way.

"Hey Angie. Granny saw you pull up and she wanted me to come over and tell you something." She bent down and greeted Dom with a rub on his head.

"Do you want some iced tea? Or a soda?" Angie motioned to the chair next to her, but Erica shook her head.

"Neither. I'm heading into town for a study group. We want to get ahead of the curve for math class this fall. The professor is a real believer in homework." She leaned against the rail. "Anyway, Granny saw a man over here at the place. He knocked, but then when you didn't answer, he walked around the house and into the barn. She thought that was weird, but by the time I got out of the shower, the guy was gone."

"Probably Ian checking on Precious." Angie smiled. "The guy is pretty sure I can't take care of one baby goat by myself. He may have wanted to see how the dehorning medicine was working."

Erica shook her head. "Granny knows Ian. He helped her harvest and sell her garden last year. This year, we decided not to plant, which is going to be easier on all of us."

"What did he look like? What was he driving?" Angie set up, wondering who was wandering through her place while she wasn't home.

"Tall guy, wore a hat, so Granny couldn't tell hair color that far away. But he drove an old truck. The kind you usually have on a farm." Erica studied her shoes. "She couldn't find her glasses in time, so she couldn't get a plate number. Frankly, I think some of her description is suspect too. If she didn't have her glasses on, she's blind as a bat."

"But you think there really was someone here?" Angie looked at the barn. "I've got to check on Precious."

They jogged to the barn where Mabel scratched the dirt near the front door. One down, one to check on. Angie walked through the open door and straight through to the one stall that was filled. Precious lay on the straw, sleeping in the sun. Angie slapped her hands together and the goat's eyes opened wide in shock. Then she jumped to her feet and came running to the gate, bleating welcome to her guests.

"I guess everyone's okay." Angie rubbed Precious's head, then looked around the area. "Nothing seems out of place."

"That's weird. Maybe he was just looking for you but when he checked the barn and you weren't there, he left." Erica glanced at her watch. "I've got to go."

Before Angie left the barn, she turned on the baby monitor and fed the goat and hen. As she walked back to her house, with Dom at her heels, she wondered who had paid her a visit and why. That second question would be much harder to find out.

She couldn't do much about it tonight. Instead, she pulled out the Bing cherries she'd had left over from Wednesday's family meal and foraged through the refrigerator until she had composed a recipe in her mind. Cooking helped her relax and she needed a break after the day she'd had. She turned up the stereo she'd tuned to a classic 70's rock station and let the worries of the day disappear as she cooked her dinner.

\* \* \* \*

Friday morning she sat at the table and crossed people off her list of Gerald's possible killers. Mildred had dropped out of the top five and Carl Simpson was off the list before she even knew to put him on. However, if Carl was right, Reana Whiting had motive to kill the guy who she'd been courting to sell his house for ever. She tapped her pen over Reana's name. The problem was she didn't feel like a killer. Which she knew was stupid, you couldn't feel your way through an investigation. You had to have facts. And there were facts that pointed to the friendly realtor.

She glanced at her watch. If she left right now, she'd probably catch Reana at the real estate office. Although she'd done this line of questioning before and the woman had stonewalled her. Worse, Reana had tried to throw her under the bus as a scapegoat for Gerald's murder. Which made her seem even more guilty in Angie's eyes.

"Dom, I'm going into town for a while. You guard the house and don't let anyone inside, okay?"

She leaned into his big ruff of fur, giving him a quick hug. The dog was all she had. Well, the dog, the goat, and the chicken. She sighed; she might as well face reality. She *was* running a small zoo. She grabbed her purse and locked the door as she left. If someone was stopping by, he'd have to get through a locked door. Then he'd have to get through Dom.

Dialing Felicia's number, she drove into town. When her friend answered, she jumped right into her question. "Hey, you going to be around in about thirty minutes?"

"Good morning, nice to talk to you. And yes, I'm at the apartment this morning and feeling much better than I did yesterday, thanks for asking." Felicia paused.

"Sorry, I've been by myself for a couple of days. I've lost my skill for small talk."

Felicia laughed. "Sweetie, you never could stand small talk. Anyway, I'll be here. Anything going on I should know about?"

Angie decided the story would be easier to tell in person. "I'll fill you in when I get to the apartment. There's a lot that you need to know."

"I'll start a fresh pot of coffee. I made peanut butter muffins this morning, you can help me eat them before I devour the entire batch myself."

Angie's phone beeped, indicating she had another call. "I'll talk to you later, I should take this."

She clicked over to the other line. "Hello?"

"What have you been doing? I've gotten a member complaint on you and Allen's been griping about having to reel you in. Reel you in from what?"

She recognized Ian's voice and with the anger she heard in the tone, also was a slight brogue he probably thought he hid most of the time. "I bet the member was Carl Simpson. The guy's a tool."

"You've already figured him out?" Ian's chuckle tempered what she'd thought had been anger, but maybe it was just emotion. "Seriously, can you stop by my office? I'd like to talk you down from your delusion you're a roving FBI agent."

"Actually, FBI can't investigate on US soil."

"That's the CIA. Even I know that and I didn't go to school in the States." He pushed on. "Anyway, I know you're in the car, I can hear the tires. Can you stop by? I told Allen I'd talk to you and make sure you weren't going off the rails."

"Why don't you meet me at the restaurant in thirty?" She glanced at the dash clock. "I've got a stop before you and Felicia has coffee and muffins waiting."

"You sure I won't be a bother?"

Angie felt the smile before she caught a glance of herself in her rear-view mirror. "I'm positive. Besides, Felicia will want to hear this too. And, I want to ask your opinion about who might have been out at my place yesterday."

"Wait, what? Are you okay? No problems with the crew, is there?"

The worry she heard in his tone made her smile widen. "We're fine, I'm just concerned and thought you might have heard something."

"Do you want me to call Allen? Maybe you should report this."

"What, that someone I don't know and didn't see came and looked around my house and in the barn when I wasn't home?" She pulled her car into the parking spot behind her building. "Look, I've got to go. Come by the restaurant and we'll talk."

"Where are you going?"

Angie turned off the car and hung up on Ian. If she told him what she'd planned, he'd tell her she was crazy and to stay out of things. She'd apologize when he came to the restaurant. Right now, she needed to talk to Reana and see if Carl Simpson's story was more than a story. She cut through the alleyway behind the buildings and went through the side door to Reana's office.

No one was in the office except Reana. The staff was tiny, but in the past when Angie would stop by, there would be at least one other person. Now, the real estate office looked as deserted as a store that was closing in less than a week. Reana looked up at her and groaned.

"Go away. I don't want to talk about Gerald anymore. You're right, it was Sunday, not Saturday." She put her head on the desk. "Go away and I'll call Allen tomorrow and tell him. I promise."

"I wanted to ask you something else." Angie sat in the visitor chair, watching the realtor. "Where is everyone?"

"The office is merging with the Meridian branch so this place will be closed soon. Everyone has moved to the new digs, but I like this space.

And I hate change. So I'll be here until they lock the doors." She lifted her head. "Alone."

"Oh." Angie winced. She didn't like to see businesses close especially since she was opening a restaurant that would depend on businesses and customers being in town. Not in Meridian.

"So was that your question? Can you go away now?"

Angie shook her head. "Sorry. One more. Was Gerald Moss negotiating with another realtor to sell his land?"

"No!" Reana leaned forward and banged her fist on the desk. "He was my client. He wasn't talking to anyone else."

"Are you sure about that?" She thought about her conversation with Carl. The man was mean and coldhearted, he could have been lying.

Reana nodded. "I mean, there were rumors, but Gerald promised me he wasn't talking to anyone else, especially not Mark Foreman. I think he was making up the rumors himself to make him look better to the developers. He's in their pocket and he's good at keeping up the public image."

She wrote the name down on a note pad she kept in her purse. "Where does he work?"

"Foreman Real Estate. Of course, he'd name the company for himself. The man is an egomaniac. It's all a scam."

"So you believed Gerald when he told you this?"

Reana stared into her eyes. "I do. Gerald was a lot of things, but he wasn't a liar. If he was going to sign a contract with anyone, it would have been me. It's unprofessional, but since Gerald's gone, I guess it can't hurt anyone. We were in love."

# CHAPTER 18

"She said what?" Felicia's eyes widened and she grabbed another muffin. "Oh, moving here was the best idea ever. This place is a hotbed of rumor and gossip."

Angie giggled and looked at Ian. "You've lived here longer than we have. So is there any truth to the rumor that Reana and Gerald were a hot item?"

Ian's face had gone stark white. "Gerald never said he was dating anyone. Not to me."

"Not even Mildred?" Angie watched as Ian took in the idea.

He shook his head. "No one. Not Reana. Not Mildred. Next you'll be telling me he dated the woman who manages the grocery store as well."

"She might be the one keeping him in Ding Dongs." Angie grinned. "Okay, so this investigation just took a weird turn. Two of my prime suspects just admitted they were sleeping with the old guy."

"Gross, now I have that image in my head." Felicia poured more coffee. "Maybe it was more of an intellectual relationship. Or they were saving the deed for marriage. Once he decided between the two of them, that is."

"It's your fictional world, you can make it any way you want." Ian unwrapped his second muffin. "So, do you know anything about this Mark Foreman?"

Angie turned the laptop where she'd been googling the guy for the last five minutes. "He's a big shot in the developing world, that's for sure. He worked several subdivisions in the river valley near Eagle. Big money in those houses."

"The ridge would be prime real estate for people with money." Felicia glanced around the table. "Then there's the matter of the treasure."

Ian scoffed. "That bloody treasure rumor is ruining my life. Allen wants me to stay out at the farm for the next few nights until they can get a security company set up. I am not looking forward to sleeping on that old couch."

"There is a bed in the house." Angie reminded him.

He shook his head. "After hearing all the stories about what the man might have been doing …"

Felicia interrupted. "Who. Not what, who."

A slight blush ran down Ian's face and into his throat. "Okay, who he'd been doing in that bed, I'm not sure I even want to consider sleeping in the bedroom."

"So you're a prude? I wouldn't have guessed that." Felicia teased as she watched Ian squirm under her gaze.

"Stop messing with him Felicia. You got him all flustered." Angie grinned at her friend. "What kind of treasure do you think is there if any?"

"My money's on nothing." Ian shook his head. "Gerald was a practical man. If he'd had access to funds, even if it was a family inheritance, he'd have upgraded the barn. He was always saving for replacement milkers and complaining about vet bills."

"I guess Kirk Hanley must have lost a good customer when Mr. Moss passed." Angie glanced toward the brick wall and his clinic, even though she couldn't see anything.

"Gerald stopped using Hanley about three months ago. Said the man was a cheat and a hustler. He had a vet from Meridian come out even though it cost an arm and a leg because of the travel time."

"As casual as Kirk is with his appointment times, I can see why Mr. Moss got frustrated with him." Angie rolled her shoulders. "I doubt he'll be in business in six months. Which will be two businesses River Vista will lose this year."

A quiet fell over the three. Felicia was the first to respond. "We'll just have to bring in better businesses to town. Ones that will stay. This could be an entertainment destination stop. Our restaurant, maybe a theatre, some upscale bars. Maybe even some designer-level clothing shops."

"Our visionary to the rescue." Ian grinned. "I've got to get going. I'm supposed to report back to Allen that we've talked and you're not totally bonkers."

"Just half." Angie's stomach growled. "I'm going to be making some lunch if you want to come back. It will give me a chance to try out a new recipe."

"As enticing as that sounds, I've got some of my own work to finish up this afternoon before I go out to the farm. I could use some help tomorrow after milking if you want to come over and have the full farm experience."

"Don't you know you're looking at the girl who had an award winning FFA steer freshman year? I'm experienced." Angie grinned.

"Then you'll be the perfect choice for getting the goats rounded up for the night." Ian glanced at his watch. "I've really got to go. Seriously, if you have time, stop by. I can do it by myself, but the 4-H group's stopping by to help and having another adult there to help wrangle the kids wouldn't be a bad idea."

"What time do you need me there? I'd like to take Dom for a hike down by the river anyway. As long as I can bring him along." Angie liked the idea of looking around Gerald Moss's place one more time. Maybe there was something she didn't see the first time she was there.

"Six would be perfect. The kids are arriving then and the milkers will be just finishing up." He tossed his keys in his hand. "Thanks for the help. I appreciate it."

After Ian had left the building, Felicia pushed a cookie over to Angie. "Okay, so spill."

"So spill what? I told you and Ian everything." Angie broke off a piece of the cookie and groaned. "Except the fact someone was at the house yesterday, looking around."

"Actually, I was asking about you and Ian McHottie. What's going on with the two of you?"

"Nothing. I'm helping him out."

"If that's the way you want to play it, but wow, sparks are flying between you guys. Anyway, who was at your house yesterday?"

Angie sighed. "If I knew who, I would have said so. According to Mrs. Potter, the guy was tall and drove an old truck." She pondered the idea. "You don't think it was Kirk Hanley, do you?"

"Did you make an appointment with him to check Precious and forgot?" Felicia broke the other cookie in half.

Angie sat down the other half of the cookie. "I don't think I even told him about Precious."

As she drove home after lunch, she thought about the things she'd learned that day. It wouldn't do any good to go to Mildred and ask her if she knew about Reana, but she might be able to get more information from her about the land. Now, instead of the cheese, she wondered if it was really about the property. Had Gerald refused to sell the farm and his goats? Ian would tell Sheriff Brown about the Mark character and what Reana had said, so there was no reason for her to report in.

Tomorrow would be soon enough to head into town and talk to the next people on her list. She'd stop in Meridian first and chat with Mildred, then go into Boise to see what this real estate developer had to say for himself. And whether or not he even knew Gerald Moss.

She pulled into the driveway and parked. Once inside, she grabbed her calendar and started to make a to-do list for tomorrow and groaned. Tomorrow was Saturday. Which meant she needed to make an appearance at the farmers' market to finalize her week's order for opening night. The County Seat was her life. This playing Nancy Drew was more of a hobby. She flipped open her computer and set up a mini workstation on her desk. First thing, she needed to review and tweak the shopping list.

By the end of the day, she'd gotten a good list going of what she would need and ordering quantity for each supplier. She had separate order lists for each farm she would be using this week which she printed out and put into her bag for tomorrow.

Then she went back to her to do list. Farmer's market 7am to 9am. Drive to Meridian and talk to Mildred 9:30 to 10am. Finally, she wrote, Drive to Boise, talk to Mark Foreman.

She'd be home with her feet up and reading a novel by three. And that was with a stop for a quick bite at one of the restaurants in Boise.

Her day was planned. What could go wrong?

\* \* \* \*

Apparently, everything. She slept through her alarm that morning so was late getting on the road. Precious decided to escape when Angie went in her pen to clean out her water dish. Angie dove for the baby goat and landed in a pile of dung so once she got the goat back into the pen and fed, she went back upstairs to take a second shower for the day.

When she came back downstairs, Dom looked at her like "I told you the goat was a bad idea."

"Don't give me that look. Precious is part of the family now, and we'll just have to get used to her antics." She gave him a hug. "We'll go for a walk down by the river when I get home."

She got into the car with her notebook and orders for the produce she needed for opening. As the actual date was getting closer and closer, she was more and more nervous for the actual opening. Maybe she should schedule another dry run for next week. She dialed Felicia's number as she drove toward town, but only got voice mail. "Call me when you have a minute. Or meet me down at the market. I'll be there in twenty minutes, max."

It was more like fifteen since she found a parking spot near the entrance. She grabbed her tote bag and locking the car, sprinted across the street to her first stop.

By ten, she'd talked to all of the producers and had a delivery schedule for Friday morning set up for all of the farms. She glanced around. Still no Felicia, and come to think of it, she hadn't seen Ian either. Maybe he'd gotten stuck out at the farm. She and Dom would stop by after they walked the river trail. She looked around one more time, then headed to her car. If she kept pushing, she might just get through everything on the list.

Mildred grudgingly gave her ten minutes. When they got into her office, she shook her head. "Carl Simpson is all up in arms about you and your rudeness."

"I wasn't rude, I just asked him some questions." Angie didn't care what the guy thought of her, she just wanted to figure out who had pushed an old man over the edge of the river canyon. "Anyway, I have a couple more questions for you. Did Mr. Moss tell you he was working with someone to sell the farm?"

"You mean a realtor? Like that Reana woman?" Mildred looked down and shrugged. "I know she spent a lot of time with him. He told me he'd never sell the place."

"So why didn't he tell Reana to stop bothering him?" Angie paused, then decided to play her card. "Or was there something else going on with them?"

"No, he said they were just friends. If he was with someone else, I would have known." Mildred flushed. "Besides, I don't think she was really interested in getting him as a client. She was just after some attention, not only a sales contract."

Angie felt bad for the woman. She could see the pain on her face as she talked about Moss and Reana.

"Look, before you think I'm going all 'Stand by Your Man' or something, I need to say something. I had a choice. Believe Gerald, or let my insecurity get me. I chose to believe the man I thought I was in love with." Mildred played with a pen as she gazed out the window. "I guess I held my own secrets. We were two of a kind, weren't we?"

"Did he ever say he was talking to anyone else about selling the farm?" Angie leaned forward.

Mildred shook her head. "He was dead set against selling. He said the dairy was bringing in good money. He'd had some sort of downturn, but he was sure he'd make it up in a few months."

"When was his downturn?"

The buzzer on Mildred's phone preceded Heather's announcement that the next appointment was in the lobby.

"Sorry, I've got to go. You might want to talk to the bank in River Vista. I know he worked with someone there with his business accounts. They might know more." Mildred stood. "I hope this is the last time we'll have to talk about this. I want to move on and put the past behind me."

"I appreciate you being candid with me."

She paused as she held the door open for Angie. "For some reason, I believe you are doing what's best for Gerald. I owe him that much."

"One more question, do you know Mark Foreman?" Angie could see the answer in her eyes before Mildred opened her mouth.

"Sorry, no. Is he one of your suppliers?"

"No. Again, thank you for your time." She walked down the hallway and met a younger man on his way into Mildred's office.

He tipped his cowboy hat as she passed by. "Ma'am."

Angie smiled in spite of herself. Cowboys were hot. Especially when they cleaned up and wore their best jeans and clean boots for an appointment.

Before she left the parking lot, she called the office where Foreman worked. A perky female voice answered the phone. "Foreman Real Estate and Investments, may I help you?"

"May I speak with Mark Foreman?"

"I'm sorry, Mr. Foreman is out of the office this weekend and unavailable. May I take a message?" The too friendly voice asked.

"No. But when will he be in the office? I'd like to talk to him about an investment property." So much for her trip to Boise this afternoon. Today was turning out to be a to-do list failure.

"Are you an existing client or a new one?"

"New, but I don't see how that changes the answer."

Now the voice didn't sound so friendly. "No need to get snippy. I'm just the answering service. The note from Mr. Foreman says if you're an existing client, I can give out his cell number and tell you he's just in Sun Valley so feel free to call. But since you are a new customer, the directions tell me to say he'll be back in the office at ten on Monday. "

"Thank you for your help. I'll give him a call then." Angie hung up the phone and made a note on Monday's page. She looked out the front window and caught Heather watching her from the reception window. When their gaze met, Heather ducked out of sight behind a wall. "Now, that's weird."

Angie put the car in gear and left the parking lot. Maybe Heather was just trying to see why she hadn't left yet. The woman seemed to have her finger in just about everything surrounding the cheese commission. Small town America. Everyone knew your business, sometimes before you even did.

# CHAPTER 19

Angie drove out to a larger grocery store and filled her cart with items she needed at the house. After putting the food away and making lunch, she still had two hours before Ian needed her at the farm. She looked at Dom who'd been watching her since she got home.

"I know, I've been gone a lot this week. But you need to get used to it. Once The County Seat opens, I'll be gone a lot more." She called the dog over to her and rubbed his huge head. "Want to go for a walk?"

The woof was louder than she expected and Dom ran to the door and sat. Angie grinned at him. "No one could tell me you don't understand what I'm saying."

He whined and pawed the floor in front of the door.

In less than ten minutes, they were on the road, a backpack with bottled water, granola bars, dog treats, her phone, and wallet. She wanted to get some pictures of the farm while she was there so she could use them in promotions in the future for the restaurant. The parking lot at the trail head was empty today. She grabbed her backpack, clipped the leash on Dom, and they headed up the trail.

As they wandered, she kept a lookout for any sign of Moss's cave. The estate needed to get in there sooner than later to make sure everything was still all right. Of course, Ian could know where the cave was and just hadn't told her.

Dom barked, bringing her out of her musing. She leaned down, trying to match his gaze. "Hey, what do you see?"

The grass by the trail had started to turn brown. There hadn't been a lot of rain in the area and the gentle sloping canyon wall where the trail led didn't hold in any moisture. A rabbit bounced away from her and for a second, it looked like it was following a trail. She inched forward, trying to find the path's beginnings.

A vibration buzzed on her back, causing her to jerk and go down on her knees from her crouched position. Dom nuzzled her face as she moved to a seated position and took her phone out of the backpack. Glancing at the display, she hit the accept button. "Hi Felicia. What's going on?"

"I just wanted to see if Estebe had gotten a hold of you."

Angie pictured her new second in command and groaned. She couldn't open without him. Or at least someone else to help. "No, why?"

"He wants to meet you at the kitchen tomorrow about three. He says he'd like to talk about the recipes again." Felicia paused. "He seemed kind of upset. I'm not sure why he didn't call you yet."

"When did you talk to him?"

"Two, no, three hours ago. I'd left my phone up in the apartment when I went down to grab something from the fridge in the kitchen. When I came back, I had three missed calls from him. I didn't even have time to call him back when my phone lit up again. If he was that insistent on talking to you, why didn't he call after we talked?"

Angie held the phone out and checked her missed calls log. Nothing. "Well, if he calls back, tell him I'll be there at three. And let's hope he's not really just quitting. I don't know how I'd pull off opening night without a sous chef."

"If that happens, we'll call for a temp. The employment agency I was working with said they could get me a temp cook, no problem. He or she probably won't have the skills Estebe has, but we'll get through. Don't worry."

That was easy for Felicia to say. Angie had worked with temp cooks before. She hated it. There was no team work or friendly banter. No, they just saw it as a job. She wanted staff that loved the place as much as she did. After she said her goodbyes to her friend, she traded her phone for one of the water bottles and Dom's dish. She poured half of the bottle into Dom's dish. Then they took a break and Angie stared down the canyon where the Snake River cut through the landscape. The sun was lower and she checked the time. Almost five. She didn't have time to try to figure out if there really was a trail here or not. At least, not today. Chugging the rest of the water, she stashed the empty bottle into her pack and stacked some rocks into an arrow shape while she waited for Dom to finish drinking. She'd come back and look harder, maybe tomorrow morning. Before she had to meet with Estebe.

* * * *

When they pulled into the driveway at Moss Farm, Angie parked by Ian's wagon near the front of the house. She figured he was in the barn, helping the milkers, but she could pretend that maybe he was in the house. She left Dom tied to the porch rail and knocked on the door. "Ian, are you in there?"

Trying the knob, she found the door unlocked and with a quick peek over her shoulder to make sure Ian hadn't heard her pull up, she slipped into the house. It was cool after the heat of the day. Tree cover replaced the need for central air. She saw Ian's bedroll still spread out on the couch. Making a beeline to the desk, she opened the roll top and sat down, flipping through papers on the top. Nothing popped out. Then she opened a side drawer and found folders labeled, bills, reports, and bingo, bank statements. She scanned through the paperwork until she found the downturn Mildred had mentioned.

Snapping a picture of the statement, she looked at the ten-thousand-dollar withdrawal that had depleted the savings down to just a couple hundred. What had Gerald paid ten thousand dollars for? She glanced around the house. Definitely not furniture or upkeep. She opened closets and doors and confirmed that the place's only heat source was a wood stove. No upgrade there. And he'd taken the money out several months ago.

Maybe there was something in the barn he'd bought? She'd look there next. But what had happened during March that had Gerald keeping that kind of money in cash? And had someone known he had the money on site? Was that why he'd been killed?

But if it was the money, why would someone wait three months? Nothing was adding up. She knew the next question she had to answer. What happened to the money?

She closed up the desk, putting away the file folders in the same order they'd been, and headed to the door to go find Ian. Dom was still sitting on the porch, watching out for stray goats. He remembered the place, Angie could tell. The fur on the back of his neck stood up. She ruffled his mane and untied his leash. "Are you afraid we're here to get Precious a friend?"

He looked up at her with fear in his eyes and she laughed. They strolled toward the barn as she snapped pictures on her phone. It would be sad if the new owner decided to subdivide and turn this into high end ranches for people who didn't ranch. But she guessed progress happened everywhere, including River Vista.

Ian was at the front table paying the milkers their weekly check. He looked up at her. "You're early. I've got about ten more people to pay out and then we can talk about how to divide up the kids."

"Okay if we sit outside? I don't know if Dom's allowed in here."

The old man in the front of the line laughed. "Dogs are fine. They are clean animals. Besides, Mr. Moss's dog, well, he's sad. Maybe he would like some company." He nodded to the corner of the barn where an older blue heeler lay in the straw watching them.

"That's a good idea." Angie turned toward the dog. "What's his name?"

"Gollum." The old man peered at his check. "Strange name for a dog."

Angie caught Ian's grin and smiled herself. Apparently, Gerald Moss had been a Tolkien fan. She hoped that didn't mean she'd be stuck with the dog as well as the baby goat. She eased Dom toward the other dog, holding his leash just in case the greeting wasn't friendly, but she shouldn't have worried. Dom leaned down, sniffed the older dog's snout, then proceeded to clean his face. She sat on the hay bale next to Gollum and petted him.

"What a good boy. You miss your guy, don't you?" Angie crooned softly to the old dog who seemed to lean into her touch. She wondered how much attention he'd gotten since Moss's death.

When Ian was finished, he walked over to her and crouched next to the dog. "I brought him inside last night and he went right to Gerald's bed, jumped on top and laid down, like this. The poor guy is grieving."

"What's going to happen to him?"

Ian shrugged. "I guess that's up to the new owners. Since an heir hasn't made him or herself known, I've been asked to see if there is a will somewhere in the house. I can't believe Moss would leave his dairy and animals up in the air with no one to take care of them."

It was hard to believe there wasn't a will, but then again, the man had taken out ten thousand in cash in the last three months from his business account. Maybe he'd been suffering from dementia. "In all the time you knew him, he didn't say anything about a relative?"

"We didn't talk about that. I asked him once what would happen to the farm and he told me to mind my own business. That he had it handled." Ian ran his hand over his neck. "Maybe me working myself to death is his definition of handled."

"Did he buy any new machinery this spring? Maybe something for the farm?" She looked around the barn. Everything seemed old, like 1950s old, but still in good shape. Moss had taken care of what he owned.

"Not that I know of. Why?" Ian's eyebrows raised as turned his attention from the dog to her. "Have you been snooping?"

"Maybe a little. Anyway, Mildred said that he'd told her the business had a downturn in March. Did he buy something that didn't work out?"

Ian glanced around the barn, taking the condition of the milking equipment into consideration before he answered. "There's nothing new here. And if he'd bought something, there'd be a receipt and an owner's manual. I swear the guy kept every owner's manual he'd ever gotten. There are things that I don't even know what they're for."

She bit her lip, wondering whether or not she should mention the bank statements. But if he was looking at why the business was struggling, he should find the withdrawal, sooner or later. And she wouldn't have to admit to a breaking and entering charge even though the door was open.

A horn sounded in the driveway. He stood and stretched. "You've been saved by the bell. We will return to this subject after the kids leave."

Ian brought the kids and leaders inside the barn where he had them sit and gave a quick rundown of a working goat dairy. Angie could see the kids squirming. One little boy hit the one next to him, and the leader/parent had to step in. The rest of the kids turned to watch the fight, and Ian talked louder, trying to get their attention.

A little girl stood up and raised her hand. Ian, looking for a lifeline, nodded toward her. "You have a question?"

"Where's the treasure?"

At her question, the kids stopped fighting and the group turned toward Ian, waiting on his answer.

"I'm sorry? What did you ask?"

She put her hands on her hips like she was talking to a child. "The treasure. My mommy said that Moss Farm holds a treasure. So where is it?"

"Maybe she meant the farm was in the Treasure Valley. That's what they call this whole area in between the mountains." Ian offered.

The girl raised her eyebrows. "I'm not stupid. I know this is the Treasure Valley. I'm in fourth grade and we've already studied that part of the history book. I want to know where the treasure is and what it's made of."

"It's probably gold." The dark-haired boy who'd hit the other one, pipped in.

"I heard it was jewels. Like the ones that kings used to hide in castles." His victim said, giving the first boy a little push. "You're so dumb."

"No one's dumb." The woman in the back moved the two boys on either side of her, keeping a grip on each one. "Let's finish listening to Mr. McNeal and then we'll go feed the goats."

Angie could hear the words the woman didn't say. *And then I can get you all back to your parents and out of my life.* She didn't blame her.

Managing ten kids with only one other parent who was on her phone the entire time must have been brutal.

"I've heard rumors of a treasure, here at the farm, but I haven't ever seen it." Ian's voice rang over the chatter that had taken over the group. "I've been all over the property and have never found a single cave."

"That's because it's hidden." The little girl nodded sagely. "You have to find the map first, then you can find the treasure."

"Okay, then I'll look for a map. But for now, let's go feed the goats. I know they are probably hungry by now." He pointed to the back of the barn. "Who can tell me what goats eat?"

As the women stood watching the group follow Ian like the children in the Pied Piper book, the frazzled mother reached down and rubbed Dom's head. "Your man is good with kids. You two have any?"

"Oh, he's not my man." Angie stumbled over the words. "I mean, we're not married or anything."

"Well, you might want to grab that one. Handsome, hardworking, and good with kids? He's a keeper." The woman sighed and shook her head. "Sorry, I've got to go. Jimmy? You hit Scott one more time and you'll be banned from field trips for the rest of the school year."

After the kids left, Ian nodded to the house. "I've got a six pack of beer in the fridge if you'd like one."

"That would be nice. Typically, I like kids, but I've only been exposed to them one at a time. In a group, they're kind of scary." She followed him toward the porch chairs.

"That Jimmy's a scamp. He's going to be a hellion when he grows up a little. I feel bad for his mother." Ian nodded to the chairs. "Sit down. I'll get the beer and I think I have a bag of chips we can break open."

"Maybe if his mother came along on these trips, she'd be more aware of the way he acts." Angie slipped into a chair and leaned back, closing her eyes. When he tapped her with the cold bottle she sat up. "They wore me out."

"Children. And by the way, Jimmy's mother was the other woman in the group. The one on her phone?" He sat the bag of potato chips between them. "Sorry, I have no dip. Anyway, I expect Jimmy acts up to see if she's even watching."

"Now that's just sad." Angie grabbed a handful of the ruffled chips. "I like plain chips. They're the best."

"I totally agree. I guess we have more in common than our love of goats." He took his own handful and threw one to Dom.

"Who said I love goats?" She glanced at her watch. Almost seven and she hadn't eaten dinner. She'd have to deal with that soon or she'd be starving and eat the entire bag of chips.

"You took Precious in without even a blink of an eye. Don't tell me you don't love goats."

"She's special. She's an orphan and, well, she's awful cute." Angie took a second handful of chips. "So tell me about this treasure. Did Gerald ever tell you anything about it? Or is it all just regional lore?"

"I'm not quite sure. I asked him about it once, but he blew me off. Said it was none of my business."

"That's the same reaction I got when I asked to see the cheese cave. You would have thought I offered to sleep with him. He told me never to bring it up again." Angie sipped her beer. "But he did say that my grandmother knew about the cave. Which was news to me."

Ian sipped his beer and then looked at her, his blue eyes intense. "Maybe you have the treasure map, as the little girl called it, somewhere in your grandmother's house?"

# CHAPTER 20

As Angie heated up some of the potato soup she'd pulled out of the freezer, she thought about Ian's statement. Could her grandmother have known not only where the cheese cave was but also about the treasure? Was the treasure actually real? She glanced around the room. Most of Nona's stuff had been either gone through and donated, or mixed in with her own stuff. But she had tucked some letters into a box she'd put in the attic. Could there be a clue there?

She decided to wait until after dinner and then she'd go pull down her grandmother's Pandora box. After the funeral, she hadn't been strong enough to sort through what was important and what wasn't, so all of Nona's writings, journals, and probably grocery lists were in that box. Or in the stacks of boxes in the attic that Nona had collected.

Dom barked and ran to the open door to look out the screen. Mrs. Potter came up the stairs with her walker. Angie held the screen door open as the woman made her way into the kitchen. She plopped down on a chair, breathing hard. Angie poured her a glass of water and she took it, then took small sips. She started choking, but waved Angie away as she pulled out a handkerchief and wiped her mouth.

"Are you all right? Maybe you should have Erica drive you over here next time you decide to visit." Angie sat down and watched her elderly neighbor as she caught her breath.

"Now, don't you start on me. Erica babies me enough. And don't tell her I came over. She's studying for her classes. She doesn't need to drop everything just because I wanted to come visit." Mrs. Potter finished off the water.

"Do you want more?" Angie reached for the glass.

She nodded. "I guess I should have hydrated before I left the house. I just wanted to tell you that man was back again today."

A chill went down Angie's back. "Did you get a good look at him?"

"I did. But I don't understand why he's showing up here. Especially since he always seems to come right after you drive off. If I didn't know better, I would say he was watching for you to leave." She took the glass that Angie offered and took another slip. Then she sat it down on the table. "That boy has nothing but bad luck. It's been that way all his life."

"Wait, you know who he is?" Angie relaxed a little. She didn't have a stalker or a potential burglar, it was just a case of bad timing.

"Of course I know him. Kirk Hanley has been my Bella's vet for a while now." Mrs. Potter pointed over toward where the soybean field sat. "He's your neighbor on the west side. He must be wanting to talk to you about watering times. Soybeans take a lot of water. Or is that pinto beans?"

While Mrs. Potter mused on the proper amount of moisture for growing the different types of beans favorited by local farmers, Angie thought about Dom's last visit to Kirk's clinic. "You're probably right, it has to be about the field and the irrigation schedule. I'll give him a call Monday when the clinic opens if he doesn't show up tomorrow."

Mrs. Potter stood and adjusted her walker. "I better make my way back home before Erica notices I'm gone. She'll go all Where's Waldo trying to find me."

"I could drive you back." Angie knew she'd get turned down flat, but the woman looked a little tired.

"No need my dear. I was just a little thirsty when I came over. I'll be fine on the way back. Besides, my doctor tells me I need more exercise. A walk isn't going to kill me."

As she walked out of the house, Angie followed her out to the porch and watched as she made her way back home. She wasn't sure Mrs. Potter was correct. But she wouldn't --no, make that couldn't-- tell her what to do either. Dom leaned on her leg and she reached down and rubbed one ear. "I know buddy. She's getting old."

Instead of going up to the attic after supper, Angie snuggled into the couch and read the mystery novel she'd been trying to finish for a few days. She couldn't think about Nona, not today. If she did, she might start crying and never stop.

* * * *

Sunday morning, she made herself waffles, bacon, and scrambled eggs. Dom sat watching her and drooling. She told him her schedule for the day as she cooked. "First thing we'll do chores, then I need to weed the garden and see if there's anything to harvest, then I'll cut up a chicken and make some soup and put part of it away for dinner." She nodded, thinking about her next menu for The County Seat. Maybe a pan-fried chicken over a bed of fried green tomatoes? It could work, depending on the spices and herbs she used. Excited to create new recipes, she sat down to breakfast, looking forward to her second cooking session of the day.

Everything came together quickly and she boxed up a sample plate for Felicia as well as a quart of the soup. Even though her friend had attended culinary school too, Felicia didn't love cooking and hated creating. Give her a recipe, and she could cook anything. Tell her to create something new and she froze.

She put the basket into the back, loaded up Dom, and headed into town. Hopefully this meeting with Estebe would go quickly and easily. She turned on the music as she tried to drown out her fears. Opening night was five days away and she needed the guy. She'd just think positive and not worry about why he wanted to talk. Or just not think at all.

He was already in the kitchen when she arrived. She sat her basket on the counter and sent Dom to his bed in the corner of the kitchen. Then she unpacked the food and put it in the refrigerator. She'd tell Felicia it was there after she dealt with whatever this was. "Good afternoon."

"You shouldn't let animals in the kitchen. The health department will sanction us for having him in here."

How do you really feel? She shook her head. She wanted her staff to be able to say anything to her, even if it was incorrect. They all were entitled to an opinion. "Actually, he'll have a bed in my office. I've talked to the health guy and as long as we're not serving, Dom can be anywhere in the restaurant."

"The government says one thing and does another. You should be careful." Estebe turned off the stove and plated whatever he'd been cooking. He handed her the finished plate. "The sauce is creamier with my recipe. We should change the process."

"Before opening night?" Angie shook her head. "Not happening, buddy. I'm more than willing to talk about this later, but we have a plan for opening night."

He nodded to the plate. His black eyes twinkled like he had a secret no one else knew. "Taste it. You'll want to change as soon as you taste. I know this is true."

The man was persistent. And asking to change a recipe was a long way from the discussion she'd worried they were going to have. She leaned against the counter and took a bite of the pasta. The smell was warm and inviting as she brought the bite toward her. Maybe with a hint of heat, she tried to identify the changes he'd made. Then she took the bite. Flavor exploded in her mouth. The goat cheese was smooth and tangy. The pasta ala dente. And there was some sort of pepper. Not cayenne. She glanced at him. "Jalapeno?"

He shook his head. "Hungarian wax pepper, minced. You like it, don't you?"

His enthusiasm made her smile. "I do. Why were you cooking the recipes?"

Now, he shrugged, looking embarrassed. "When I left here on Wednesday, I felt like something was missing from the pasta dish. I started playing with it at home and came up with this yesterday."

"You've been cooking this same recipe since Wednesday?"

He filled a second plate with the rest of the pasta and took both plates to the chef table. "I wanted it to be the best. Come sit and eat with me. I want to learn more about you. Where did you learn to cook?"

The impromptu lunch went on for over an hour. Finally, Estebe pushed away from the table, picking up the empty plates. "I have to go cook for the family tonight. Thank you for considering my change to your recipe."

"No, thank you for the twist. I want this to be an open and creative kitchen. The only way that will happen is if we talk to each other." She took the plate out of his hand. "Family rule, you cook, I clean."

A real smile curved his lips and not for the first time, Angie was struck by his looks. "It's a good rule. One I will have to remember."

And his accent didn't suck either. Angie headed to the dishwasher station. "See you bright and early on Friday. I'll update the recipe book with your changes."

After he'd left and the dishes were washed and put away, Angie texted Felicia to see if she was in the apartment. When she responded that she'd be right down, Angie grabbed a soda out of the bar fridge and sat at one of the tables, looking out toward the veterinary clinic. There was no sign of life at the building across the street, but that didn't mean Kirk wasn't there. Maybe she'd go knock on his apartment door and ask why he'd been visiting her house for the last two days. Dom lifted his head as Felicia made her way down the stairs.

"Hey guys, how long have you been here?" She grabbed her own drink and sat next to Angie. Then she looked at her watch. "Oh, yeah, the meeting with Estebe. Do I need to call the temp agency first thing in the morning?"

"No, he's not quitting. He just wanted to tweak the pasta recipe. And I have to admit, it's better."

"Okay..." Felicia turned and stared out the window. "What are you looking at? Did I blink and miss the parade?"

"No." Angie shook her head. "I'm just remembering something Mrs. Potter said. I think Kirk has been showing up at my house when I'm gone. Don't you think that's strange?"

"Honestly, I think everything about that man is strange. I'm so glad I dodged that bullet. Once you let the crazies into your life, they're hard to get rid of." Felicia glanced out the window again. "Did I ever tell you about that guy Randy who stalked me for two weeks after I smiled at him in the grocery store?"

"I remember him. He was one of our best customers for those two weeks. He ate at the restaurant three times in one day." Angie turned back to her list. "If we're done talking about your love life, are we ready for Friday? Anything you need me to do? Are the deliveries set?"

"Yes, no, and yes." Felicia shrugged. "We're good. Stop worrying. This isn't our first rodeo." Felicia stood. "Do I have to get the menus reprinted because of this change?"

Angie thought a moment. She hadn't considered the menus. "No, I think we'll just alert the servers that the dish is a little spicy. Not on the extreme level, just a little."

"I'll put it in the notes I'll go over with the servers this weekend." Felicia nodded toward the upstairs. "I'm watching *How to Lose a Guy in 10 Days*. Want to join me?"

Angie stood and picked up her tote. "I better get back to the house. By the way, I have a test dinner in your section of the fridge and some soup if you get hungry."

"Perfect. I was going to go salami and crackers tonight. A real meal will be amazing." She turned and headed up the stairs. Just before she disappeared from view, she paused. "Are you sure you're okay? You seem a little off."

"Just ready for this opening to be done and over with. I'm not sleeping well." Which wasn't a total lie. Angie had already brought her into her worries about Gerald Moss's death. Now with the possible connection to

Nona, it just seemed too overwhelming, even for her. It was all in the past and they needed to focus on the present and the future.

Leaving the restaurant, she started toward the vet clinic to talk to Kirk. No need to wait until Monday. But as she started to cross the street, Kirk's old pickup pulled out of the back-parking lot and wound its way through the small city park, a short cut to the road to Meridian. Or Boise. Or even Jackpot, although that would be a long drive to go and come back before tomorrow. One more thing she didn't get to cross off on her list.

* * * *

The next morning, she made a quick list of must-get-dones. She wanted to spend some time in the restaurant's kitchen before Friday. She planned on having 'office hours' for all the non-cooking tasks on Wednesday and Thursday, but she wanted one day just to cook and play. She marked up her planner for the next four weeks with the times she would be at the job. Checking the time, she called and made an 11 am appointment with Mark Foreman, claiming to be a new client. He didn't need to know she didn't want to expand The County Seat to a second location. At least not yet. But first, she'd stop at the local bank and pay a visit to her loan officer. Maybe she'd have some insight on why Gerald took out such a large sum in March. But did they have confidentiality issues, like lawyers? All she could do was ask.

She tapped her pen on the page. She still hadn't looked through Nona's papers. She was avoiding it, she knew. Touching the things her grandmother touched, delving into what she thought, it would bring Nona back to life, if just for a minute. Then Angie would feel the pain again. But it had to be done.

Angie put her pen down and, grabbing a to go cup of coffee and her phone, headed up to the attic to search. Knowing Nona's box 'filing' system gave her an advantage this time. It shouldn't take long to find what she was looking for—a box filled with papers she'd put in the attic after she'd moved back home. She also wanted to go through Nona's own boxes, just in case.

She quickly found the one she'd packed and with a pang of grief, sat the box near the attic stairs. Then she went to Nona's stacks. It took two hours for her to go through everything. Mostly because an item would catch her eye, evoking a memory and she'd follow the trail. But finally, she had two more boxes of papers and journals stacked with the first one.

She carried all three boxes down to the kitchen as Dom followed her out of the dusty attic. The dog hadn't left her side, but had been extremely quiet during her search. Had he felt the emotional undercurrents? Or had he just been sleepy? She made another cup of coffee and started going through the papers. By the time she found Nona's diary, she had an hour to get to Boise for her appointment with Mark Foreman. The good news was she would be able to throw away most of two boxes as they were old utility bills. She kept the bank statements to make sure she'd found all of Nona's hiding holes. The woman liked to open a new account for every new goal or project. Sometimes, there was less than a hundred dollars in an account. A few months ago, she'd found one with a different bank near the shopping center in Meridian with several thousand dollars in it.

As she drove past Mrs. Potter's, she waved at Erica, who was pulling weeds out of the flower bed. She'd have to warn Erica to question her own grandmother about possible accounts, but Nona hadn't had anyone here to watch her as she slowly lost her grasp on reality. There could be money stuck in the walls for all Angie knew. And besides, Mrs. Potter didn't have even a little sign of dementia. The woman was as sharp as a tack. It was her body that was failing her.

By the time she found street parking and coins for the meter, she only had a few minutes to dash into the large tower. She paused at the large marble reception desk. "Foreman Investments?"

"And you are Miss Turner, correct?" The woman looked up from the computer screen that must have shown her appointment as well as her name. "Fourth floor, Suite 402. Go to elevator D."

Computers would take over the woman's job in less than ten years, Angie mused as she headed toward the bank of elevators. You'd walk into somewhere like this, they'd do a palm print and retinal scan, and you'd be directed to the correct floor. Or you'd do the entire visit virtually, which was more likely.

She stepped out of the elevator into a cream and oak hallway. A small sign directed her that suites 400 and 401 were on her left and 402 and 403 on her right. The padding on the carpet was thick and her sandals sank with each step. She was glad she hadn't worn heels, that would have made the walk dangerous.

She opened the doors into 402 and found another smiling woman waiting for her. "Miss Turner, come this way. Mark's waiting for you. May I get you some bottled water, soda, or a coffee?"

"A Coke would be great if you have one." She could use the sugar since she hadn't eaten since breakfast. She'd find something on her way back to town before she visited the bank and tried to find Kirk Hanley. She knew she got grumpy when her blood sugar was low, and she didn't want to snap at someone when she was trying to sweet talk information.

"Not a problem, I'll bring it right in." The woman held the door to an office open and motioned her inside. "Mark, Ms. Turner is here."

The man who turned around looked better than his photo Angie had found on the company website. Tall, dark, with a touch of silver at his temples. He wore a suit that looked like it cost more than Angie spent on clothes during an entire year. He stepped toward her, his hand outstretched. "Miss Turner. So nice to meet you. I've heard good things about your new restaurant, are you already thinking of expanding?"

"Actually, no, since we haven't opened yet." Angie shook his hand. She tried to size the guy up as she sat. How would he take her direct manner of questions? Just because he was in an amazing suit didn't mean he wasn't a killer. Finally, she decided that playing a little dumb about everything might be the way to go with this guy. "I'm afraid I have some strange questions I need to ask you."

He laughed. "Strange seems to be my niche. Come on in and take a chair." He nodded to the receptionist as she brought two glasses, Angie's can of Coke, and a Dr. Pepper. "Sit, let's drink and talk. You have my curiosity piqued."

And that was what she'd been hoping for. Angie eased onto the orange leather visitor chair. "I'm in the same situation. I'm curious about a few things."

He poured her soda over the ice and handed it to her. Then he poured his own drink and settled into a chair next to her, rather than on the other side of his desk. "Now that we're comfortable, tell me what you need."

"There's a farm on the canyon's edge in River Vista. I've heard that you were courting the owner to agree to a possible sale." She sipped her soda and watched him for a reaction. There was nothing, except a mild confusion.

He paused before he spoke. "You're right, I was interested in the property. The Moss dairy farm, correct? It would be an amazing place for an exclusive subdivision for maybe ten houses, but I didn't have to do any courting. The guy came me to and practically begged me to sell the land for him."

# CHAPTER 21

"He initiated the sale discussion?" For the first time, Angie was truly surprised. It didn't seem like Old Man Moss was even considering selling that Sunday morning when they'd had coffee and breakfast together watching the morning arrive at the canyon's edge. "Gerald Moss called you?"

Mark sipped his soda, obviously thinking about his answer. "No, it wasn't the actual owner—Gerald Moss, right? He had an intermediary reach out. A relative, if I remember right."

"I'm not sure Mr. Moss had any relatives." The man seemed nice and up front, but maybe he was playing with her. Or he might be mixing up the property with someone else. Before she jumped to conclusions, she wanted to make sure they were talking about the right property. "This is the farm right on the canyon edge?"

"Yes, I know what property you're talking about." He snapped a little impatiently at her. "My memory for land is much better than my memory for people. Hold on a minute, let me check."

As she drank more of her soda, Mark stood and hit a few keys on his computer. She didn't respond to his comment, giving him the silence he'd requested.

Finally, he nodded and pointed to the screen. "I knew I still had that listing in my pending folder. I printed out the forms and gave it to the guy to have the owner sign. I told him he could either bring the guy in, or have the forms signed before a notary. Any listing with over a 7-figure asking price, I make sure we have exclusive rights to sell the property."

"But the guy never came back with either the owner or the papers." Angie filled in the ending.

"No. And I reached out twice, then moved the contact to my assistant for another month." He finished off his soda. "It happens. People talk about selling, but then can't get past the sentimental value of the place. I'm sure when this guy passes, the family will come back to me for the listing."

"He's already gone. Gerald Moss was murdered last week." Had it only been a week since this all started? "I take it no one has contacted you since?"

Mark shook his head. "The guy said he was a nephew. Have you talked to the family?"

"I'm going to pass this information over to Sheriff Brown. Do you have a number for this guy? Or a name?"

"Sure." He wrote something down on a slip of paper with his company logo and phone number on the top. "Here's his name and the phone number he gave me. I never could reach him directly there, so I'm assuming it's going directly to voice mail."

She took the paper and after reading the name, she froze. "That's impossible," she whispered.

"I'm not sure what you mean, but that is the guy who came into the office offering to list the property. Let the family know I'm very interested in helping them get rid of the place." He glanced at his watch. "Sorry, I have another appointment now. I'm going to have to cut this short."

When she left the offices, she felt a little shell shocked. She climbed into her car and called the River Vista police station and asked to speak with the sheriff.

"Sheriff's out on a call this morning. Some kids decided to sneak off and spend the night out at the cave. He's out there with some volunteers trying to get them out so their folks can tan their hides." The overly chatty receptionist offered. "I can tell him you called, unless this is an emergency? I've heard you've had some unexpected visitors out at the old Turner place."

"No emergency." Angie wasn't even sure she had anything other than a name. And she hadn't thought to ask Mark to describe the guy. Which she should have if she'd been thinking straight. "Have him call me on my cell when he has a minute. I'll be back in town in less than an hour and I'll stop by."

"He should have the kids up from the cave by then. I'll have him give you a call if I hear it's going to take longer."

Angie heard a series of clicks on the line.

"Sorry, I've got to go. Monday mornings are usually dead. I don't know why my phone's blowing up today."

And with that, the officer disconnected her call. A bang sounded on her window causing her to jump. A meter checker stood there with his machine in one hand. She rolled down her window.

"If you don't want me to give you a ticket you either need to feed more money into the meter, or take off now." The young woman looked at her with concern. "I can't tell if you're coming or going."

"I'm going. Sorry for the delay." She started up the car, checked her seatbelt and then eased into traffic. She'd stop by the bank, see if she could find out anything else, then head straight to the police station to wait for Sheriff Brown. If what she was thinking was right, she needed someone else to handle this. Playing Nancy Drew was one thing, dealing with a killer up close and personal was out of her pay grade.

The trip back to River Vista took longer than she'd planned. She was starving and had to pass up all the fast food places. If Sheriff Brown was still out, she'd stop by the restaurant and cook up something. The bank parking lot was empty when she pulled in and parked. She looked around, checking to make sure no one had been following her. "Paranoia strikes again," she muttered as she stepped into the bank. The branch décor was 1970's modern. It had looked this way when she and Nona had come to set up Angie's first bank account when she turned 16 and took on a summer job topping corn.

The teller, Martha Fields, an older woman who'd worked there since Angie could remember, motioned her to the window. "Miss Angie, what are you doing today? Mr. Fields and I are so looking forward to visiting your restaurant. We couldn't get reservations until the weekend after next. Your place is so popular. Your grandmother would have been so proud."

Angie felt her shoulders relax. She was back home, with friends. And as soon as she talked to the sheriff, she'd retire from playing Nancy Drew and just be a chef. "Make sure you let your servers know you want to talk to me. I'd be glad to come out and see you guys."

"We wouldn't want to bother you at work." Martha's face broke into a grin. "Unless you insist. Maybe we could get a quick picture with you that night? I just started posting on Facebook and you'd be my first celebrity."

"I'm not much of a celebrity, but I'd be glad to stand for a couple of shots." Angie looked toward the offices. "Hey, is Tyra in? I have a couple of questions for her."

"Sorry, no. She works Saturdays so she gets Monday off. Mr. Harrold is available though. He's in there doing reports." She glanced behind her as a car came into the drive up. "Looks like I have a customer. Go knock on his door and he'll help you."

Angie nodded her thanks, then went to the offices. Mr. Harrold was behind a large wooden desk, staring at his computer screen. She'd seen him in the same position years ago, but then, he'd had a pile of papers in front of him. She knocked. "Mr. Harrold?"

"Angie Turner, come on in. Mrs. Harrold and I will be there first thing on Friday to welcome you and your restaurant into the River Vista community." He stood and pointed to a seat. "Can I get you some coffee?"

"No, I just have a quick question." She pulled out her phone and blew up the picture of the statement she'd snapped from Gerald Moss's desk. She went with an almost truth, hoping it would ease her path. "I'm looking into a few things for Sheriff Brown and wondered if you could tell me who that check was made out to? The copy just says Cash."

"We can't release information about one account holder to another without the permission of the account holder." His face turned from welcoming to stony. "And you don't have permission."

"You do know Mr. Moss is deceased, right? That he was murdered?" Angie pushed. "He *can't* give me permission."

"Of course I know that. The missus and I were very sad to hear about his untimely death. But that doesn't change bank rules. I'm sorry, there is just no way I'm going to tell you anything about Gerald Moss's account. And if Sheriff Brown wants to know more, he can get a warrant." He stood, indicating the chit chat was over. "I'm sure you understand. We'll see you on Friday."

Angie tried to think of something to say that would change his mind, but finally, she stood and smiled. "I'm sure you'll love The County Seat. We're excited to be a destination restaurant for River Vista."

And with that she left Mr. Harrold's office. She'd tell Sheriff Brown about this when she met with him. As Angie passed by Martha, the woman held up one finger and whispered, "Wait for me outside."

Angie nodded and went out the front, standing by the side of the building without any windows. When Martha emerged less than a minute later, she beelined straight to Angie. "I only have a minute. I told him I needed to use the little girls' room. Which I do, so I can't be long here."

"What's going on?"

"I heard you talking about Mr. Moss and the check. He came into the bank and cashed it at my window. I tried to talk him out of it, but he was so mad." She shook her head at the memory. "He took the money, shoved it into the other man's hands and said 'We're done. You have your inheritance.' I thought that was really strange, but Old Man Moss did some strange things, you know."

"He gave ten thousand dollars in cash to who?" Angie thought she knew, but she wanted to hear the name. "Did you recognize who it was?"

"Of course, I tried to get him to just transfer the money into the other account, but he said he wanted cash. It almost emptied the vault, but it was close to end of day so Mr. Harrold said go ahead." Martha looked at her watch and turned toward the entrance. "I really have to get back inside before he notices I'm gone."

"Wait. Who did Mr. Moss give the money to?" Angie grabbed Martha's arm as she started to turn.

"Why, Kirk Hanley. I'm sure you'll meet him soon, if you haven't already. He's the veterinarian in town. I thought I said that."

Angie dropped her hand and watched as Martha scurried inside the bank. The clues were adding up. And Kirk's had been the name Mark Foreman had written on the sheet of paper.

She dialed the police station. "Is Sheriff Brown back yet?"

"Not yet, Angie." This time the person on the other end of the line didn't try to hide his impatience. "It's been a crazy morning. He said he'd stop by your place as soon as he can."

"Okay—wait, no. Tell him I'm at The County Seat. If he's not there by the time I leave for home, I'll call and let you know where I'll be."

She hung up the phone and drove to the parking lot behind her building. This didn't prove Kirk had murdered Gerald Moss, but it was the most likely scenario. Had Kirk lost his inheritance and come back for more? It explained why Moss Farm had hired a new veterinarian. Things were clicking into place, but she knew it was all a theory. That she couldn't prove.

Instead of worrying about it, she went to her kitchen and did what she always did when the world didn't make sense. She cooked.

\* \* \* \*

"I didn't know you were down here until I smelled the food. What are you making?" Felicia made her way across the kitchen to sit on a stool next to the expediter station.

"Chicken tacos. There was a couple of breasts in the fridge from my last experiment. How did you like the dish, by the way?"

"Yummy. Definitely a keeper." She took a water out of the fridge. "You look stressed. What's up? Is it the opening? I keep telling you that we'll be fine. We have good people working for us. And you make amazing food."

"I am nervous about the opening, but no. That's not what has me cooking." She pulled a rack of chocolate chip cookies out of the oven and set four on a plate. Then she turned down the heat on the chicken strips and sat the plate at the chef's table. She waved Felicia over. "Come and sit. We'll have dessert first while I tell you what I think happened to Gerald Moss. Then we can eat lunch and hopefully, Sheriff Brown will be here by then."

She made two mochas as she told Felicia about what she'd found out that morning. By the time she was done, they'd eaten most of the dozen cookies.

Finally, her friend sat back in her chair. "OMG. And I thought about dating the guy. Do you really think he could have killed Mr. Moss?"

"I don't know, maybe it was an accident. Maybe he went back for more money and the old guy tried to run him off." Angie went over to the stove to finish up the tacos. "All I know is if Ian didn't know this, Sheriff Brown probably didn't either. Those two seem to talk about everything."

"I'm not sure how hungry I am." Felicia took the cookie plate to the dishwasher station. "Those cookies were amazing."

"We need real food too." Angie thought about the many times her grandmother had told her the same thing. "Oh, and Ian thinks that maybe Moss told Nona where the treasure is at the farm."

"Wait, there's a treasure out at the farm?" Felicia grabbed another cookie and leaned against the counter, watching Angie cook. "And when are you going to tell me what's going on with you and Ian? I need to know if it's serious or not because a certain other someone asked me if you were dating anyone."

The spatula hung in the air. "Who asked you about me?"

Felicia shrugged. "I didn't tell him I wouldn't say anything, so I guess I can spill. Estebe asked when he called to talk to you. I wasn't sure if he was quitting or wanted to ask you out on a date."

"Neither of which happened. Maybe he just wanted to be prepared in case he did consider asking me out." Angie finished up the plates, slicing a fresh tomato and avocado on the side for a small salad. "Did you know they grow avocados here? I'm so excited for them to come into season later this summer."

"You're taking this farm-to-fork concept literal." Felicia took her plate to the chef table. "So, now that you've solved the mystery, you're going to focus on food?"

"Definitely." Angie picked up the taco in the homemade tortilla she'd made earlier. "As of now, I'm back to being a chef, twenty-four seven."

# CHAPTER 22

When the Sheriff still hadn't shown up after lunch, Angie called the station and asked to be transferred to his voice mail. She went through the basics she'd discovered. Then she told him if he wanted to talk to her, she'd be at home. After finishing that, she locked up the downstairs and hugged her friend. "Tell me you're staying in tonight."

"You know me, Monday night is when I catch up on the shows I missed during the weekend." Felicia paused on the stairs. "I could pack a bag and we could do a girl's night."

"I'll be fine. Besides, you do know I have a guard dog, just in case?" Angie pushed aside the fact it just took one person to casually mention she was looking into Moss's murder and the small-town gossip chain could get the news back to Kirk

"Dom's more likely to lick someone to death than actually protect you."

Angie paused at the door. "His superpower is sitting on people. I can have the bad guy cornered and I'll just have Dom sit on him until the police show up."

When she got home, she saw Erica out in the yard, mowing. She parked and ignored Dom's quick barks and crossed the street.

Erica turned off the mower when she saw Angie crossing the road. "What's up neighbor?"

"Nothing much. I just wanted to let you and your grandmother know if that guy Kirk Hanley comes by when I'm not here, call the Sheriff. I think he's looking for something."

Erica's eyes widened. "You think he's trying to steal something? But he's the vet!"

"I may be wrong, and if I am, I'll be the first to apologize to him, but I don't want him at the house if I'm not there. And you guys shouldn't approach him either. I don't think he has the best of intentions. So can you just keep away from him?" Angie hoped the woman wouldn't ask more questions, and to her surprise, she didn't.

"If you don't trust him, I don't trust him." She grinned at Angie's surprised look. "The residents of where the sidewalk ends have to stick together. There's bad people out there in reality world."

"Thanks and tell your grandmother hello." Angie headed across the street to get her lecture on being gone too long from Dom.

He was at the door waiting when she unlocked the house. Then he greeted her with a yelp and as she bent down to his level. "Hey buddy. Have you been a good boy?" She followed him out to the back yard through the mud room. She sat on the step as he wandered through the yard and watched the butterflies flock around the flowers.

Standing, she popped back into the house and grabbed a bottle of water and Nona's diary. She took a sip and opened the aging book. Nona had always kept a diary, since she could write. There were several journals in the box, waiting to be read. Sometimes the entry was just date, weather, and farm stuff. Often, Angie found a recipe. She took her own notebook and tore out a sheet of paper ripping out slips to mark the recipes.

Were there enough recipes to make an actual cookbook? That would be an amazing project to work on and a beautiful tribute to her Nona. As she flipped through the pages, she wondered why she hadn't read these journal entries before. They made her feel closer to Nona, not overwhelmed with grief, like she had been when she'd first come home.

She opened another journal and a piece of paper fell out. Glancing at it, she realized it was a map. She ran her finger down the river, then up the cliffs to a big X. If she didn't know better, this looked like the trail where she'd been walking Dom. And the X was placed right at the spot where she'd seen the bunny disappear into the wall. She turned over the page. On the back, in Nona's cursive handwriting was two words. Moss Farm.

"I think I found the treasure map." Angie glanced at Dom who looked up from his nap he'd been taking at the bottom of the stairs while she read. She glanced at her watch. 4:00 p.m. If she hurried, she'd still have time before the sun set to see if the map really directed her to Gerald's secret cheese cave.

She grabbed her backpack, shoved a couple of water bottles and a flash light, just in case and shot Felicia a short text. Taking Dom for a walk down on the canyon trail. I'll text you when I'm back home.

Her phone beeped back Felicia's response. HAVE FUN AND BE SAFE. I'LL BE WATCHING FOR YOUR TEXT.

"Yes, mother." Angie chuckled and tucked her phone into her pants pocket. She put Dom's leash into the pack, just in case the trail was busy, but being a Monday, she didn't think she'd run into anyone. Most of the trail runners were weekend warriors and back to their day jobs and weekday routines today. She, on the other hand, worked weekends and took off early in the week for her personal time. Or at least that would be the pattern once The County Seat opened on Friday.

Rolling her shoulders, she decided this was a great idea, even if the map didn't prove to be anything. She needed the exercise after a long, crazy day. Carefully folding the map and tucking it into her pocket she grabbed her keys and they headed out for a quick walk.

Kirk Hanley's warning about it not being safe the first time she'd met him echoed in her head. He'd been right, it hadn't been safe, but she hadn't known at the time that he was actually the bad guy.

As she'd figured, the parking lot at the trailhead was empty. She unloaded Dom, grabbed her backpack, and remote locked her car. The beep echoed against the canyon walls and a startled bird flew up from a bush near the trail.

Dom gave a quick woof to let the bird know that he hadn't been scared at all and they started hiking. Ten minutes later, she thought she was at the switch back where she'd made the rock arrow, but she couldn't find it. She slowly walked up to the next turn, and then the next, scanning the edge of the trail. Finally, she found the pile of rocks that looked nothing like an arrow now. She took out the map and glanced at the markings, then compared them with her current location. It looked like the same place.

It was time to go off trail and see if she was right. But as soon as she pushed through the bushes closest to the trail, she realized she was still *on* a trail. Not one used a lot, but one that had been carved out of the dirt years ago.

Following the trail and remembering where she saw the bunny disappear, she approached the rock wall. If you just glanced at the rock wall, there was no opening, but going around the stone edge, you came into a large entryway. She grabbed her flashlight out of the bag and shined the beam on the edge of the opening. It seemed solid enough. Then she shone it on the stone floor. No sudden drop offs like in the River Vista cave. She'd seen drunk kids fall into the creek there when they'd gone down to the cave to party.

She eased herself around the rock and into the cave. The air was cool and the temperature dropped from the high seventies outside on the trail to a balmy sixty, maybe sixty-five. A large temperature gauge was hung on the entrance of the cave with a table underneath it. In Gerald's scrawled handwriting, dates and temperatures had been recorded. Sometimes twice a day. The temps never got over sixty-five or under sixty from the pages she scanned. Two flashlights sat on the table next to the notebook.

She shined the light farther into the cave. There were wooden shelves lining each side of the cave. Wheels of cheese sat with a label on the shelf with the create date written in ink. Some of the first ones were so faded she couldn't read the date, but as she went further into the cave, she realized some of the dates went back five, ten years. Why wouldn't he just let the cheese commission certify the cheese and sell it? Why did he keep this a secret from even the woman—or women—he'd been courting?

Questions she'd probably never get answers to, as they died with Gerald Moss. Ian needed to see this. She'd call him when she got home. Or maybe stop by the farm. He could be still sleeping on Gerald's couch, hoping to deter local treasure seekers or teenage kids looking for a new place to party.

She wandered farther back into the cave and realized she'd run out of shelving. She swung her light over the back of the cave and saw something on the wall. Curious, she stepped closer and realized it was drawings. Not just drawings, petroglyphs that must have been from the original Indian tribe that ran this area before the first white settlers came in from the west. The park that lined the canyon walls following the river had two examples of Indian art, but they looked old and weathered. These looked like they had just been painted, the coolness of the cave keeping the colors bright.

She took out her phone to snap some pictures and noticed she had two missed calls and a text from Felicia. Where are you?

She hadn't been gone more than an hour, had she? She checked the time. Angie didn't think she had cell service, but just in case, she responded back. I found the cheese cave and more. I'll call you as soon as I'm in the car.

She opened the camera app and snapped several pictures of the walls. She was just getting ready to leave when she heard Dom's low growl. Fear ran through her and for the first time, she was hoping she'd see coyotes when she turned.

"You have got to be kidding me." Kirk Hanley stood watching her and staring at the walls. "This is the so-called treasure? The only thing this does is mess up the sale of the property. I'm sure the biddies at the historical society will put this place under a no-build order, until they decide what to with the cave."

Angie felt a chill go through her body as she eased toward the cave entrance. Her legs were shaking so hard, she thought she might fall before she even got close. Trying to keep the waver out of her voice, she said, "I don't know. Maybe the cave isn't that special."

He shook his head and pointed a revolver at her. "Nice try, but you and I both know that's not true. I've been hearing that you're quite the little detective. What exactly do you think I did?"

"You mean, besides holding me at gunpoint?" She tried to think of a way to get out but she didn't think she could win a footrace against him or a bullet. She'd have to talk her way out of this. "I'm not sure what you're talking about. I just saw the cave from the trail and decided to come explore."

"And you just happened to have a flashlight?" Kirk shook his head. "I followed you from your place out here. You took out of there like a bat out of hell. I knew you'd found your grandmother's map."

"How did you know she had a map?"

Kirk shrugged. "My mom always talked about how stingy Moss was with her, yet he and your grandmother had some sort of relationship. Mom said he told her that your grandmother was the only woman he trusted. Mom saw the map once, but then he just handed it over to your grandmother. He was probably sleeping with her. He should have put family first, don't you think?"

Angie thought about arguing for Nona's virtue, but honestly, she couldn't think of anything to say. Her mouth felt dry and she could feel Dom shaking beside her. She didn't want to work Kirk up, not when she could still talk him into letting her leave. She had to.

"You're related to Gerald? Why haven't you told anyone? They're looking for a relative to take over the farm and the inheritance." Angie decided this was her chance. "Let's just go outside and you can call Sheriff Brown from my phone and let him know you are the legal heir."

"I was the legal heir until that old man decided to disinherit me. I got a letter from some attorney working in Nevada telling me I was out of the will. Seriously? All I get is a measly 10K? That didn't even last me the weekend on the tables. I had some bad luck."

"Ian told me Moss didn't have a will. No one needs to know." She took a step toward the entrance. A tiny ray of hope filled her as she could see the light from outside. "Let's go outside and talk this through. I'll keep my mouth shut about the lawyer and you'll be a rich man."

"With an old goat farm? Seriously? All that land is worth is to sell it off to a developer." He waved the gun at her. "You move again and I'm going to shoot you. Or maybe I'll shoot your dog first. That should keep you still."

Dom growled again at the threat. Angie slapped her leg. "Come here."

"See you can follow orders. Training people is just like training dogs. You have to have an incentive to follow." He nodded toward the wall. "Go sit down there. I need to make sure the guy didn't hide anything else in here before I deal with you."

Angie found a blank wall and slid down to the floor. Dom laid his head on her lap. Tears filled her eyes as she rubbed his ears. Kirk was going to kill her and probably Dom too. And no one knew they were in a hidden cave on the Snake River. She should have left him at the house. She should have stayed at the house and let Sheriff Brown deal with this. She should have never started investigating. She wasn't made for this. Instead of listing off more shouldn'ts, she buried her face into Dom's fur. "You're such a good boy. I love you."

All of a sudden, the cave was lit up with bright lights and people rushed inside. She kept her head down and held on to Dom's collar, keeping him beside her. When she looked up, Sheriff Brown was cuffing Kirk and Ian was standing over her.

"Are you okay?" He held out a hand to pull her to her feet.

Shaking, she took in a breath. "I am now. How did you find us?"

"Let me get you out of here, then we'll talk." Ian put his arm around her and led her out of the cave. They paused at the entrance and moved out of the way when officers came up the trail.

Angie glanced behind her to see where her dog was but Dom padded behind them. She wanted to cry, but not here. "There's too many people here. It's going to excite Dom. I'm not sure I'll be able to keep him quiet."

"I'm going to take you down to your car and drive you home. Allen can come talk to you there." He walked her down the trail and to the passenger side of her car. "Give me the keys."

She did as she was told. She wondered if she was in shock. Even though it was still warm, she grabbed the hoodie she kept in the car and covered her upper body with it.

"Do you want me to turn on the heat?" Ian sat beside her and adjusted the arm of the hoodie. Dom was in the back seat, leaning his head over her shoulder.

"I'm not hurt." She said, taking a deep breath. She put her hand on Dom's head and pressed it into hers. "I think I was just scared. He would have killed us."

"I believe you're right. Something's off with that guy. If anyone stands in the way of what he wants, he feels justified in getting rid of them." Ian started the car and pulled out of the now crowded parking lot.

"So you think he killed Mr. Moss?" Angie thought about the way he discarded the value of the petroglyphs. "All he wanted was money."

"I don't know if Allen has enough evidence to prove the guy killed Gerald, but he has enough to lock him in a cage until he can prove it." He rubbed her hand. "We heard him threaten you. That was enough to lock the guy up for kidnapping and attempted murder."

"He didn't kidnap me, he followed me. I led him right to the cave. I should have realized he was watching the house, but I assumed he was in Jackpot gambling." She took a bottle of water out of her pack.

"Which was a good assumption, but I guess someone tipped him off that you were looking into who killed Gerald, so he started watching you." Ian turned the car down the road that led to her house. "And he made you stay there against your will. That's kidnapping. Tell me he touched you and Allen can add assault to the charges."

He sounded so earnest, so angry that Kirk had done this to her. It made her feel warm and cared for, even if it was just in the heat of the moment. "He didn't touch me, but thank you for this. I needed someone to lean on for a few minutes."

Ian smiled, his blue eyes twinkling. "I'm always here if you need a shoulder."

They rode in silence for a few minutes. Then she looked at him. "How did you find me? Find us, I mean?"

"Allen got your voice mail and came out to the house to talk to you, but according to Mrs. Potter, you'd just left. Then Erica told him she'd seen Kirk's truck following you down the road." He glanced at her. "She was really worried. She told him you'd said to stay away and call the police station if she saw him. I guess she was coming inside from a walk to do just that when Allen showed up."

"And you?" She narrowed her eyes. "Where were you? And why did you get involved in this whole take down?"

"Superman to the rescue." He shot her a quick grin. "Actually, Allen called me after he talked to Felicia. He knew I was over at the farm. You're going to have to take me back to my car in the morning."

"You're staying the night?" Angie didn't know how to react to the news.

Ian laughed. "Don't look so stricken. I'll be sleeping on your couch tonight. I know the killer is going to be behind bars, but until Allen makes sure he was working alone, I'd rather not take a chance of you being out here by yourself."

"I could call Felicia to come stay over." She sank her head into the headrest.

He snorted. "Two girls? That's just a serial killer movie waiting to happen."

"Okay Mr. Male Chauvinist, I'll have you know, we 'girls' can take care of ourselves." Anger flared up inside her.

"Now there's the fight I expected to see." Ian smiled. "Let me rephrase. Would you mind if I slept on your couch tonight? I'd be less anxious there than home in my bed wondering if you and Dom were all right."

"Since you asked so nicely, I accept your offer." The anger was gone as soon as it flared. All she felt now was bone-dripping tired.

He pulled the car into the driveway and parked. "Thank you. Let's get you inside. I'll handle feeding your zoo and if you feel up to making some, I'd love a cup of coffee when I come back."

"Coffee coming up." She looked down at Dom. "And several doggie treats for you, Mister. You were amazing in there."

Dom woofed his agreement and ran inside to his bed where he did two circles and lay down. He was asleep before she finished setting up the coffee pot and got his treats out of the cupboard. She sat the treats next to him and lightly stroked his head, hoping not to wake him. "Thanks big guy. I appreciate the backup."

Then she sat down with a plate full of cookies and waited for Ian to come back inside. Her body started to relax and she thought she'd need a cup or two of coffee to keep her awake until bedtime. The adrenaline of the situation having totally wiped her out.

The good news, she thought as she munched through a second cookie. She'd figured out who killed Gerald Moss and probably why. She wasn't half bad at this investigating stuff. But she was amazing at this cooking thing. She figured she'd stick with that.

# CHAPTER 23

Angie had guessed right on needing the caffeine because before she was able to climb into bed that night, she'd had to field a phone call from Erica and Mrs. Potter and once she got off the phone with them, Felicia was at her door.

Felicia insisted on cooking dinner for the three of them, but before she finished, Sheriff Brown was there, wanting to interview Angie for the record. She invited him to stay for the meal, but his wife had supper waiting for him at home.

She slept through the night and late into the morning. When she woke, she made her way downstairs, Felicia was working on her laptop and something smelled amazing. She went straight to the coffee pot and poured a cup. When she sat down after a few fortifying sips, she asked "What are you still doing here?"

Felicia didn't look up from the screen. "Good morning to you too. There's some strata in the oven. I ate with Ian before I drove him back to the park to get his car. He's an interesting man."

"He's overbearing and chauvinistic." Angie stood and dished up a plate of the breakfast casserole. Grabbing a fork, she returned to the table. "But I have to admit, I appreciated all he did last night. I'm not sure I wanted to be out here alone after the day I had."

"From what I saw, you weren't alone. We had to tell Mrs. Potter and Erica not to come over more than three times last night. They were worried about you." This time she did look up. "You're an important part of the community. I've been dealing with calls all morning from town folk wanting to make sure you were okay."

"It's because I'm Nona's granddaughter. The woman was loved. And really, they just wanted to hear the gossip." She took a bite of the food. "This is great. And just what I needed."

"Thanks, but I think you're wrong on why they were calling. They like you." She went back to her computer. "I hate to bring up work after yesterday's situation, but do you think we'll need to push off the grand opening? I've had several emails asking if we were."

"No." She waved her fork for emphasis. "I'm not dead and people need to eat. Besides, I want something good to focus on. And opening The County Seat on Friday will keep me so busy, I won't be able to even think about what could have happened."

"I'm glad you're okay." Felicia stood and gave her a quick hug. "I would have been really ticked if you'd had me move all this way to open a restaurant and then got killed the week before we opened."

"Sensitive, are we?" Angie smiled, knowing her friend was really saying how scared she'd been.

"Not that I'm admitting." Felicia poured another cup of coffee and then sat down to talk. "And that's the last we're going to talk about the ultra-scary thing that didn't happen."

"Then let's pull up the to-do list and see what we can knock off remotely before we go into town to work." Angie finished her breakfast and went to the sink to wash off her plate. Mabel was in the herb garden pulling up a large worm. She could see Precious in her pasture, munching on grass. And Dom was snoring in his bed. All was right with the world. "How's front of the house set up going?"

* * * *

The white lights twinkled over the redwood pergolas set up in the dining room, making the restaurant look almost magical. White tablecloths covered the tables and red napkins added to the festive flair. The bar gleamed with the deep polished wood and a mirror backing where the liquor bottles set. A tall dark and handsome bartender, in a white dress shirt, suit vest and black jeans was filling the ice well. Jeorge was his name and Felicia had stolen him from one of the Boise restaurants. Angie thought he made the bar look even more perfect.

Estebe had run the prep time with a kindness and efficiency she hadn't expected. The kitchen crew were ready, if a little nervous. The prep work was completed, and it was time to open.

"It's real," she whispered to Felicia who walked up in a floral dress and stilettos. Angie was dressed in chef whites with her hair pulled back into a low bun.

Felicia hugged her. "I told you we could pull this off. Of course, don't expect me to wear these heels every night. My feet are already killing me. I have cute flats back behind the hostess stand so if I lose a few inches later, don't complain."

"I'm just so excited to be starting up The County Seat here. I wish Nona was here to see this. She would have loved everything about it." The door swung open and their first customers came into the foyer.

"I'm sure she's looking down from Heaven and blessing you right now." Felicia squeezed her arm. "We have guests so I'm up. Stay out here and mingle for a while. They'd love to see you."

Angie thought the town folk would probably love to see her alive and find out how she found Moss Farm treasure cave as it was being called by the media. Even the woman who'd come out to interview them about the restaurant opening had started with questions about how she'd escaped being killed by a mad man. But she followed Felicia's directions, visiting each table as they sat, popping into the kitchen to make sure they were okay without her, and then coming back out to mingle again.

Appetizers started flowing along with the drinks and then there he was. Ian McNeal walked in the door dressed in a suit with a blue shirt. He took her breath away and when he saw her, he smiled. Then he turned back to the door and held it open.

What had she been thinking? That he'd come stag? Of course he'd brought a date. Her chest tightened, but she took a deep breath and pushed the pain away. This was her night. And she wasn't going to let him hurt her. But when he helped the woman inside, she thought her heart would burst.

Mrs. Potter and Erica were on both sides of Ian as he escorted them up to the hostess stand. Angie stepped closer and heard him tell Felicia. "I believe we had both a table for one and a table for two, but could we combine those reservations into a table for three?"

"Of course, let me just get it set up." Felicia and a server went to set up a table near the exit so Mrs. Potter wouldn't have to walk far.

"You look lovely tonight." Ian whispered as he leaned over to kiss her cheek. "But I didn't expect to see you out here. Shouldn't you be cooking?"

"Felicia wants me to do the dog and pony show for a while. She says everyone here wants to meet me." She looked up at Ian. "Thanks for bringing them."

"Not a problem. I figured I could do the run in my wagon better than that little car of Erica's. Besides, now I have company for dinner." He turned and looked at Mrs. Potter. "And two lovely ladies at my table. A man could die happy."

"You are a charmer, that's what you are." Mrs. Potter shook a finger at him. Then she waved Angie over for a kiss on the cheek. "You need to watch that one carefully. Before you know it, he'll have a ring on that finger of yours."

"Grandma, I don't think Angie and Ian are even dating." Erica greeted Angie with air kisses. Then she grinned. "Yet."

"You all are terrible." Angie glanced back at the kitchen. "I've got to go, we'll be firing main courses soon and I want to be there to expedite. Enjoy your meal."

"You can bet on it." Ian nodded toward Felicia. "Looks like our table is ready. May I escort you?"

Angie left the trio as they were slowly making their way to the table. Opening The County Seat felt different than el pescado had. There, it had been fun and exciting getting to know new people. Here, it was like having family over for dinner. The County Seat felt like home. She stepped into the kitchen and took over expediting from Estebe. She turned on her CD of classic rock and turned up the volume. "Let's get this kitchen rocking!"

After they'd served the last dessert and had shut down and cleaned up the kitchen, she sat at the chef's table. Estebe was the only one left of the kitchen staff. "Well, tonight turned out amazing."

He brought over two bottles of beer from the fridge. "You did great. This is a happy place and we serve happy food."

She took a long sip from the bottle and held the cool glass on her head. "*We* did great. And we get to do it again tomorrow night."

"You make that sound like a bad thing." Estebe clinked his bottle on hers. "To The County Seat. May this be the first of many years of exceptional nights."

They chatted for a while about the details of the night, what slowed down service and ways they could speed it up. Finally, she glanced at the clock. "It's almost eleven. I've kept you way too late. You go home and I'll see you tomorrow."

He paused, looking at her. "I could make you something to eat before I go."

She rubbed her face. "I'm not hungry. Besides, I need to get home to Dom. He's probably wondering what happened to me. This working late is going to mess with his bedtime routine."

"The dog loves you. He'll manage." Estebe stood and paused at the table. "I enjoy cooking with you, Angie."

And then he left through the back door. She realized that was the first time he'd called her by her first name. Smiling, she went to lock the back door. Then she checked the stoves, and turned out the lights. Time to go home and fall into bed.

Felicia stood at the bar, closing up with Jeorge. She patted him on the back and said her goodbyes. As he walked out the front, she strolled up to Angie, shoeless. "What an amazing night. We did close to fifty covers, all the servers went home with a wad of money in their pockets from tips, and no one sent back anything. I think we did all right."

"I think we did fantastic." She peeled off her chef coat, exposing the glittery tank underneath. Pulling her hair free from the bun, she sighed. "This is why I love running a restaurant. Feeding people, providing a food experience, and being done at the end of the night. This is the best job in the world."

The door opened and they both called out, "We're closed."

Ian peeked inside. "I kind of figured that, but I wanted to talk to Angie if possible."

Felicia squeezed Angie in a big hug. "That's my cue. I'm going upstairs and soaking in a hot bath until the water turns cold or my bottle of wine is gone."

"See you tomorrow." Angie smiled toward her friend then walked to the front where they had benches for early arrivals and waiting customers. "Come sit if you want to talk, I don't think I'll last long standing up. And thank you again for bringing Mrs. Potter tonight. I can't tell you how much it meant to me for her to be here."

"All in a day's work for Superman." He sat next to her and loosened his tie. "Besides, it was my pleasure."

"You may be the only one who thinks of you as Superman, but I think you're pretty amazing."

"Do you now?" He turned toward her. "Then this next thing I'm going to ask will be a walk in the park."

"What do you want? I already told Sheriff Brown I'd testify against Kirk. I hear they found the lawyer Gerald was using." Rumors had been flying for the last few days and since they all wanted to hear Angie's side, she heard all the gossip.

"Yes. And he it turns out he did have a will. He left everything to Mildred. When Allen told her, she broke down sobbing." He looked at his hands. "She really loved him."

"I got that impression too." Angie wished the best for the woman who had to go on without the man she'd come to love. All because of money. She glanced at her watch. "I really have to get home. I'm going to be beat tomorrow."

"One more thing. I know you can't go on a weekend, but would you have dinner with me on Tuesday night?"

She turned toward him. "You want to have dinner with me? Is this about the market? Should I cook?"

"No, this isn't about the market, and no, you aren't going to cook. I thought we'd take a drive up to Sun Valley and eat at the lodge. I can have you home at a decent hour if we leave here about two. And it's a beautiful drive."

"I don't understand." Angie felt like her brain was foggy.

He took in a breath. "Angie Turner, I'm asking if you want to go on a date with me?"

She grinned. "Just because Mrs. Potter said that thing, doesn't mean… "

Interrupting, he shook his head. "I've been planning this for weeks, but thought after you opened would be a better time. You might be less distracted. But then, when you were with Kirk, I realized time is the one thing we aren't promised. So will you go on a bloody date with me?"

Angie smiled. Now, it was a perfect night. "Yes, Ian, I will."

# And now, a note from the author

Potato Soup.

My comfort, go-to food of choice.

Whenever I'm feeling sick or lonely or anxious—yes, I'm an emotional eater—this is my go to recipe. When I went back home a few years ago for my mother's surgery, I found it was a family tradition.

My oldest sister started the potatoes, celery, and onions cooking, chatting as she peeled and chopped. Then, the second in line, took over, mixing in milk and the egg dumplings we'd all come to expect in the creamy goodness.

When it was served, the resulting goodness filled us with a warmth that highlighted the fact that most of the family (I have two sisters, two brothers, one half-sister, and one stepbrother) was sitting at the table, brought together from four different states to support Mom. I wasn't sure when the last time we'd all been together was and we were afraid of what the next time would be, but no one spoke of that. Instead, we talked about happy memories and the different versions of this family classic we made in our own homes.

My version doesn't have goat cheese, which Angie would probably find a way to incorporate during her experiments, but we love it.

Chop one onion and mince a clove or two of garlic. Brown this in a large heavy stockpot with a couple tablespoons of olive oil. Crumble a pound or so of a fresh sausage into the pan. I like the spicy Italian sausage my grocer makes for this. Sprinkle in a teaspoon of red pepper flakes.

Cook until the meat is done but not overcooked and dry. Then set the mixture aside in a colander, draining out the fat from the olive oil as well as the sausage.

Pour a box of chicken stock into the empty stock pan. Don't worry that there might be bits and pieces from the sausage mixture still in the pan.

Peel 4-6 large russet potatoes, chopping into small pieces. Add these to the stockpot along with two stalks of celery chopped into small slices. Add the leaves and chopped stalks into the pot. Add enough water to cover the potatoes, add in salt (I like a lot of salt, so I'd say at least a teaspoon here, but this can be adjusted up or down for your own salt liking) and pepper and let the mixture boil for thirty minutes, checking the water level at different times. You don't want this to dry out and burn. When the potatoes are soft, mash up some of the potatoes. Not all of the pot.

You can also do this by inserting an immersion blender, but it seems a bit fancy for the recipe.

Add back in the drained meat mixture, a cup of heavy cream, and enough milk to make the soup appear creamy.

Then in a separate bowl, add a ½ cup of flour, and generous sprinklings (or dashes) of salt, pepper, garlic salt, seasonal salt to the dry mixture. Then crack an egg in the middle. Mix together in the bowl, then drop by spoonful into the soup. If there are left over crumblings, add those as well as the flour/egg mixture will thicken your soup.

Put a lid on the soup, heat until the egg dumplings are cooked through, and serve.

My husband, who's a meat-and-potatoes dinner lover, finds this soup perfect for a weekend meal. I like to add some fresh rolls to the mix (yes, more carbs) but he likes the soup all by itself.

Enjoy.

Lynn

Got a craving for more Angie Turner adventures?
Be sure to keep an eye out for more
Farm-to-Fork Mysteries
Coming soon from

Lynn Cahoon
And
Lyrical Underground

And don't miss her other series

The Cat Latimer Mysteries

And

The Tourist Trap Mysteries

Available wherever books are sold!

# ABOUT THE AUTHOR

*New York Times* and *USA Today* best-selling author Lynn Cahoon is an Idaho expat. She grew up living the small town life she now loves to write about. Currently, she's living with her husband and two fur babies in a small historic town on the banks of the Mississippi river where her imagination tends to wander. *Guidebook to Murder*, Book 1 of the Tourist Trap series, won the 2015 Reader's Crown award for Mystery Fiction.

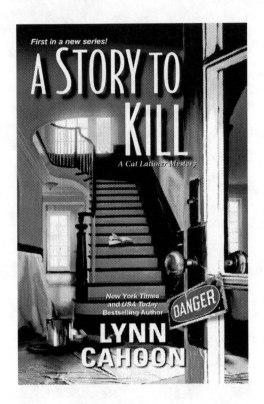

## A STORY TO KILL
### *A Cat Latimer Mystery*

***Former English professor Cat Latimer is back in Colorado, hosting writers' retreats in the big blue Victorian she's inherited, much to her surprise, from none other than her carousing ex-husband! Now it's an authors' getaway—but Cat won't let anyone get away with murder...***

The bed-and-breakfast is open for business, and bestselling author Tom Cook is among its first guests. Cat doesn't know why he came all the way from New York, but she's glad to have him among the quirkier—and far less famous—attendees.

Cat's high school sweetheart Seth, who's fixing up the weathered home, brings on mixed emotions for Cat...some of them a little overpowering. But it's her uncle, the local police chief, whom she'll call for help when there's a surprise ending for Tom Cook in his cozy guest room. Will a killer have the last word on the new life Cat has barely begun?

## GUIDEBOOK TO MURDER
*A Tourist Trap Mystery*

*In the gentle coastal town of South Cove, California, all Jill Gardner wants is to keep her store—Coffee, Books, and More—open and running. So why is she caught up in the business of murder?*

When Jill's elderly friend, Miss Emily, calls in a fit of pique, she already knows the city council is trying to force Emily to sell her dilapidated old house. But Emily's gumption goes for naught when she dies unexpectedly and leaves the house to Jill—along with all of her problems...and her enemies. Convinced her friend was murdered, Jill is finding the list of suspects longer than the list of repairs needed on the house. But Jill is determined to uncover the culprit—especially if it gets her closer to South Cove's finest, Detective Greg King. Problem is, the killer knows she's on the case—and is determined to close the book on Jill *permanently*...

Printed in the United States
by Baker & Taylor Publisher Services